SIEGE AT HAWTHORN LAKE

Murder on the Mountain

Paul G Buckner

Edited by: Jody Kirchner

To my supportive wife, Jody, and inquisitive son, Chase

Table of Contents

Siege at Hawthorn Lake

Chapter 1

Troy Turner sat at the kitchen table drinking a cup of coffee, and watching the sun make its appearance over the snow covered mountain ridges. The warm, orange glow revealed a beautiful panorama of Lake Hawthorn below surrounded by tall, majestic pines and mighty oaks standing guard around the crystal blue water. As the sun continued its grand ascent, the small valley slowly awakened with the sounds of wildlife. Shrill cries of black birds could be heard calling out, echoing across the water as if to warn all that winter was coming fast. Squirrels were waking up hungry and barking at each other. Soon, they would be tunneling through the snow searching for the prized nuts, seeds and other goodies they had buried to fill their empty bellies.

Troy had been up since 3:17 a.m. The bright-red numbers of the digital clock beside his bed was the first image he saw through his blood-shot, sleep deprived eyes. He could still see that image of the clock clearly in his mind. He had awakened by what he gathered was a bad dream - a nightmare rather, with details that he couldn't remember once the cobwebs of sleep faded away. He remembered hearing a blood curdling scream that actually woke him, which he believed to be his own once the morning grogginess wore off. He half-heartedly laughed to himself. *Too real*, he thought, not remembering any solid details about the dream, but still feeling a cold chill from it.

He was forty-two, but had the body of a thirty-year-old, a product of good genetics, exercise, and healthy living. People referred to him as a ruggedly handsome man. His dark and weathered skin tone was a sharp contrast to his light colored hair that had gotten a bit darker as he aged, but his steel gray eyes had never changed. He took pride in his appearance, but lately he hadn't been sleeping well and it showed in his features. Two days growth of dark beard stubble adorned his face and added years. He was a writer by trade and bought the cabin only a few months back during the summer. He hoped that the solitude would not only be relaxing, but productive for his work. Perhaps too much quiet is what kept him from sleeping well. His thoughts drifted away from the lack of sleep and to his earlier days.

Born an only child to a family from Cincinnati, he was mostly raised in the city, but loved being in the country. The family would take trips often to visit his dad's parents in Albany on their little farm. Troy spent many weeks during the summer months on the farm and helped his grandparents with chores. What he liked most, however, was walking out to the fields, catching up a horse with nothing more than a hackamore, and riding down to the creek bareback. There he would take the bridle off and let the horse graze while he fished or explored, depending on his mood. Sometimes the horse would still be grazing nearby and he would ride back, but more often than not, he would have to walk.

His grandparent's farm was a small dairy farm with several milk cows. His grandfather was up every morning by five o'clock for the milking - rain or shine. When Troy was there, he would help in the mornings. He was supposed to help in the evenings too, but there were so many things for a young boy to do in the country that, sometimes, he lost track of time, and failed to make it back.

His grandmother would scold him when he finally showed up for dinner.

"Did you help your grandpa this evening with the chores?" She'd ask, knowing the answer before he said anything by how he hung his head, and looked away. She would chuckle a little and tell him to make up for it by feeding the chickens, or tending to the horses. It was a great way for a young boy to grow up and he always looked forward to those summers.

Tragically, he lost both of his grandparents in an automobile accident shortly after he began high school. It was a very difficult time for him, and his grades in school suffered for it. He became broody, and began keeping to himself more, turning away from friends. He would have gone down an entirely different path had it not been for his football coach who also happened to be his freshman English teacher.

Coach Bradley saw his potential not only on the football field, but as a writer. He would have all of the kids write short stories and essays. He was most impressed with Troy's writing and encouraged him to use it as a way of dealing with his feelings. On the football field, he could take his aggression and anger over losing his grandparents out on the opposing team. Troy's success on the football field got him the scholarship he needed for college, but his writing skills gave him goals and a successful career he loved.

Troy moved east with his bride shortly after graduating college. She was determined to live in New York City in order to pursue a career in theater. Her goal was to one day perform on Broadway. He wanted to support her dreams, but he also longed to live in the country. He truly wanted nothing to do with city life, but he stuck it out for several years in an attempt at making the marriage work. That wasn't the only difference they discovered. As time went on there were many things that the couple never saw eye to eye on and eventually they divorced. Troy had lost his parents during those years, which was hard on him. The stress of losing them, and not being happy in the city, caused more insufferable arguments between him and his wife. He believed it was simply due to the fact that they had grown so drastically apart. They tried for a long time to keep the marriage together, but in the end, divorce was the only sane thing they could do. His memories of those days slowly faded away as he came back to the present. His coffee needed refilling.

Troy loved the way his cabin rested comfortably on the gentle slope of the foot hills of the mountain. Located only about a hundred yards from the edge of the water on the west end of the lake, it was the perfect, picturesque setting. The two-story log cabin had an amazing view from the upstairs master bedroom that led out onto a beautiful red-wood deck. The veranda was quite large and contained a variety of lounge chairs and a small grill. He sat out there many times to watch the sun rise and light up the valley with its bright red, welcoming radiance.

Just below the house was a boat dock that ran about fifty feet out into the crystal clear water where a fourteen-foot V-bottom boat floated silently in Hawthorn Lake. The small gasoline engine hanging on the transom was old, but ran well, and was strong enough to push the little boat across the lake under most circumstances. If, however, the wind was really howling down from the mountain passes it always proved to be a struggle. The landing deck of the boat dock was a perfect twenty feet by twenty feet square. Troy knew this because he had measured the old one and bought new material to rebuild it with even before he closed on the property. He was confident the paperwork would go through and simply couldn't wait to get moved in to begin creating his own space.

As he sat quietly sipping his coffee, the sound of a loon could be heard echoing across the lake. The water was fairly smooth and calm this morning so he thought it may be a good day to take the boat out on a short fishing trip. The lake was large with several inlets from the mountain runoff that kept it cold and full year round. The water would be icy cold, but at least it wasn't completely frozen over yet. He would have to remember to haul the boat out before that happened. The freeze was still another month or so away, and even then it wouldn't freeze over entirely.

The fishing on the lake was excellent as was the hunting in the area. The realtor that sold him the property mentioned that during season he could practically hunt from his porch. He warned Troy that even though most hunters never venture this close, he should still make sure to wear his hunter safety orange if he was out in the woods during hunting season. Sometimes, out of state hunters got lost or turned down wrong roads.

"There's a lot of public hunting land in these mountains. Easy to get lost," the realtor said. "It never hurts to be cautious."

Troy finished his coffee and climbed the stairs to his bedroom to get dressed. He opened the veranda doors wide to let the cold morning air invade the room as he pulled on a pair of Carhartt jeans. Thick wool socks would keep his feet warm for the morning, but as the sun warmed the day the wool would also breathe well. He opted for his hiking boots instead of the deck shoes he normally wore. Next, he pulled a red plaid flannel shirt over a long sleeve thermal under shirt followed by a light jacket. A Kansas City Royals baseball cap hung on a nail near the door. He grabbed it and haphazardly put it on his head as he closed the doors behind him.

He left the cabin by a staircase that led down from the deck, and walked through the thin layer of snow to the shed that doubled as a garage. His fishing gear was stowed in the back. The wide double doors were made of thick, rough cut wood and were strong and durable. There was no need to open the big doors so he went in the walk-through door on the side. The shed was large enough for two vehicles and had an upstairs loft for added storage. The former owner had left some boxes up there, and Troy had told the realtor about it. The realtor said that he would be glad to let the man know, but still had not followed up with Troy to tell him if the man would be coming back to get them or not. *Another item on the to-do list*, he thought.

Troy grabbed a couple of his fishing poles, a tackle box and a small Styrofoam container with big red night crawlers inside. The few times that he used the worms for bait, the catfish in the lake devoured them. The fishing was great here due, in large part, to the absence of a lot of fishermen. Troy's land encompassed the lake on all sides, though sometimes locals liked to come up to fish. There were many streams below that held beautiful trout and brownies that were excellent eating, but the lake held everything from walleye, perch and crappie to Kentucky's and steelhead.

He closed the door to the shed and walked down to the boat dock. He set his fishing gear on the edge of the dock before stepping into the boat. He had to be careful not to slip on any snow or ice that had frozen in the bottom. After he had boarded, he grabbed his gear off of the dock and stowed it. He spun around to the engine sitting behind him and after a few squeezes on the fuel bulb to fill the lines with gasoline, he turned the choke on and cranked the motor. It took a few pulls, but it kicked off without fail, and puffed out bright blue and white smoke as it warmed up. He slowly opened the choke of the little two-stroke engine as it began idling on its own, untied the boat, and pushed off with a paddle. Once he was out a few feet from the dock he grasped the throttle handle and puttered out across the peaceful lake.

Troy guided the boat across the inlet and out into the main body of the lake staying fairly close to the shoreline opposite the cabin. His destination was a spot a few miles away from the house, to a small creek that flowed out of the lake. The creek itself ran almost the entire length of the valley getting very small in some areas and rather wide and deep in others. He had boated quite a ways down it exploring one day, but didn't know if he would have enough fuel in the tanks to go very far. He would remind himself later to make sure to put the spare tank in the boat as he had yet to do so. As a matter of fact, he remembered that he hadn't thought to refill the tank from the last time he went out and reached down to check it now. He picked the tank up and sloshed it about. Figuring it to be about a half of a tank, he thought it would be plenty to get him there and back with no trouble.

The mouth of the creek was fifty yards wide with soft grass banks along the sides. Tall pines dotted the land near the lake, but an overgrowth of scrub brush obscured any chance of a view into the woods. Troy had found the spot last weekend and caught several nice sized catfish that he fileted and deep fried along with some crispy hush puppies. That sure sounded good again for dinner this afternoon, he thought.

He guided the boat close to the shoreline for a mile or so in until he found the familiar tree that had fallen from the edge of the creek out into the water. It was a huge birch that had grown too close to the flowing water. The edge of the creek bank finally eroded from flash floods and over-flows and the giant tree no longer had a good foothold and eventually gave way to the forces of Mother Nature. The tree itself covered almost the entire width of the creek leaving only a small gap on the other side to slide a boat through. He reached back to the engine and hit the cut-off switch. He didn't want the sound of the engine to spook the fish away so he paddled the remaining distance to the tree.

Troy wasn't born and raised a country boy, but the many summers at his grandparents' farm taught him a lot about country living. What he didn't know, he could certainly figure out on his own. If he had not had those experiences growing up he never would have bought such a remote place. When the realtor first told him about the cabin he almost bought it without seeing it. He joked about it with the man later as he signed the paperwork. A very secluded cabin on a beautiful lake with all the hunting, fishing, and solitude a writer could ever ask for was cliché, but nonetheless an incredible opportunity.

As the boat glided up to the tree, Troy reached and grabbed one of the lower hanging branches that looked strong enough and tied the bow line to it. As he did so, snow from the overhead branch fell down into his jacket collar and melted into an icy, cold rivulet down his back causing him to scrunch his shoulders. The cold, windy weather made Troy cringe a bit so he pulled his collar up and around his neck a little tighter. He then let the anchor down to keep the boat from moving around and drifting off his fishing-hole. He took one of his rods, pulled the hook free and put a fat, juicy worm on it, dropped the line in the water and kicked back in the padded boat seat to relax and think about nothing at all. Within a short time the rod tip bounced and Troy perked up. He picked up the pole and waited for the fish to hit the bait again. He felt the strong thump on the line, set the hook and reeled in a nice four-pound catfish.

"That'll make a couple of nice filets," he said out loud, as he put the fish in a wire mesh basket and dropped it over the side. He didn't like to clean the fish, but it was a necessary evil, he supposed, that couldn't be avoided. It could be a nasty job, but he learned how to filet from his grandfather long ago so he didn't have to get too messy. He put another worm on his hook and re-set the pole. He figured a few more of these beauties should keep him stocked up for another week.

+++

A crow cawed loudly overhead as it flew to its unknown destination stirring Troy out of a sleepy, lazy haze. He realized he had been asleep, but didn't know how for how long. He never wore a watch, not since he moved in. The Sun was still low in the east so he surmised he had slept for a half hour. He laughed out loud and thought that maybe he should start sleeping in the boat, he might get better rest. He had caught a few more fish earlier, but hadn't had a bite in a while now. He figured that the fish had moved on to deeper water or weren't biting anymore. He made his mind up to move a little further into the creek and try to catch a few more before returning home.

He untied the boat and pulled the anchor up. He paddled out around the tree and floated silently past the overhanging branches. Just a little further up he passed a bend in the creek where a small beaver lodge was built on the edge of the shore. He knew that fishing near the lodge wouldn't be productive because of the beavers, but there was a spot a ways on up past it that opened wider and much deeper where it should be better. There were a few natural laydowns and buckbrush growing at the edges where bass and channel cats like to hide out and ambush their prey. That's where he was heading. He soon reached the area where he wanted to try his luck and stood up to get the anchor to drop. When he bent down to pick up the nylon rope attached to it, his hands slipped on the wet rope as he hoisted it over the side. The heavy weight plunged into the creek with a loud WHOOSH! He wasn't ready for it and the sudden shift in weight rocked the boat causing him to lose his balance. He fell heavily in the boat among his fishing gear and paddles. At that same moment, he heard another large splash in the water somewhere just ahead of him and then a heavy crashing in the brush that startled him. A loon standing in the water not far away suddenly flew off with a loud cry and wings beating hard on the air. Troy struggled to sit up in the boat, but where the water had dripped on the aluminum hull it had already frozen making his attempt even more difficult. By the time he was able to gain his balance and sit up, whatever had caused the splashing was gone. Must've been a beaver, he thought, as he laughed out loud. Surprising, was all. The poor beaver was probably more scared than he was.

After his nerves calmed, Troy picked up his fishing pole and put a worm on the hook, cast it to the edge of the buck brush and set the rod back down between his feet. As he sat there watching his bobber float in the water, the area grew strangely quiet. He began to feel a bit uneasy the longer he sat there, like there was someone or something watching him. He knew it had to be his nerves just settling after his tumble in the boat, but he still couldn't shake the feeling. It was too quiet now and it seemed that all of wild game had stopped everything they were doing for the day and were holding their collective breaths. The eerie silence pervaded the area and made Troy feel even more uneasy the longer he stayed. He decided the fish had stopped biting so he might as well head back to the cabin anyway; mainly as a defensive justification to his male pride.

Chapter 2

It was late in the evening by the time Troy got back to the cabin and put his things away. He filleted the fish at the cleaning station in the back of the cabin that was set up with running water and sinks. After washing up, he decided to make some hush puppies and deep fry the fish with a cornmeal and egg batter. The smell of the fish was titillating as it wafted through the cabin. The deep fried cornmeal and buttermilk hushpuppies with chopped onions made his mouth water. He was famished and couldn't wait for them to cool down as he popped one in his mouth. The hushpuppy immediately burnt the roof of his mouth and he sucked in air grabbing for a glass of water to ease the pain.

After dinner Troy cleaned up the kitchen and decided to grab his laptop to check his emails. He didn't have a phone line yet, but he did have a satellite dish for internet that enabled him to use his phone as long as the signal was strong enough. It wasn't exactly high-speed internet, but it was better than dial-up and helped him stay connected. He could Skype and download music, which is mostly what he would do if he wanted entertainment outside of what Mother Nature offered here in the mountains.

Dozens of spam emails littered his inbox with an occasional one from someone he actually knew. He hadn't checked it in a few days so it was rather bloated with junk. He had one from his publisher that asked him to give him a call, one from an old colleague asking him to visit her the next time he was in New York, and one from his buddy Craig asking him about the hunting there. Obviously, hinting to his old friend that he'd like to stay at the cabin soon and do some hunting of his own. Opening day of deer season was only days away. "Those northern deer get big as hell up there I hear and rifle season opens in just a week or two," his friend wrote. Troy laughed out loud as he read Craig's email.

His friend from college was from Oklahoma and a serious deer hunter and fisherman. Troy had called him some time ago, before he bought the cabin, and invited him up once he got settled in. Craig wasn't going to let him forget it either. He would try to give him a call tomorrow and ask if he would like to come up and hunt. They had a mutual friend named Phil Jackson that was sure to come if Craig asked him to. The two grew up together and were inseparable. They had been on many hunts together and Troy counted them both as his closest friends.

Troy had first met Craig in college where they both were scholarship football players. Craig was a big bruiser of a tight end and Troy was a strong safety. The two were first introduced when the team began spring practice. The offense had been running drag routes and the linebackers weren't picking it up correctly. The Coach brought in Troy as a freshman eager to listen and learn. On the first play, Troy picked it up and tackled Craig hard enough to cause him to fumble. That was one of the rare times he ever fumbled a carry. After practice, Craig, a sophomore, sought the young freshman out. After ribbing each other about practice for a few minutes the two players learned they had a few classes together along with Craig's buddy from back home, Phil Jackson. Over time, the three men became very good friends and stayed in touch with each over the years.

Troy dragged his laptop upstairs when he decided to get ready for bed. He thought he might get a few chapters in before his publisher actually showed up at his house looking for the manuscript! Troy's last book was on the New York Times Best Sellers list for several weeks and made his publisher a lot of money. Not that he was complaining because he certainly made his fair share, but it also landed him a new publishing deal asking for more novels. Now, he had actual deadlines. It netted him a good income, but deadlines on creativity weren't something that he necessarily loved. As he began typing he soon fell asleep.

+++

A thunderous boom shook the entire cabin and woke Troy out of a deep sleep. The glass in the windows rattled and something crashed to the floor downstairs. The bedroom was dark except where the moonlight had found its way in through the windows of the doors. He quickly sat up remaining still and quiet, holding his breath as he got his bearings. His ears were straining, listening for any sound that may come again. He scanned the room intently, but could see nothing except the dark shapes of his furniture. After several seconds passed with no further sounds, he slowly slipped out of his bed and made his way over to the dresser where he kept a handgun; a Colt 1911 that belonged to his grandfather. He opened the drawer as quietly as possible, pulled the loaded pistol out of its case and moved to the top of the stairs. He was slow and deliberate as he crept down the stairs being sure to stop and listen every few feet. He could see very well into the living room as one of the lamps was still on. A photo frame lay in glass shards on the floor next to the wall it had previously hung on. The writer reached the lamp, switched it off, and grabbed a flashlight from the table. It was a powerful flashlight called a Stinger that many law enforcement officials used because it could light up an area like a spotlight. He had used it quite a few times and it always came in handy. This moment was no exception. He checked all of the rooms one by one and made sure the front and back doors were still secured.

That told him that nothing could have gotten in to the house. The front door to the cabin was a huge solid oak door with three small windows at the top that formed the shape of a half-moon. Know the solid structure of the log home helped to calm his nerves. He was secure knowing that whatever it was, it was outside of the walls of solid pine that were almost a foot thick. His first thought was that it could possibly be a bear. In which case, he could probably scare it off if he turned on the outside lights. He might even fire a few rounds in the air. He didn't want to shoot it unless he absolutely had to and certainly not with a pistol. He laid the pistol down on the sofa, reached up to the gun rack and pulled down his Marlin 45-70. It was the biggest caliber he had and at close range, it was a very lethal round.

Suddenly, the cabin walls shook from another jolt surprising Troy. It came from the side of the house and sounded like a dull thud against the wall. Whack! Another hit, but this time further up on the roof and whatever it was rolled down the metal and clattered all the way to the ground. There was no tree close enough to the house so he knew it wasn't dead limbs or acorns falling. Someone was throwing something at the cabin!

Troy flipped the main breaker for all of the outside lights in the yard and the ones that hung from poles leading down to the boat dock before hurrying up the stairs. He cautiously walked out on to the balcony and looked around. A separate pole beside the garage had a large outdoor yard light that came on automatically when it became dark enough for the sensor to trip it. He fired two shots into the air and hollered, "I know you're out there so knock it off before someone gets hurt!"

Whack! Another rock landed on top of the roof not far from where he stood and bounced harmlessly to the ground.

"Stop throwing rocks or I'll start shooting," he yelled, just as another rock bounced on to the deck close to his feet. Troy aimed his flashlight in the direction he thought it came from, but the light revealed nothing more than the snow covered yard and trees. He aimed the rifle in the air fired a round. The blazing report of the big caliber rifle exploded and echoed through the cove. He stood there for several minutes longer watching intently. Then, silence.

+++

He shined the powerful flashlight all around the yard, but didn't see or hear anything else. After a few more minutes of looking around from the upstairs deck, he realized that he didn't have on any shoes. The adrenaline had slowly left his system, leaving him shivering from the cold. He turned and went back in, securing the door behind him. He normally left the French doors closed and the inner solid wooden doors flung open so that the morning sun could wake him in the mornings. He could use the heavy wooden doors for bad storms or as a way to keep bears out as they had a huge crossbar beam that lowered down across them like both of the doors downstairs. They folded back against the interior wall and remained there unless he needed them. Tonight, he closed them.

Troy sat up the rest of the night drinking coffee and nervously keeping his rifle within reach. He didn't see or hear anything else. When morning light came, he pulled on his boots and grabbed a coat. He walked over to the front door, opened it, and cautiously stepped out. He took a long look around then checked his rifle once again to make sure it was loaded and headed down the steps. He walked slowly around the house watching for any signs that someone may still be around. There was snow on the ground, but there were no tracks near the cabin that he could see. He walked over to where his jeep was parked and gave it a thorough going over. Nothing had touched the vehicle. After several minutes of investigating, he felt comfortable that whoever or whatever was there last night was gone and he made his way back inside. Once inside he checked his internet connection. It was solid so he made a call to the sheriff's office to make a report. The lady that answered the phone sounded pleasant, but still half asleep.

"Sherriff's Office, this is Lindsey," a lady answered.

"Good morning Lindsey, This is Troy Turner. I'd like to make a report," he replied.

"Good morning Mister Turner. What's the nature?" She asked.

"Well, I'm not sure of the nature, but harassment comes to mind," He went on to explain about the events that took place while Lindsey seemed to be writing it all down.

"Uh huh, yeah, okay, uh huh, did you get a look at them?" She asked.

"No, I never actually saw them. They stayed in the woods hiding in the trees," he replied.

Troy had the feeling that she was either very bored with his story or she just didn't believe him. He was sure that, as a dispatcher, she's heard more crazy calls than she cared to recall.

"Any idea how many there were? Could you hear any voices?" She asked.

"No ma'am, I didn't actually get a look at them or hear anything other than the rocks bouncing off my house so I couldn't tell you. It may have been one or a half dozen. Truth is, I didn't see so much as a glimpse of movement," Troy answered.

"You use the word 'them' like you think it was more than one person. What makes you think that?"

Troy said, "I'm not sure why I decided to say that to be honest. Like I said, I never heard or saw anyone in particular, but there were a few rocks that came pretty quick leading me to believe that there was more than one person throwing them. For the life of me though, I can't figure out why anyone would be out there at that time of night in the first place. It's not like my house is easy to get to and it's not close to town."

The lady was nice, but sounded uninterested when she told Troy that she would let the sheriff know and that he may send someone out this morning so he should expect them.

Now that it was a little warmer, Troy decided to take another look around the cabin. He wasn't doing anything at the moment except worrying about who could be out there anyway. He put his coat back on and slipped the handgun behind his back tucking it away neatly in his jeans. Walking around to the side of the cabin he noticed the rocks lying on the ground. He had missed it this morning when he first took a look around in the daylight, probably because he was more worried about the person that did it may still be out there, but these were what had apparently been thrown at the cabin. One of the rocks was the size of a football. About ten feet up the wall was a huge gash in the wooden logs, the obvious result of the projectile. Troy reached down to pick it up, but was amazed at the sheer weight of the rock. It had to weigh more than ten pounds!

"Holy hell," he said out loud.

Who could possibly have thrown the rock? He wasn't a weakling by any account, yet he couldn't imagine anyone being able to throw it! He stood up and looked around at the woods with his hand instinctively reaching for the Colt.

Chapter 3

It was midday when the sheriff's deputy drove up to the cabin. Troy had checked all around the property, but could see no other damage or signs of the intruders. There were no footprints in the snow at all. He even thought that it could have possibly been a rock that fell from the chimney, but the damage was done to the side of the house making that theory impossible. He said as much to the deputy after their formal greeting.

"I don't understand why anyone would want to drive all the way out here just to harass me. I don't really know anyone around here. I just moved in this last summer," Troy said.

Deputy Billy Larson was a small man standing barely five and a half feet tall with a shock of blonde hair and wearing a uniform that seemed two sizes too big for him. He said, "Well, it may not be you that they're harassing. Maybe someone had a mad-on for old man Reed. The guy you bought the place from. 'Course, I couldn't imagine anyone wanting to scare the old goat, though. He never bothered anyone and was always a nice guy."

"I've no idea, but let me show you something," Troy replied.

Troy took the deputy around to the side of the house and showed him the rock and the spot on the side of the house where it hit.

"Whew," the deputy let out a whistle. "That's a hell of a rock."

"That's a hell of a man that could throw a rock that size that hard against the house! I didn't see any footprints at all the way around the cabin. That tells me whoever threw it had to be hiding in the woods," Troy said.

The two men walked around the property, but saw no other signs other than the few rocks lying by the cabin. The deputy checked out the woods with Troy in tow. Not finding any more evidence they made their way back to the cabin. Deputy Larson told him that he would write up the report, but for him to be sure and keep a gun handy in order to protect himself. It took too long for anyone on patrol to drive out here especially in bad weather.

"As remote as this place is, I can't imagine that they'll be back, but I wouldn't be caught off guard. And, honestly, I doubt that it was a bear. I never heard of a bear that could throw rocks. Whoever it was probably wanted to give you a good scare and most likely high tailed it out of here covering their tracks. I doubt you have any more trouble." the deputy stated.

"I don't plan on leaving the cabin without a gun any time soon, Deputy. I appreciate you driving all the way out here - I know it's quite a ways for you."

"Think nothing of it and if you need us again, give us a call. Wish I could be more helpful, but that's about all I can do for ya right now. Besides, nothing like a little windshield time. It beats pushing a pencil around back at the office. Take care now."

The deputy paused when he got to his car and turned back to Troy.

"I don't think I need to reiterate just how remote you are out here. The nearest house is on the other side of the mountain; The Denizen's. Mountain folk. They're a bit odd, but otherwise harmless. But, like I said, it's pretty far away. As the crow flies probably only about ten miles, but if you were to drive it, you'd have to go all the way around the mountain and that'd take you the better part of two hours on these roads. I hear there's a pass that'll take you over, but who knows if that's true or not. You'll probably live here all your life and never run into 'em. They're just not the overly friendly type at all and keep to themselves."

Troy had not seen anyone out at the cabin or on the lake since he first moved in. He had driven into town on several occasions and had met several folks, but none that lived out this way. Some had mentioned that they would come out and fish the lake sometimes, but there were lakes all over the county. The deputy told him that most folks in the county were pretty friendly and would help anyone. The locals respected the mountains and they knew how important it was to be able to rely on one another.

The deputy continued through the rolled down window once he climbed inside his vehicle, "Well, I'll be heading back now. I'll follow up with you, but call in the meantime if you have any more problems."

Troy waved as he watched the deputy's four-wheel drive truck disappear down the road. He could catch a glimpse of it through trees along the lake road as it wound around the edge for quite some distance and then crossed a bridge. From there, the road continued for several miles before coming to the county highway. It was only an hour's drive into town when the weather was good. If the weather was bad, as was often the case during the winter months, it could take twice that if it were even possible over some of the passes. Troy remembered joking with the realtor that he could probably make it to town quicker on a horse than in a car.

The small town of Hawthorn was a very friendly locale. The population wasn't more than about 4,500, but there were many families that lived outside of town up in the mountains. It was a beautiful area full of wildlife that fishermen and hunters sought regularly during season. The town also thrived on outside money that came from the skiing population. The many businesses did very well when the weather cooperated.

Troy spent the rest of the evening piddling around outside. The grass had gone dormant long ago and snow now covered the ground. At this particular altitude it snowed often, but it shouldn't get bad for a few more weeks before heading into the heart of winter. He busied himself picking up dead limbs and rocks out of the yard and cleaning up around the place. He thought about tackling the shed in order to make room to park his car inside. He drove a 4X4 door Jeep Wrangler so it didn't need a lot of room, but still the shed was piled under with all of his things from the move. He meant to have it cleaned out long ago, but never got around to it. A few boxes at a time got unpacked, but mostly as he needed something out of one. He kept his Colt on his side the whole time…just in case.

It was dinner time and his stomach told him as much. Troy knocked off for the day and went inside. Rummaging through the pantry he decided on something easy tonight. He found some pasta and a jar of spaghetti sauce. Once he put the noodles in a pot of water and set it on the stove, he cut up some onions, peppers and mushrooms and put them in a pan with some olive oil. He would add them all to the jar of store bought sauce that he started in another pan. The smell of the onions and peppers was tantalizing and made him realize that he had hadn't eaten anything all day and he was starving. It wasn't anything like his mother's homemade spaghetti sauce, but it would do for a bachelor. He wasn't a gourmet chef by any stretch of the imagination, but he liked to be in the kitchen. He was good with creating dishes from whatever he had on hand at the time. He referred to it as cupboard cooking.

After dinner he decided to check his emails and turn on the TV. While surfing channels he deleted junk email and flagged others that he intended to read later. He flipped the channel just as a news reporter was signing off from a story about an 18-wheeler that had wrecked out on the interstate. No injuries reported, but it shut the highway down for a few hours, and had traffic backed up. The next channel a weather reporter was standing in front of a map talking about what to expect over the next few days. The meteorologist said to expect an early season snowstorm that shouldn't be much to worry about at this time. Not surprising and Troy didn't pay much attention to it. Snow would be in the forecast now until spring. He pushed the button on the remote control again and continued to surf until he found a movie that he wanted to watch. It wasn't going to come on for a few minutes so he turned back to his emails. He opened another email from his publisher reminding Troy that he still hasn't called him back. He deleted it. I'll call him tomorrow, he thought, just as a vibrating buzz began in his jeans pocket alerting him to the fact that he had a call. There was no cell tower nearby so the phone could only work when the wireless internet router was open. He left it on all the time, but it only worked about fifty yards out from the house. Past that distance, it was too weak for a phone call to go out or come through. He reached in his pocket and looked at the caller id to see who it was. A big smile came over his face. It was his friend Craig so he slid the green square on the touch screen to answer.

"Hey, Craig, how are ya?" Troy asked.

He hadn't seen Craig in a few years, but the friends kept in touch regularly. It had been more than twenty years past now since they had roomed together in the athlete's dorm. Both were good players and had much in common even though they came from different backgrounds. Craig's family was farmers and he grew up knowing that hard work sometimes paid off, but many times didn't. He knew heartache and struggle and worked for everything he ever had. He worked so that he could live whereas, it seemed to him, that many people simply live to work. Troy, on the other hand, came from a family of white collar professionals. His father was an electrical engineer for a large company that built military wiring harnesses. His mother was a physician's assistant at the local hospital and volunteered regularly at a downtown mission that fed and housed the homeless population. The family lived in a moderate home in the Cincinnati suburbs.

"I'm doing good, Troy boy. How's life in the big woods?" his friend asked.

Troy replied, "Quite honestly, Craig, it's incredible out here! You should see the lake. Deep blue and crystal clear and the fish practically jump in your boat."

Troy laughed out loud as he excitedly talked about the beautiful setting in the mountains. It made Craig all the readier to pack up and head out on the road. Ever since Troy first told him about the place, he had wanted to visit and see it for himself. He imagined the views were spectacular and he knew were mostly unseen by people as the road to the lake and the cabin wasn't heavily travelled. Troy had told him before the road was built a few years back, the only way in was either on a four wheeler or snow mobile. Some hunters that may have ventured into the area could have walked or ridden hunting mules, but it was rare they would go into that area since all of the public hunting lands had much easier access.

"Man, that's what I'm talking about! How's the deer population? You ready to let me help you manage the herds yet?" his friend asked.

"Are you not packed up yet," Troy joked. "What about Phil, he coming too?"

Craig laughed, "You know he stays packed and sitting on go."

The men were always ready for a big game hunt, and the mountains where Troy lived certainly provided their fair share of big game. The men had spent many hunting seasons together and had traveled to several places for camping and hunting. They spent another hour on the phone talking about everything from hunting to work and just catching up. Troy told him what to expect as far as the terrain and winter clothing.

"I bet I can manage that. I'll give Phil a call and make plans to be there sometime on Friday. Opening day is that Saturday so we'll be ready. I'll load the Razor up too and a couple of Yeti coolers for all that meat I'll be bringing back. I can't wait to see some of them big northern whitetails and muleys," Craig said.

Troy knew how much his buddies loved the outdoors and neither of them would miss an opportunity to hunt whitetail deer here and possibly be mentioned in one of Troy's freelance stories that he wrote for various outdoor magazines. There weren't many places that out of state hunters could get access to that wasn't public hunting. Public hunting meant camping and roughing it which wasn't all that bad of an experience, but it also meant several other hunters could be in the area. What Troy offered was a nice warm cabin, hot food, and hot showers every night. It would be like staying at a Holiday Inn for them.

Craig and Phil would arrive at the end of the week before the opening day. Back in Oklahoma, the deer were relatively small and lucky to weigh more than a hundred pounds dressed; they didn't provide much meat to put away for the winter. Up here in the north, the deer were much larger and could weigh upwards of 200 pounds dressed with some going well over 250. Mule deer could weigh as much as 300 pounds. Troy was getting excited about his friends' visit and ready for the hunt. He had spent so much time talking to Craig that the movie he had set to watch was almost over. He clicked over to the old west channel and found a rerun of Gun Smoke on and settled in.

Chapter 4

When the show was over, Troy was getting sleepy. He turned the TV off and went to make sure everything was locked up for the night. The front door had a huge security bar lock on it that could only be used from the inside. It had to be lifted up and dropped into two iron braces on each side of the door. This was bear country. Though they rarely attacked humans, it was still entirely possible. He placed the heavy board into the metal pocket braces and then made his way to the back door to bolt it. Once he felt the house was secure he turned in.

The next few days passed without incident and Troy felt much better about being alone at the cabin, though he didn't venture far, and he always took a gun with him when he was outside. Occasionally, he glimpsed a deer in the meadow behind the house. There seemed to be an abundant mule deer and white tail population here in the mountains, though Troy had only seen a few elk since he moved in. He was told that in some instances a Shiras moose may be spotted, but a rarity. He had never seen one.

Early Friday morning Troy was startled awake by a honking horn. He rolled over and looked at the clock - 6:37a.m.; the sun wasn't even up yet. He groaned as he rolled out of bed and walked to the veranda doors. He opened the door and walked outside to see who it was - it was freezing cold. The wind was blowing down from the mountain and along the lake chilling the cove with a wintry blast. He quickly ran back in and grabbed a coat. When he came back out he could see a black Ford F-250 with a camper and trailer hauling a Polaris RZR tied down on the back. The RZR, also called a Razor, was a four door all-terrain vehicle more than capable of traversing incredibly diverse and rugged environments. The Razor was Craig's baby. The doors opened and two men stepped out of the truck.

"Hey there you lazy, good for nothing," Craig shouted with a huge smile on his face when he saw his friend on the top deck. "Rise and shine and cook us some breakfast! We just drove eighteen hours straight through with nothing more than truck stop sandwiches along the way. We're starving."

"How about I go back to bed and let you sit outside and wait until I'm ready to get up," Troy sleepily replied, but he was genuinely happy to see that his friends had arrived. They always had a good time together.

Phil laughed and joined in, "Well, there ya go, Craig, that's what you get for waking a man up out of his obviously much needed beauty sleep. Starvation!"

Troy laughed and told the men to grab their gear and he would be down to let them in. He turned and went back in, found his socks and slid them on, then pulled on his jeans and boots. He found a gray flannel and buttoned it up while he walked downstairs. Troy unlocked the front door and greeted the two men just as they climbed to the top of the steps of the porch.

"Good to see you boys! It's been way too long. Come on in here out of the cold."

Troy stepped back out of the doorway, reached down and grabbed a couple of their bags. Carrying them inside, he asked about their drive up. Craig said that he had done most of the driving and the weather was good all the way. They made exceptionally good time once they were packed up and loaded. This wasn't their first hunting trip and had it down to a well-oiled system. They stopped as soon as they crossed the state line to buy their out of state hunting licenses and tags.

"Right this way, fellas, and I'll show you where you're bunking. You can stow your gear while I get some grub on. Coffee will be ready in a jiff. I might even be persuaded to make some biscuits and gravy."

Troy helped the men get their gear stowed away in their rooms. Craig would be sleeping in the front bedroom just off the kitchen facing the lake and Phil would take the room in the back. Each bedroom had a three-quarter bath and plenty of room for them to lay out all of their gear. The closets were large and the men were able to get all of their hunting clothes hung up and put away by the time Troy had breakfast started.

Phil Jackson was the first to arrive back in the kitchen and helped himself to a cup of coffee. The shortest of the three men, he was still a large man at two-hundred and twenty pounds and a little over six feet tall. He had a dark brown complexion and black hair cut short to reveal his brown eyes, eyes that seemed to have a permanent squint due to the many long days in the Midwest sun. He was Native American, and of the A-ni-a-wi Clan of the Cherokee. A-ni-a-wi means deer in his native language and the clan was known as fast runners and hunters. He was very proud of his heritage and was, indeed, a very skilled hunter.

The two men talked about the area and the layout while Troy got out plates and silverware. Phil said that he and Craig had used Google Earth before they left and printed out a few maps of the area that they could use. Troy also wrote down the Wi-Fi code for them and explained how the telephone worked. They could both set their cell phones to use his internet in order to get service for texting or for using their built in GPS. Without the satellite receiver dish, neither would work.

"Your cell phones won't get any reception here until you get out to the state highway, but as long as the Wi-Fi is on, you can use the Wi-Fi cell phone app to make calls," Troy said.

Craig had just walked into the room as Troy was explaining how the system worked. He opened his cell phone and tapped in the code for the Wi-Fi and the connection was made. He tested it and then closed it out. No reason for using it now, he thought. Neither Craig nor Phil were married or had families they needed to contact. Craig always insisted that he would never get married and miss out on all the fun of these hunting trips. He referred to himself as a professional bachelor.

"Man that sure smells good! This is quite the setup, Troy boy. That lake is incredible."

Troy finished cooking eggs, hash browns, and biscuits and gravy for the men and told them to help themselves, they all dug in ravenously.

"If for some reason the weather turns bad, we'll probably be out of luck with the internet. You may have seen the satellite dish on the house when you drove in. It looks good, but when it's snowing, iced over, or storming hard, the signal fades to nothing. I've called the phone company and they said it wouldn't be anytime soon that they get a land-line out this way. One house just isn't a priority to 'em I suppose," he laughed.

Craig Morton was a tall man standing just over six foot four inches with broad shoulders and was strong as a bull. In college, Craig played tight end for the Wildcats and even though that was several years ago, he certainly maintained himself well with a strict workout routine. He walked back to the counter and refilled his coffee cup. When he sat back down on one of the bar stools he asked Troy about the fishing in the lake and mentioned that he'd love to have some fish for dinner. Troy told the men that he had some catfish in the freezer, but he had planned on going back out one day and catching a few steelheads.

"Sounds good to me," Phil said, as he looked to Craig for agreement. "Though I wouldn't mind dropping a line myself while I'm here. That lake sure looks tempting."

"Just one thing I need to tell you fellas," Troy said. He went on to explain to them about the rock throwing incident and what the sheriff's deputy had told him. After listening to the story both men wanted to check it out. Troy took them outside and pointed out the damage on the side of the cabin where the rock had hit it.

"Wow," Craig exclaimed. "That's freaking crazy! That's obviously what shook the house and knocked the picture off the wall. Was anything else torn up?"

The men looked around the house and all through the yard for any indication of the intruder, but came up empty. Coming back around to the front of the house Troy said, "I'll tell you, it was a little spooky. 'Course I had my Colt and I loaded every other gun I have in the house and had all of my ammo handy," he laughed.

Phil asked, "Have you recently pissed anyone off enough to try and scare you or do you think it might have been some punk kids being jackasses?"

"I really don't think it was any kids because that rock must've weighed ten pounds and I never heard any voices. I've not been here in this town long enough to have pissed anyone off, let alone enough for someone to drive all the way out here, sneak into the woods and throw rocks at the house in these freezing temperatures in the middle of the night. I turned the lights on and never seen anyone or anything and the lights around the place will light up the entire yard all the way out to the tree line," Troy explained.

Craig asked, "I'm curious now, how far do you think it is to the trees from this side of the house?"

"I don't know, maybe a hundred feet or so, why?" Troy replied.

Craig turned and jogged to the house saying over his shoulder, "I'll be right back."

While Craig went off on his sudden errand, Troy pointed out a few things to Phil around the place such as the fish cleaning station he had set up in the back and the shed where he still had all of his things stored from the move. He was explaining the backup generator to him just as Craig came back around and held something up to his eye.

"Living out here like this, it's a smart idea to have one of these bad boys hooked up on the system. Grid ever goes down, I still have power. Fifteen kilowatts and it'll run the entire house on propane with no problems. That tank sitting out there is fifteen hundred gallons and it'll last me all winter. Expensive as hell, but I wasn't taking any chances," Troy explained.

Craig shifted a few more times before moving back over to the other two men.

"Boys, I gotta tell ya. I just used my range finder and at the closest point, it's fifty-three yards to the house."

"Yeah. So what," Troy asked.

"Think of it like this, you can throw a baseball that far with no problem right?" Craig began explaining.

The others nodded in agreement.

"But throwing a ten-pound rock a hundred and fifty feet? That's not freaking possible even for an Olympic athlete throwing a shotput! Whoever threw that rock had to be standing only a few feet away, but if so, why didn't they leave any tracks. You said that what woke you up was when the big rock hit the house and shook it, but the next morning when you looked around you didn't see any tracks and neither did the deputy when he came out. I'm sure you must have spooked them off when you got up and turned on the lights. I think it was some kids like Phil said that were just messing with you and then when you fired a couple of rounds off they knew the joke went far enough and got out of here in a hurry." Craig said.

"Could be," Troy pondered. "I've not heard anything else the last few nights, so maybe."

Phil pointed out that daylight was wasting and he wanted to do some scouting before deer season opened the next day. The men went back inside and the two visitors pulled out the aerial photographs and maps to pin point some locations for scouting.

"So, Troy boy, what are your property border lines here?" Craig asked.

Troy explained to the men that he had more than twelve hundred acres that surrounded the lake area. He showed them on the map and pointed out the fence that surrounded the bottom meadow where the previous owner kept some cattle and horses. The men mentioned that they had seen a lean-to and a couple of loafing sheds on the way in and then, of course, the hay barn with the corral.

"From the hay meadow, the boundaries go up to the ridge and basically wrap around the mountain to swing back to the lake on the eastern edge. Even though my property stops at the ridge, you can hunt just about as far as you would like to have to drag a deer back because the land that butts up against me is federal and it's public hunting. You're just not allowed to build any permanent structures or have any motorized vehicles up there," Troy explained. "There are trails that go all over my property and you can see it better from the Jeep or your Razor if you're ready to go look. I'll show you where the main section lines run and from there we can scout some good locations."

The hunters readily agreed and made their way back in to get some gear. Once they had gathered what they needed they climbed in the Jeep with Troy at the wheel.

"Are you going to hunt with us any?" Phil asked Troy.

"I'll probably do some tomorrow for opening day, but I've got some work to catch up on or my publisher is going to kill me. But, I'll get out there and hunt quite a bit though."

The morning air was crisp and cold and the skies were an overcast gray. The sun was probably not going to show itself for quite some time now. It could stay this way for weeks. The weather was turning colder now and the men wore heavy coats over their Scent-Lok under clothes. Troy showed them where the trails were and had them mark them on their GPS units they each carried. The trip around the property almost two hours and he pointed out interesting topography that might yield good hunting results. He admitted that he hadn't been able to go over every acre of the place yet, but expected to in due time.

Troy stopped the Jeep midway up the rugged trail and said they would have to walk into a few areas on foot. The men split up to scout for good places to start their hunt the next morning. They agreed to meet back at the Jeep in one hour.

Troy walked with Craig up to the ridge line to look around while Phil set out on his own. After seeing where the game trails came down off the mountain Craig was satisfied that he knew where he wanted to hunt the next morning. He marked a couple of trees that he thought were good candidates and then marked his trail on the way back out as they made their way back down the mountain. As they neared the Jeep they spotted Phil making his way through the woods. Troy got in and started the engine to wait for him as Craig climbed in the front seat beside him. When they were all settled inside Troy backed up and turned the Jeep around.

"See anything interesting," Troy asked as they bounced along.

"Yeah, I found a great spot not far from where a couple of game trails cross. They come down off the ridge and make their way down to a small clearing near a mountain stream. Found the perfect tree and marked it for in the morning," Phil replied.

Craig said, "I found a nice place too with lots of tracks and rubs all over the place. I may come back out on the Razor in a bit and look around some more. I need to unload it and get everything ready for morning anyway."

The men discussed the different aspects about the weather and deer movements on the way back to the cabin. Troy told his friends that once they returned, he had planned on going out on the lake for a couple of hours and catching some fish for dinner. Troy invited them to come along, but Craig declined as he wanted to unload his ATV and scout the terrain a bit more before resting up a bit. Phil said that he'd love to go out for a bit.

"Sounds good to me, just make yourself at home, Craig. Mi casa es su casa,"

Craig laughed and said, "Now, that is a deal, Troy. Be sure to catch a lot because there may not be any food left when you guys get back!"

+++

When they returned to the cabin, Troy dropped Craig off then he and Phil gathered up the fishing gear and made their way down to the boat dock. Once they reached the dock Troy realized that he had forgotten to refill the fuel tank and put it back in the boat. He set his gear down on the dock, quickly got the tank out, and walked back up to the shed to refill it. He told Phil to just hang loose and he'd be right back. When he got to the small side door of the shed he noticed that the door was not shut all the way. *Hmmm,* he thought to himself.

Maybe one of the fellas forgot to close it when they were looking around. He found the fuel for the tank and filled it up. It was much too heavy to lug all the way back down so he sat it on a hand cart and wheeled it out. The snow next to the door had been trampled into a small brown patch of mud and as he turned to close the door he noticed something shiny lying on the ground. He reached down and picked it up, flipped it over a few times and knew exactly what it was - the broken tip of a pocket knife. He returned to the dock and loaded the tank into the boat reconnecting the fuel line. After getting settled they decided they would fish nearby for walleye since they didn't have a lot of daylight left.

While anchored just out from the dock a hundred yards or so Troy deliberated on the situation about the knife tip he found. No way had one of the fellas done that and the tip was still shiny so it must have been fairly recent. As a matter of fact, it was probably as recent as within the last few days. He knew that he was just in the shed only three days ago to retrieve a couple of boxes. He knew it wasn't his so maybe it was a bunch of kids after all that had been harassing him.

After catching several nice fish, the two men headed back in to the dock and unloaded the gear. Troy wanted to leave the fuel tanks in case they wanted to fish the next few weeks. They made their way up the gentle slope to the cabin and dropped the fish on the cleaning station. Troy went back around the house, collected the gear where they had laid it down, and took it to the shed. Meanwhile, Phil began cleaning the fish. While at the shed, Troy wanted to do a little more investigation on the door. Mainly he wanted to see if anything in the shed was missing. He stepped into the shed and flipped on the lights. He went to the large garage doors on the front and opened them to let even more light in. He checked all of his boxes and found everything in order. Nothing seemed to be missing at all.

"Why would anyone bother to break in and not take anything?" he asked out loud, to no one in particular. He thought that maybe he had scared the intruder off when he came outside for something. He searched a bit more and then noticed the stair case that led up to the loft. He didn't keep anything up there because it was still full of boxes from the previous tenant. If the realtor could get in touch with him maybe he would come back to pick them up. Troy never looked through any of it, he felt it wasn't any of his business and didn't want to intrude on another man's privacy. He climbed up, took a quick look around, but saw nothing of interest. He came back down and made his way to the side door. Just as he stepped out and closed the door, Craig pulled up outside in the Polaris. He climbed out when he saw Troy and walked over to him just as Phil walked around from the back.

"How was the fishing, Buddy?" Craig asked.

"Not bad at all. You're just in time to help us filet 'em," Troy laughed.

"Not a problem, Troy boy," Craig said. "Just let me get squared away and I'll be right over to help."

Phil told them that he needed to run inside and get the filet knives so Craig asked him if he would mind taking a few things inside while he put the Razor away. Phil turned and carried an armload of gear into the house then met the others behind the cabin at the cleaning station and pitched in. Soon they had all the fish cleaned and Troy made a batter with the beer, eggs, and cornmeal to dredge the fish in. He also made his special hush puppies for his friends. The men deep fried the fish outside in a fish fryer with a small propane bottle attached to it. They built a small fire in the pit and settled down in comfortable, wooden Adirondack chairs. The wind had quit blowing hard and it was nice sitting next to the heat of the fire.

"Fellas, I'm beat," Phil said. "Think I'm going to turn in after a good hot shower and get my stuff together for the morning. I can't wait to get in the woods tomorrow!"

Phil got up and started walking inside when Troy asked him, "Did you decide where you were going to start out?"

"Yup, I'm thinking the area on the west side up by the ridge looks like an awesome place. When we were scouting I saw quite a few signs up through there. Pine trees were torn up with rubs and I saw several scrapes," Phil replied.

The men chatted a bit longer and considered a few different options before deciding on exact locations of their opening day deer hunt. They told Troy that they had seen several deer when they were on the Razor. A few were really nice looking bucks; the kind they were after. Craig soon followed suit and got up to help extinguish the fire and head inside.

"I saw at least five deer when I dropped Phil off. I went on up and around due west of where the cabin sits. There are several game trails up there and lots of signs. One of the deer I seen was a pretty nice buck, but I couldn't tell just how big it was from where I was at. He was running at a good clip when I glimpsed him," he continued. "If you hunt that last spot, we can go in kinda backwards. You can drive the Razor, drop Phil off where he wants to hang his stand and then drop me off above that area. After that you can circle back down to your tree stand where you can hide the ATV in that clump of cedars we spotted. I think we will have a nice chance of seeing some game."

"That sounds like a good idea to me," Troy replied, as the pair walked in to the warmth of the cabin. Troy grabbed some more firewood and built the fire up for the night.

Craig said, "Ya know, I can't think of anywhere in the world I'd rather be right now. I always get excited the night before a hunt. Good night, buddy. See ya in the morning."

Chapter 5

Sheriff Blaine was of average build, wore a gray felt cowboy hat, green jacket, and boots. A scar ran across his left cheek; the result of a knife fight he broke up in a bar years ago. He was fifty-two years old, but seemed much younger yet was wiser than his age led one to believe. He sat alone in his office reading the morning newspaper, the Hawthorn Post, and drinking a cup of coffee when Deputy Billy Larson knocked.

"Come on in," the sheriff called out.

Billy greeted him, "Morning, Sheriff. Anything exciting in the paper today?"

"Nah, same ole stuff," the sheriff replied. "Mostly church gossip. Seems Twyla Dougherty's daughter Brenda is finally marrying that Jones boy."

Deputy Larson scoffed, "Bout time. They've been shacked up since they graduated high school." He thought a moment, "Seems like that's been about two years now if I remember right."

"Yes, that seems about right."

The sheriff folded his paper and set it aside. "Read your reports this morning. What do you make of that rock throwing incident out there at Isiah's old place?"

Billy helped himself to a seat before answering, "Honestly, Sheriff, I'm not sure. Who in their right mind would drive all the way out there, park where they couldn't be seen, walk around through those woods at night and pelt the place with rocks? It's too damn cold for one thing, but why would anyone want to do it? What's the motive? A prank maybe? Seems unlikely," He went on, "It just doesn't make a bit of sense to me. I think the rocks just fell off the top of the chimney."

The sheriff listened to Billy give his thoughts then replied, "I'm not at all certain about that either. I've not met the new owner yet. I hear he's a writer or something. What's your read on him?" The sheriff continued, "I mean, do you think he's a bit sketchy or is he straight up? Maybe trying to get a story out of it or something?"

"Nah, seems pretty honest to me, Sheriff," Billy explained. "'Course I was only there for about half an hour or so, but he seemed genuine; a real likable guy. Early forties, average height, blond hair, medium build. Very polite. He doesn't seem out of place like you might think a newbie would be. I really can't see that he's the type to make it up."

"I might drive out there in a few days and introduce myself. Check on things and make sure he's doing okay," Sheriff Blaine replied. "I doubt he'll have any more problems, but it may help put his mind at ease if he knows we're not far away. Besides, we don't want to lose any new residents. This town can use a few more tax payers."

+++

Troy's alarm clock woke him up at 4:30 to a tune by Reckless Kelly called Crazy Eddie. He reached over, turned the alarm off, and slid out of bed. He had time to take a quick shower before he got dressed in his hunting clothes and headed down to the kitchen to put the coffee on. He could hear the other two men rustling about in their rooms no doubt excited about the impending hunt. He turned the coffee pot on and as it brewed he looked in the freezer and pulled out some frozen breakfast sandwiches.

"Morning, Phil," Troy said as Phil walked into the room. Phil was fully dressed and carrying a backpack in his hand. He was covered in arctic camouflage from head to toe.

"Morning, Troy, coffee smells good," Phil grumbled. He was not much of a morning person, but he was always ready to go when it came time to get up.

"Where's mister sunshine? He got his lazy butt up yet?" Troy asked.

"Yeah yeah yeah, I'm up," Craig complained sleepily as he came down the hall and entered the kitchen. "Who could sleep with you two caterwauling around?" he joked. "Nah, I've been up since three. Didn't get much sleep at all last night thinking about this hunt. What time does the sun come up around here?" he asked.

Craig was also dressed in arctic camouflage. He carried a backpack slung over one shoulder. He tossed it onto a chair near the front door before walking back over to join his friends at the kitchen counter.

"Not for a couple of hours yet," Troy said. "We should be able to get out to our hunting spots about a half-hour before daylight. That is if the sun even comes up and gives us much daylight at all. I'm sure this gray overcast will linger with us for quite some time; may be weeks before we actually see the sun again."

"As long as I can see the deer I'm good to go," Phil laughed. "What's that rifle you're using, Troy?"

"This here is my trusty Marlin three-thirty-six CS in 45-70. I aim to make sure that whatever I shoot goes down and stays down," Troy answered as he held up his rifle for closer inspection.

The three friends drank their coffee and ate the breakfast sandwiches while excitedly talking about the upcoming hunt. When they finished eating, Troy sat his empty cup down on the counter.

"Are you boys about ready to head out?" Troy asked.

"I'm ready soon as I fill up my thermos," Phil said.

"Hah, you open up that thermos of coffee out there and every deer in the county will turn tail and run out," Craig laughed out loud while slapping Phil on his shoulder.

"You and your stink factor, Craig. Let me ask you something, how many trophies do I have hanging on my wall and how many do you have?"

Craig scoffed and shook Phil's hand off.

"Ah, there it is! You always go back to that don't ya? Doesn't matter that you go out hunting twice as much as I do and you take other trips without me too. So if you factor in the amount of time actually spent in the woods hunting then it's fairly obvious who the expert wild game hunter is around here. Don't ya think?" Craig said.

The two had the same friendly argument over and over throughout the years they'd hunted together. Craig stuck to his theory of buying the most expensive hunting clothing on the market because it worked better to block his human scent. Phil was of the notion that no matter where one hunted these days, the deer are not distracted by human scent. He always said that he'd taken more deer than anyone else wearing a pair of jeans and a jacket and never bought into the hype of the more expensive it is, the better it is.

Troy laughed at his two friends and said, "Boys, you haven't changed a bit. Let's hit the woods before you two square off. We better put our hunter safety vests on here fellas. Once we get out in the woods you don't want to be digging around for it and put it on in the dark."

The men gathered their packs and rifles and left the warm confines of the cabin stepping out into the frigid Rocky Mountain night air. The cold air stung their lungs and their breath hovered a moment before floating silently off into the darkness. They put their ear buds on for the short wave radios and pulled their balaclava's down over their heads. Each of the men carried a flashlight in their pockets, but also one that strapped around their heads that would shine a flood light a short distance. They used these for finding their way through the woods in darkness. After they loaded the Razor with their gear, Craig climbed in beside Troy and then Phil jumped in the only back seat that still had room. All three men carried metal tree stands made for climbing up trees and stowed them on the rear of the vehicle. They could climb as high as they wanted to, using them to get well above the game trails and out of site. They had used these literally hundreds of times over the years.

The Razor purred along the snow covered terrain with no problems. When they got further up the trail and deeper into the woods, Phil leaned forward and tapped Troy on the shoulder. He spoke in low tones to keep his voice from carrying.

"This is good right up here by that big oak tree," Phil said as he pointed to the tree.

Troy pulled the Razor over and let Phil grab his gear and rifle and jump out.

"Good luck buddy. Radio me if you see anything," Craig said, as Phil headed off to find his hunting spot in the darkness.

"Will do. Good luck you guys," Phil whispered just loud enough to be heard over the purr of the engine. He walked into the woods using his head lamp. The sun wouldn't be up for another hour.

+++

Phil made his way slowly through the woods and found the game trail that he had marked with reflector buttons. He quietly made his way up the game trail pausing every few minutes to take a breather and listen for any sounds that might alert him to deer moving in the woods. He didn't want to give away his position and spook the deer that may be bedding nearby. Hearing nothing, he pushed on. He wanted to reach the tree before daylight. Twenty minutes later he reached the tree he had marked for his hunting stand. He had scoped out a narrow-leaf cottonwood the day before that would be good for climbing. He liked to be as high as possible and the cottonwood seemed like the perfect tree to get him up fifteen to twenty feet with minimal limb cutting. The bark was a smooth pale green and turning grayer. The climber stand that Phil used could climb a grease slick telephone pole easily, so the smooth tree trunk presented no problems.

+++

After dropping Phil off Troy gassed the Razor and moved off at a safe clip. The spot where Craig wanted to hunt was quite a ways off and they would have some rough trail to get over, especially in the dark. The lights on the ATV were super bright LED's, but the men did not want to use them all so they opted for the smaller red fog lights. Occasionally, the men would stop and switch on the overhead spots when they came to a particularly rough patch in the trail. The cold air wasn't really a worrisome problem with the cold weather clothing they wore. The men knew how cold it could get up in the mountains and dressed with layers of thermal underwear, wools socks, and light to heavy outer wear. They knew the only worry would be any exposed skin areas so they each wore neoprene masks.

When they reached the next drop off point Troy decided to do a radio check and make sure that Phil was set in his position. He whispered into the lapel mic, "Phil, this is Troy. Do you copy?"

"Loud and clear, buddy. Just got to my tree and getting ready to climb up. Sun should be up soon. You boys set yet?"

"Just now dropping Craig off at his spot," Troy said. "It will take him about a half an hour to get to his tree stand. I should be at mine down by the barn about that same time. I'll holler back on the radio when I get there. Let me know if you need anything."

"Roger that fellas, good luck." With that, Phil had signed off and continued getting his gear ready. He used a climbing stand that allowed him to literally climb straight up a tree. He preferred being about fifteen feet off the ground. Most game would never spot him as he sat quietly watching the trails below. It was a great vantage point when hunting in the woods.

"I figured he would already be up in the tree by now," Craig said softly as he lifted his tree stand up on his back, picked up his rifle and stepped back from the Razor.

"He's probably walking slowly since he's only seen the trail during the day time. Once he gets his bearings he'll be okay," Troy replied.

"Probably so. I'm gonna slip on down to my spot. I marked the tree good so I can find it in the dark. Call me on the radio when you get set." Craig turned and trudged off into the woods.

Troy put the Razor in gear and cracked the throttle to move out slowly. He switched on the normal driving lights since he no longer had a co-pilot. After about ten minutes of motoring through the rough terrain he stopped the vehicle and got out to relieve himself. The ATV was still running and the driver side door hung open. When Troy finished his business he turned to walk back, but stopped short. Just out of range of the driving lights stood something very large!

Troy's chest tightened and his breathing suddenly came in short gasps. His pulse quickened and adrenaline pumped through his body. He could literally feel himself shaking as it coursed through his veins. He didn't know if he should stay still and silent or if he should jump in the ATV and edge up closer. He realized he was frozen in place and he should get back over to the quad where he could get his hands on his rifle. He started edging slowly to the vehicle, but didn't take his eyes off the giant figure on the trail. The figure moved again ever so slightly. Troy could make out the silhouette moving in the dark fringe, but still had no idea what it was. As he stepped over an old tree that had fallen he suddenly tripped and almost fell. He took his eyes off the dark mass for only a moment, but when he looked up, it was gone.

The animal had slipped off as silently as it appeared. Troy was even more nervous not knowing where it went. The forest was thick with underbrush in this area and he couldn't see more than a few feet past the trail. He reached the vehicle and pulled his rifle out of the case and checked to make sure it was loaded. He also reached into his pack and pulled out his Colt 1911 and made sure he had two full clips. Laying the rifle in his lap and the pistol in back in the paddle holster at his side, he moved forward. He reached the spot where the massive figure had been standing, stopped the quad, and looked around. Seeing nothing close, he switched the engine off so that he could listen more clearly.

After a few minutes of intense looking and listening, he reached in and turned on all of the lights in the quad and switched his head lamp on as well. The sun was beginning to come up by now, but in the woods it was still dark enough to need the lights. Troy investigated the ground in the area thoroughly, but found no tracks of any kind. He had hoped to see the tracks of a heavy white tail, but the trail was very hard and rocky here and not much good for tracking anything. The little amount of snow on the ground never penetrated the floor in this location deep in the woods. He walked up the trail on both sides for quite a ways, but could find no traces of the animal whatever it was. He motored on down the mountain and found the spot where he could park the ATV and hide it in cover. From there he would walk in with his own climber tree stand. He turned off the motor and hid the key in a magnetic box under the dash. Next, he checked his pack to make sure it was secured to the tree stand and slung it on his back. He snapped the closures around his chest and settled the weight. Satisfied with his packing, he grabbed his rifle and headed to a stand of tall pines overlooking a very well used game trail.

+++

Phil had been in his tree stand watching the game trails that crisscrossed below him for about half an hour when he heard a call come through the radio. He had the ear pieces lying close to each ear, but not in so that he could hear the ambient noises from the woods. He reached up and put one of the ear buds in and keyed the mic open.

"This is Phil, what was that again?"

All three men were approximately a half mile apart from each other in their hunting stands. "Hey Phil, Craig, this is Troy. Just letting you boys know that I'm in my tree stand now. Sun's up, but with this overcast weather it sure doesn't seem like it."

Phil was the first to reply, "Hey T, Phil here. I'm settled in. They should be on top of us soon!"

A moment later Craig chimed in, "Copy that. Damn, it's cold sitting up here in this tree stand. Looks like more snow coming in."

The temperature had dropped over night down into the single digits, but at least the wind wasn't blowing too much in the deep woods.

"Ah suck it up, buttercup," Phil replied. "You've been begging Troy to come up here to hunt these big mountain deer and now you're bitching like a little, whiney girl."

Troy keyed his radio, "Knock off the chatter you two and start watching for trophies that are probably walking all around you."

+++

Craig was sitting perfectly still, intently watching the game trails when he heard a soft rustle in the leaves behind him. The animal was slowly making his way toward him, but Craig dared not turn his head fully around in case he may spook it away. At this point, he had no idea of what it could be. As the animal moved closer to him Craig checked his hands on his rifle to make sure that he could throw the safety off and take aim if it was the trophy buck he wanted. The animal seemed to have veered off to his left and was now moving away so Craig decided to take a look. He turned his head very slowly with his eyes wide to see as much area as possible on his peripheral. He spotted the big bodied buck about twenty yards away from his stand. It was a good eight-pointer that probably would go about one-eighty, but it wasn't the one he was after. He had spent a lot of money to come up to Troy's and he wasn't leaving with anything less than a nice, big buck. He let this one go thinking there would be another one soon.

+++

A half-mile away Phil sat comfortably in his tree stand twenty feet off the ground. He was an avid hunter and had been on several big game hunts including a trip to Alaska to hunt Dahl sheep. The weather there was much more intense than the range where they now hunted. In

Alaska, he was guided across mountains of incredible, frozen terrain that only wild animals had ever walked. The day treks covered several miles on foot and many more on horseback. He was accustomed to roughing it in the wilderness, but nothing could compare to the frigid temperatures and harsh conditions he had faced there.

Like the others, Phil was statue still as he scanned the woods while only moving his eyes. His breath could be seen floating away and disappearing into the tree branches. He was thinking about one of his hunting trips a few years back. He had hunted hard for several days and it was the last day of the hunt. He had thought for sure that he would be leaving empty handed on that trip. He was climbing out of his hunting blind and no sooner had his feet hit the ground when he heard a sound on the trail not forty yards away. When he looked up he knew it was the buck that he had been waiting for. It turned out to be one of the biggest ones he had ever taken.

About mid-morning Phil saw a movement out of the corner of his eye. He unhurriedly reached down and took his field glasses out of his coat where he kept them and scanned the area. He kept the binoculars inside his first layer coat to keep them from banging around making unnecessary noise or getting caught on a limb; also to keep them from fogging up in the weather. As he scanned the area, he caught site of the animal. He knew it was a whitetail deer by the markings of its tail, but he couldn't make out if it was a buck or a doe from where it was standing in the brush. He could see its tail clearly through his binoculars. One of the most identifiable characteristics of the deer is their tails. They are fringed in white and they run with their tails up in a very distinct way. Mule deer have black tips on their tails and run with their tails down. Typically, the mule deer will run in a very distinct pattern that makes them look like they are hopping on all four feet. The ears of the mule deer are much larger and distinctive, but Phil had not had a chance to see the deer's head well enough yet.

He waited patiently as the deer moved around, foraging. Finally, he saw it. It was a beautiful buck moving closer his way. Suddenly, a flutter of sound came from the leaves off to his left. Phil glanced over and saw two smaller does scampering through the brush playing with each other. The buck looked back down, but was hidden by trees. Phil waited patiently for the buck to move in closer so that he could get a better look. Finally, it stepped out from the trees and he was able to see it was a very nice buck though he still could not make out its antler points. Legally, he could only take a whitetail buck if the deer's antlers were at least five inches in length. This one had no problems with that minimum requirement, though he still wasn't able to get a positive look at how big and how many points it carried.

The two deer below him were mostly playing and in no way concerned that Phil was camouflaged only twenty feet above them nor were they seemingly aware of the buck nearby. One of the does pranced directly beneath Phil's tree stand and stopped to sniff around. He could hear it bleating. Ba'eh , Ba'eh! The buck was moving closer to check out the doe. Phil still had his field glasses in hand with his rifle resting on his stand across his lap. He moved very slowly to put them away. From this distance he could see the buck move in cautiously. This was a trophy worth taking and he wasn't going to pass it up. Adrenaline pumped through his body and his ears seemed to block out every noise around him in a deafening silence. He moved his hands gingerly to his rifle. The rifle was a Winchester Model 70 Safari Express 375 H&H Magnum. He was shooting a 235 gr load which was more than capable of humanely bringing down these northern bucks. At a velocity of almost 3,000 fps the round was perfectly suited for the task at hand. Phil brought the rifle up to his shoulder, careful to not let the deer see his movement. Looking through the Swarovski Z5 scope on the rifle, Phil could see the buck clearly. He put the reticle directly over the deer's vitals, took a deep breath and let half out, paused and slowly squeezed the trigger.

Chapter 6

The wind had picked up considerably and it was getting much colder now. Troy thought that he probably should have layered up a little more, but he was still fine with his artic camo hunting clothes he had on. His base layer kept him snug and he also wore a full face cover that not only protected his skin, but was also camouflaged. In the spot he had picked out, he was able to overlook an open field where a small pond stood near the edge. The pond itself was obviously used by deer and other wild game and the trails all converged near it. It was a great vantage point for hunting, but unfortunately it was also open to the cold wind that came whistling across the field. As he scanned the area from one side to the other he had seen a couple of small bucks and several does step out into the field to munch on the grass. The sky had become more white than gray and soon it began snowing, small flakes at first, but soon becoming the size of a quarter. Troy had not watched any weather reports so he wasn't sure just how much snow was expected, but up here it could be a lot in a short amount of time.

The radio had been silent all morning. None of the men wished to try and chit chat for any reason. They were too busy concentrating on watching for game. Troy was looking at the pond when he noticed a new comer. A lone elk cow appeared and sauntered over to the pond for a drink of the cold water. She was huge and must have weighed in at a good four-hundred pounds or so. As Troy sat there watching her it occurred to him that she could've been what he saw on the trail earlier that morning.

Troy heard the crack of a rifle shot echo through the woods. The cow he was watching looked up and then quietly moved off into the cover of the brush. He could no longer see her at all now. When he heard the shot his body automatically stiffened and his pulse raced. He knew it was one of his friends and if they had missed their prey then perhaps the sound of the rifle would scare the game in his direction. He waited and watched intently for several minutes.

+++

Craig, a silent sentry on the game trail not far away, heard the report of the big bore rifle. From the direction of the sound he knew that it would have been Phil shooting. In his excitement, he thought about radioing him immediately, but figured he had better wait until Phil called for them first. He didn't want to disturb him if he was still in hunter mode. He knew his buddy would call when he was ready. Craig sat motionless, the only sign of his presence being the heated breath that vaporized every few seconds. He had his binoculars up to his eyes scanning in the direction from which the shot was fired. He was experienced hunting with a group in this fashion and he figured if Phil had spooked anything else with the shot then it may come past his position. He was ready.

+++

Phil's shot was perfect! He saw the buck jump and arch its back as it spun away and quickly loped off into the brush. The other two deer beneath him heard the loud explosion of the rifle and with raised white tails, flagged out of the area as quickly as possible. Phil's heart was racing and felt as if it would literally jump out of his chest. He knew he made a good, clean shot. He would be patient, though, and wait for a bit before he started the climb down to go track the animal. The deer may lie down nearby, but if for some reason the shot was off even just a little, it might be spooked to jump back up and run off again. Phil patiently waited and knew not to push too soon. He would wait for twenty minutes or so before going after it. The buck would eventually lie down and Phil would have no problems retrieving his game.

Craig waited for ten minutes, but couldn't stand it any longer and radioed Phil.

"Hey, Phil? Did you get one?" Craig asked.

"Yeah boy and he's a nice one. At least a ten pointer and huge! Wow, what a deer."

"Do you need any help?"

"Not yet, he ran after I shot, so I'll let him go lay down and bleed out. Don't want to pressure him back up. If he runs off up that mountain we may never get 'im. I'll get down in about twenty or thirty minutes and go track 'im. I'll holler if I need ya when I do."

"OK, buddy, congrats! I'm gonna wait right here then and hope his big brother comes by me," Craig laughed over the radio as he scanned the game trails beneath him. He was glad for his friend and would be the first to offer assistance.

Troy chimed in, "Congratulations, Phil. Can't wait to make some of that deer jerky! I'm gonna wait 'til you give me a holler and I'll bring the Razor up to drag it out."

Troy then signed off and remained diligent of the trails in his watchful gaze. It may take a few minutes for the forest to quiet back down, but he knew it wouldn't take long. He had been hunting many times when shots rang out nearby and deer that he'd been watching never even looked up.

Phil waited patiently and allowed his heart rate to slow. After twenty minutes, he unloaded his rifle, slipped it into a rolled up soft case and lowered it softly down to the ground. He stood up and spun around in his tree stand, adjusted his safety line and inched his way to the ground. It took another ten or fifteen minutes to climb down, but once he reached the forest floor, he wiggled out of the stand and left it attached to the tree. Picking up his rifle, he pulled the cover off and reloaded the gun as a precaution. He wanted to make sure that he was ready if for some reason his first shot didn't take the deer down cleanly. He would be able to get another shot. He certainly didn't want a wounded animal out there.

Phil made his way over to the spot where he had shot the deer and found blood on the ground. He was a highly skilled tracker, but in the snow the animal wouldn't be difficult to track at all. He started slowly walking down the trail being as silent as possible. About twenty yards further along he found more signs in the snow of the deer's path and knew he was on the right track. Every few feet he spotted signs and now the crimson trail was obvious to spot. Tracking the animal was simply a matter of following it. He stopped and scanned up ahead and spotted his prey. "Woo hoo," he shouted excitedly as he hurriedly walked to the downed animal.

Phil looked at the buck's eyes and could see them wide open and glassed over. He knew the animal was down and it was a quick and clean kill. He excitedly checked the buck's rack and counted twelve points. The animal was massive and should provide a hundred and fifty pounds of meat or more. He did not hunt for the sheer sport of it. Fact is he hunted venison as a main source of meat for the entire year. It wasn't simply about a trophy on the wall for him, though it was certainly nice to have taken such a beautiful animal.

He removed his warm hunting gloves and set his pack on top of a large boulder with a flat top overhang on it. The rock was huge and rested just above a slope where a game trail wound around it and down towards an arroyo in the ridgeline. Next, he opened one of the pouches on the pack and took out his field dressing kit and a pair of latex gloves. He used them to keep as much blood off of his clothes as possible. As he bent down over the huge animal he was surprised to hear a massive crashing noise behind him. He quickly spun around to see what it was. Suddenly, everything went dark and he slumped to the ground.

+++

Troy realized that it had been over an hour and still had not heard from either of his buddies on the radio.

"Hey, Phil, have you fallen asleep or did you just plain miss?" he asked with a chuckle.

After a short moment he called again. "Phil? Do you copy? How about you Craig?"

"Yeah, I can hear ya, Troy," Craig responded. "I heard something earlier in the brush, but couldn't make out what it might have been. Thought he would've called by now though."

"Me too! Guess I lost track of time. He's probably tracked that buck all the way out of range."

"That's my guess," Craig said.

"OK," Troy said, "I'm climbing down and heading your way. We better go give him a hand before this snow really starts piling up." He began stowing his rifle and lowering it to the ground. Once his pack was lowered he keyed the mic once again.

"I don't think it's supposed to get too bad, but it could still cover up our tracks. If you aren't too familiar with the area, it may be pretty easy to get turned around."

Craig replied, "Alright, buddy, I'll climb on down and be waiting for ya."

Chapter 7

Craig had just reached the ground when he heard the Razor coming down the trail. He left his stand hanging on the base of the tree and made his way out to meet Troy. He had called on the radio a few more times for Phil, but never received a reply. He was certain that the radios were just out of range or the weather was keeping them from transmitting very well. The terrain also would play a factor in the distance the radios could work. If Phil had gone down into a ravine or over the ridge, then he probably couldn't receive or transmit far at all.

Troy could see Craig's bright orange hunting vest and hat as he walked through the woods to meet him. He stopped the Razor and got out to help Craig put his pack away in the back.

"Still no sign?" Troy asked, as he pulled his balaclava down under his chin.

"No, and I've been calling for him. He may have gone over that ridge and out of range of the radios. I think we can find his tree stand and may be able to track him. He said his tree was about a hundred yards straight in from where we dropped him off. It's not too rugged so we can probably get the Razor through without too much problem. From there we can track him down."

Long as this snow doesn't cover up the trail, he thought silently to himself.

Troy climbed into the passenger side and let Craig take control of the ATV once they had secured their rifles. The Razor purred down the trail and in a few minutes had reached the area where they had dropped Phil off that morning. The men watched the snow falling through the trees to the ground get heavier and with a silent look knew what the other was thinking. If they didn't find him soon, things could get bad!

Craig turned and guided the ATV through the woods toward the area where they thought Phil's tree stand may be. With the snow coming down so heavy now it would be easy to miss it so they had to go slow and stop every so often to look around. The tree stand would most likely still be attached to the tree with a cable lock on it. The men were very familiar with this routine. They would hunt the same location for a few days leaving the tree stands attached to the base of the tree. The problem was locating the exact tree. In the thick brush, they could pass right by it and never know.

About a half hour later Troy gave Craig a nudge.

"Hey that might be it. Let's drive over that way." Troy said as he gestured off to the right.

Craig turned the Razor in the direction Troy was pointing and pulled up to the tree. Attached to the base about three feet off the ground was Phil's climber tree stand just as they had figured. Unfortunately, the snow had started coming down much heavier now threatening to cover any tracks the man may have left. They climbed out of the ATV and looked around. Troy gave another call out on the radio.

"Phil, this is Troy. Do you copy?"

His request was met with silence.

"His pack isn't here and from the best I can tell he went off in that direction." Craig was pointing toward a large pinion tree. He knew from the way Phil left his tree stand and the heavy boot tracks leading off, that this had to be his trail. As they climbed back in the Razor and headed in that general direction Craig reached down and turned the heater on. If nothing else, it would keep their feet warm even though they wore plenty of layers of clothing, along with neoprene face masks and ski hoods.

"We'll have to hurry if we want to find him before the weather really gets bad. This snow is getting heavier by the minute and once it reaches the ground in these woods it'll get tough as hell to find any tracks underneath it."

"Who knows," Troy said. "Maybe we'll come across fresh tracks in the snow and it'll make it easier. Surely he still has his orange vest and hat on."

"We can hope!" Craig replied as he started off in the direction he indicated.

+++

The snow falling on his stocking cap melted and ran down his exposed face. He was groggy and his head was pounding. Phil moved his hand to his head gingerly pulling his cap off and felt sticky wetness in his hair. He hoped that it was just the snow and sweat, but as his vision cleared, he could see the blood stain on his hand. He rolled over to his side and tried to sit up.

"Ahh, damn!" he said, and lay back down. He waited a moment before slowly sitting back up. This time he had more luck. He ran his hand over his head a few more times and felt around. Satisfied he was otherwise in good shape, he staggered to his feet. He still had his radio ear buds around his neck, but the radio was nowhere to be found. He must've dropped it somewhere. He searched his pockets and discovered his GPS unit was also missing. "What the hell! Where's my gun?" he asked out loud. His vision had cleared, but he was feeling dizzy and a little disoriented. He looked around trying to get a bearing on where he was. The last thing he remembered was taking a shot at a really nice buck.

He made his way over to a fallen tree and sat down on the log to gather his thoughts. He rubbed his aching head as he sat in silence and watched the snow falling all around him. He simply could not remember anything after shooting the buck. He rested for a few minutes as he scanned the area for anything familiar. The snow had been falling and covered any tracks that he may have left and nothing seemed familiar. He stood and decided to make a sweep of the area to search for his pack and rifle. He knew he would never leave that behind, no matter what.

After fifteen minutes of searching he stopped and made note of his current location and familiarized himself with it as best he could. He decided he should try to find his way back to the game trail and that, he knew was going down the mountain side and definitely not up. He was confident he wasn't lost. From there he should have no trouble finding his way off the mountain. The snow was beginning to fall more rapidly as well as the temperature. He looked around one last time for his backpack, but had no luck. Unsure where he was exactly and no sun to guide him, he started off in a direction he thought was east and heading down. The terrain was unfamiliar to him, but he wasn't worried about finding his way out. He was more worried about losing his rifle.

+++

Troy called out on the radio repeatedly, but heard no reply from Phil. He and Craig had been searching for a few hours and it was beginning to get darker from the winter storm. The two had separated and were combing the area in a crisscross pattern.

"Craig, do you copy?" Troy called out on the radio.

"I gotcha, Troy," Craig replied.

They were about a hundred yards apart and the snowfall was heavy, even under the dense canopy of trees and scrub brush. It had already covered the ground completely now and they were finding no new tracks.

"I wonder if Phil decided to walk back to the cabin," Troy speculated. It was more of a question than a statement. "He's good out here in the woods even though this is unfamiliar territory." Craig said. "I bet he's already hiked back to get the truck to haul that buck outta here. Don't know why he wouldn't have waited on us though!"

"Maybe so, but I hate to just head back without knowing. I think one of us should stay here just in case he comes back," Troy said.

"Good idea," Craig replied. "Let's head back to the Razor."

Soon the men had made their way back over to the ATV and from there decided that Craig would drive back to the cabin and look for Phil while Troy waited in Phil's spot in case he returned.

+++

The sheriff drove along the state highway and turned off onto a blacktopped county road. He followed it until he reached an old barn that had fallen years ago from neglect. There, he took a county road that wound up through the mountains toward Troy Turner's cabin. The snow was coming down much heavier now, but he wasn't worried in the 4X4 Excursion he drove. It shouldn't take more than half an hour to get to the place now.

The big vehicle bounced along the old dirt road when the sheriff suddenly slammed on the brakes. It took the big truck a few seconds to come to a jolting stop due to the wet snow on the road…

+++

Troy had waited at Phil's tree stand for the better part of an hour before Craig returned. He pulled up on the ATV and left all of the lights on to shine as brightly as possible. Maybe Phil would see the lights and know where to come.

"I looked everywhere at the house. He wasn't there and doesn't look like he has been either," Craig shouted through the stocking cap he wore over his head and face. He was nervously revving the engine as well. "The truck's still parked in the front and I didn't see any tracks in the snow. I drove all around the perimeter of the yard, nothing!"

"Where in the world could he be?" Troy questioned aloud.

"I don't know, buddy, but it's not like him," Craig said worriedly.

The storm had set in and caused a premature nightfall to take hold. The men couldn't see anything in the woods without the use of lights. Neither of them ventured a guess that something terrible could have happened to Phil, yet each knew in the back of their minds that he could have been tracking the wounded animal over the mountain ridge and gotten lost. If that were the case, it would be incredibly lucky to find him before the storm had cleared.

"It's getting dark and I hate to leave here without him!" Craig exclaimed. "Why don't I take you back to the cabin? I'll stay in the Razor and search for him and you can take my truck. Turn on all the LED's and let 'em shine. Hopefully he'll see 'em!"

Troy jumped in beside Craig and together they drove away in a mad rush throwing snow out from under the all-terrain tires of the Razor and sending it flying behind them.

+++

Phil was a skilled woodsman, but he was disoriented from the blow to the head. He was weak, thirsty, and hungry and had a terrible headache. He had lost his backpack which had food and water in it. Everything he had in the way of survival was what he had on him. He decided to try to find his tree stand, but the terrain itself wasn't familiar and the snow had covered his tracks completely. He looked around, but could not see very far in the distance as the snow was heavy even in the deep woods. He couldn't see any of the mountain peaks in order to orient himself so he used his feet to feel the ground beneath him and guessed at the direction that he thought felt sloping down and started walking. Eventually the terrain turned more drastic in a downward slope and he knew he was headed on the right path.

The sky was getting dark and the snow still coming down. He had no idea how long he had been walking. At least a couple of inches covered the ground now. Phil trudged along a game trail in the woods and felt very alone. He was angry more than he was afraid, and the anger drove him forward. He had no idea what had happened. Had he slipped and fell? Maybe hit his head on a rock? He just couldn't remember! When he looked up from the path he saw headlights! Phil half ran and half stumbled through the woods as quickly as he could in the direction of the headlights. They were getting closer to him so he took off his orange stocking cap and started waving the driver down.

+++

Sheriff Blaine threw the gear shift into park and jumped out of the big four-wheel drive. Just off to his right a man had staggered out of the woods wearing hunter safety orange with blood on his face. He was only about ten feet from the road and waving an orange cap frantically to get his attention. The sheriff ran over to meet the distressed hunter. "What the hell happened to you, son?" he asked.

"Not sure exactly, but sure glad you came by when you did!" Phil panted… "Was hunting with some buddies, shot a nice buck and then…well, can't remember a damned thing after that! My rifle's gone, my pack is missing. I have no idea what happened. All I remember is shooting that buck. After that, it's all black."

"Let's take a look at that injury." The sheriff moved over to Phil and began to triage him.

"I've got a first aid kit in the truck. Let's get you cleaned up a bit and we can take a closer look. It's too damn cold to stand around out here in this snow and we need to get you warmed up."

The two men climbed into the truck and as the sheriff cleaned Phil's wound he began to inquire for more detail. "Looks worse than what it really is. Who are ya? What's your name?"

After a few seconds Phil responded. "Phil. Phil Jackson, sir. I'm staying with a friend, Troy Turner, up at his cabin not far from here."

"Head wounds tend to bleed a lot. Tell me, do you have a headache? Are you dizzy or nauseous?"

"Yes sir, my head is pounding…ears are ringing too."

Phil felt like his head was the size of a basketball. As hard as he tried, he could not remember a thing after tracking the buck he had shot.

"Have you been throwing up any?" Blaine asked him.

"No, not really. Just dizzy as hell."

"Well, I'm no doctor," the sheriff paused, "But I think you may have a concussion. I know the cabin where you're staying, but we need to get you to the ER first. I'll send a deputy out to let your buddy know where you're at."

The radio signal was weak as far out of town as they were because of interference from the mountains. After driving for thirty minutes, the sheriff was able to reach his deputy and explain the situation to him. The deputy assured him that he would get in touch with Turner and have him pick up his friend at the emergency room in town. On the trip in, Phil relayed everything that he could remember, but it wasn't much more than he had already told the Sheriff. He simply couldn't remember anything about what happened. It was a long drive, but the sheriff made good time and pulled into the hospital emergency room entrance just as it was getting dark.

Deputy Larson had been patrolling the county road near Troy's turnoff, locally known as Reed Road, when he received the call from the sheriff. He turned his truck around and headed for the cabin. From his location it wouldn't take him more than half an hour to reach it even in the snowy weather.

Chapter 8

Troy had been slowly driving along the property edges in Craig's truck searching for Phil when he saw the headlights approaching. He drove back out to the driveway to meet them at the cabin. It was Deputy Larson. He pulled up beside him and the deputy rolled his window down.

"Hey, Mister Turner, Sheriff sent me out here to let you know he found a guy that says he's a friend of yours. He's taking him to the ER in town. Nothing serious, but the sheriff found him walking near the county road not far from here with a concussion. Must've fallen and banged his head or something. Should be alright, but he's taking him in to see the doc just as a precaution."

"Wow, that's good to hear! We've been looking for him since this morning! Hang on a sec deputy I need to radio..." He trailed off just as he noticed the Razor's headlights coming up the road behind him. "Well, there he is now. That's our friend Craig on the ATV there."

Troy explained to the deputy that he had two friends from Oklahoma that were staying a couple of weeks to do some deer hunting. They talked a few minutes about the rock throwing, but Troy assured him that they haven't seen or heard anything else the last few days. Troy got out of his truck and greeted Craig as he parked the Razor close to the driveway and walked over to the pair.

"Craig, this is Deputy Larson. He said the sheriff found Phil. Apparently he has a concussion and he took him to the ER. We can follow the deputy back to town and go meet them there."

Craig shook hands with the deputy.

"Where did he find him? Any idea what happened?"

Deputy Larson said, "I'm not exactly sure yet, but once we get to town I'm sure we'll get some answers."

"We'll follow you, Deputy," Troy said as he climbed in on the passenger side of Craig's truck. Craig jumped in behind the wheel, put his seat belt on and followed the deputy's truck out of the drive.

"Damn!" Craig exclaimed. "What in the world could've happened? I bet the goofy bastard didn't put his safety harness on when he was climbing out of that tree stand and fell. Sheriff probably found him walking around out in the woods like a nut job after banging his head."

The two men traded theories on the way into town about what could have happened. Troy speculated that Phil simply got turned around when the sheriff found him. They hoped though, that Phil at least had his hunting license on him. Troy took the opportunity to show Craig around as they followed the deputy. He pointed out the ski resorts and the roads that led the hotels and shopping centers. They pulled up to the hospital and parked. Troy climbed out of the truck and walked around to the front where Craig waited on him.

"I'm guessing this hunting trip will leave a lasting impression on him and the sheriff."

Craig suddenly had a puzzled look on his face.

"You don't think that whoever attacked your cabin the other night could also have attacked Phil in the woods? I'd sure like to find out just who the hell it was!" He continued, "I just hate a coward that hides."

"Nah, no way," Troy said. "I can't imagine anyone doing something that stupid with a man that has a rifle and watching everything that moves in the woods. That's just asking to get shot."

"Yeah, you're probably right. It's just weird as hell. I've hunted with him ever since we were kids and

I've never known him to fall out of a tree stand or trip and fall to the extent of getting his ass lost. I don't know what to think really. I guess we'll find out soon enough."

+++

Phil sat on the edge of an examining table in the emergency room of Hawthorn County Medical Center. The sheriff stood in the corner of the room listening to the doctor as he examined Phil. The physician was asking him a series of questions about his name and dates, obviously looking for signs of a concussion. After a few minutes, a nurse returned with a set of x-rays.

"Good news and bad news for you, Mr. Morton." The doctor looked intently at Phil over the top of his bifocals for a brief moment and then turned to Phil and said flatly, "The good news is it's only a mild concussion. The bad news is you're probably going to have a hell of a headache for a while. I can give you something for that, but you're going to want to lie down and rest. That means no hunting for a few days. I don't want my handiwork to pop loose for any reason. I only had to use a couple of stitches so they shouldn't leave much of a scar. We can take them out in a week to ten days."

"What? No way, doc!" Phil pleaded, with a look of total disappointment on his face. "I've come all the way from Oklahoma to hunt with my buddies! These out of state tags and licenses aren't cheap! I'll take it easy I promise, but I've only got a few weeks before I have to head back for work. I planned on hunting and doing some fishing."

"I understand, but as a doctor I'm recommending a few days of rest. Your pupils aren't dilated and you seem to be walking just fine. No other issues I can see, but it's going to take a little time to recover completely. So, do this for me because I know you're not going to stay out of the woods. At least be sure to come back and see me in a few days and when you leave here today if, for any reason, you don't feel right, if you start having vision problems or more headaches get here right away. No alcohol and no driving either. Got it?"

Just then Deputy Larson, Craig, and Troy walked into the ER.

"Sheriff, I rounded 'em up and brought em in," the deputy said with a smile as he stepped into the room.

"Hey Phil, what in the world did you do? Fall out of your tree stand?" Craig asked him when he saw him sitting up.

"Nah, no way! I'd never fall out. I always use my climbing harness... unlike you," Phil replied.

"Well, what did happen to you?" Troy asked.

"That is the million-dollar question," Sheriff Blaine interjected.

Troy and Craig only then noticed the sheriff and introduced themselves. "Sheriff, I'm Troy Turner and this is Craig Morton. I live out on Hawthorn Lake. Phil and Craig got here yesterday to stay for a couple of weeks to do some hunting. Appreciate you bringing Phil up here. We've been out in the deer woods looking for him all day. Got pretty worried when we couldn't find him."

"Pleasure's all mine, Mr. Turner." The sheriff shook the men's hands and continued, "Seems your friend took a bad lump on the noggin. I found him wandering around in the woods out by the county road that leads up to your place. He had ad blood all over his face and head. From the way it looked, I thought he had been in an argument with a mountain lion or something!"

"I must've been a sight to see," Phil said. "I can't remember, but I swear someone must have hit me from behind!"

"I'll say!" Craig joked. "You're a sight to see when you 'don't' have blood all over your face. And besides, who could have sneaked up on you in the woods?" Craig asked incredulously as he turned to the sheriff.

Troy turned to the sheriff and asked, "Sheriff, not sure if you know anything about a report I filed the other morning about someone throwing rocks at my cabin in the middle of the night, but I wonder if this might be related? Any idea if these two things could be linked?"

"Oh, I don't think so. I'd be at a loss for motive. I'd think if it were an attack by an animal he wouldn't be here right now to tell about it. He doesn't have any other signs of an attack by a bear or lion. Nah, I'm betting that your buddy here tripped and hit his head. I might come out there tomorrow and take a look around if you don't mind though...long as this snow will let up a little anyway. The weather reports said we could be getting a foot or two of fresh powder."

"I don't have a phone at the cabin yet, but my cell works through my internet when I'm there. As long as the dish isn't frozen over with snow or it isn't raining too heavily anyway. That keeps it from working. The weather plays hell with it."

"I understand. I have a dish for my television too. Cable doesn't go out of town very far and without my dish I'd go nuts," the sheriff laughed.

"Just let me know when and I'll make sure I'm there to meet you," Troy replied. "The boys came up to hunt whitetails so we may be out in the woods. Probably come in about noon for some lunch though. Why don't you come out about then and I'll have something for us to eat and some coffee on."

"Sounds like a plan to me, Mr. Turner. Appreciate the offer."

"Please, call me Troy. Mister is way too formal for me." Troy laughed then turned to his buddy, "So, when are they springing ya, Phil? Where's your gear?"

"That's something that's really bothering me! When I woke up, I didn't have it with me and I looked everywhere for it! I just can't remember what happened exactly."

The doctor finished up with dressing Phil's laceration and turned to the men. "He's about ready to be released now. The nurse will have a few papers to sign first and then you can get him home. Now, as I told him, my orders are plenty of rest, but I know you hunters all too well. At least rest as much as possible and nothing too strenuous or that headache might get a lot worse."

"Thanks, doctor. We appreciate your help patching 'ol Phil up. He's getting older so he's obviously getting clumsier every day," Craig joked.

The doctor turned and walked out the door speaking over his shoulder, "You bet, fellas. That's what we're here for. The nurse will be right back. Take care, gentlemen."

As the sheriff and Deputy Larson left the room the nurse came back in with the necessary paperwork. Phil signed where she asked him to and then told him that he was free to leave. Once the nurse left the room Troy looked intently at Phil.

"What the hell really happened out there? I know better than you tripped and fell"?

"I gotta tell ya, buddy - it beats the hell out of me. I'm not lying about not remembering what happened. I don't think I tripped!" Craig exclaimed. "I mean, think about it. If I had tripped, most likely I would've landed face down with my arms out to break my fall. Right? Unless I possibly slipped going down a slope and fell backward, but I just don't remember anything at all."

Craig walked over to the window and opened the blinds to check out the weather.

"I don't know, man. It's just weird as hell. I've taken plenty of falls before, but never cracked my head on soft, damp dirt enough to get knocked out!" Phil said.

Troy replied, "I think someone or some 'thing' cracked your ass! The question is who or even why? We need to go back out there and take a look around in the morning. We need to find your rifle too."

"Damn! I completely forgot about that! That's my baby. We've got to find it. Maybe we can find it tonight?" Phil asked.

"I'm thinking we had better get on the road real quick if we want any chance of finding that rifle tonight! The snow has let up, but still, even out there in the thick of the woods it'll be heavy in places. Let's get going," Troy said.

The men quickly headed for the door as Phil put on his coat. They climbed into Craig's 4X4 and sped out of the parking lot making a beeline for the cabin to get the Polaris. The snow had stopped, but it was dark and cold. The men would have to hurry to find any tracks in the snow at all. They talked about where to start looking and agreed that the best place would be at Phil's tree stand.

Chapter 9

The county road out to the cabin was fairly empty and the men passed very few vehicles along the way home. Phil kept repeating the story of shooting a really nice buck, climbing down to track it and then nothing, but pitch blackness. After a few minutes they all sat in silence thinking about what may have happened and hoping that they would be able to find Phil's rifle. Troy was the first to break the silence.

"Well, maybe we'll get lucky and find that rifle tonight. Craig, let's get back and jump on the Razor and head out to Phil's tree stand. Phil, do you feel up to leading us out there? Maybe it will jog your memory when we get there?"

"Oh yeah, I don't think that'll be a problem. That's a very expensive rifle and I'm not about to let you two knuckleheads go it alone. Besides, the headache is mostly gone now and I'm afraid if we let lay there all night the scope may freeze up and break some of the optics."

"It's going to be a pretty tough go of it to find it at all," Craig chimed in. "No telling where you were when you fell. The sheriff said he picked you up on the county road and that's got to be at least a half a mile from where you were hunting if not further. The way I figure, we could start at your tree stand and see if you maybe remember where you shot that buck and go from there. If you can't, then we look for signs of blood on the ground. The snow isn't too deep yet out here in the open areas so maybe deeper in the woods it will be more sparse and easier to see."

The three friends agreed that if they concentrated their search efforts between Phil's tree stand and where the sheriff picked him up they should have a pretty good chance of picking up Phil's trail and finding the rifle. They knew the only thing that could prove to be a hindrance was the fact that driving around in the Razor through that area could scare the game away for the hunt the next day. They could also possibly run over the rifle in the dark and bust the stock or the scope.

"Why don't you and I walk in front of the Razor and let Phil do the driving?" Craig asked Troy.

"Sounds like a plan to me," Troy replied. "I still have my stinger flashlight with me. Do you have yours?"

"Hey, fellas, I remember something!" Phil suddenly exclaimed. "I think I know where that buck was down. I remember seeing a big rock with a tree growing on the side of it and it looks like it's almost a part of it! I can see it in my head. When I went over to the buck I remember laying my rifle there propped up against it. I'm sure it's not too far from my tree stand."

"Awesome," Craig said. "That narrows it down some. Maybe we won't have to worry about trying to track your footsteps. Especially since we've already driven all over the place in the Razor! We can just look for that big ass rock then."

The truck turned down the lane that led them across the lake. They could see that the lights from the cabin were still on when they crossed the bridge. Troy had left them on when they went looking for Phil thinking that it might help to lead Phil home if he could see the light. Craig maneuvered the truck up to the cabin. The Razor was still parked in the driveway where he had left it earlier to climb in with Troy. It had some frozen snow piled in the seats, but it was an ATV designed for the elements. It was nothing that couldn't be knocked off. The men climbed out of the truck as Craig said, "Hey, if you boys want to grab us a thermos of coffee I'll go over and get the Razor warmed up and cleaned off. I put my rain poncho down across the driver's seat when I parked it earlier, but there's nothing except snow in the other seats. It'll take me about fifteen minutes to get it heated up and ready."

"That'll work, Craig. It'll take about that long to get some hot coffee ready," Troy replied.

Phil went inside with Troy and sat down on the couch in the living room while Troy busied himself in the kitchen making coffee. He wasn't feeling bad, but he had mentioned a few times that he was feeling a bit weakened by the ordeal. He could see that Troy was keeping a watchful eye on him so he reassured him that he was feeling fine. After a few minutes, Troy brought him a cup of hot coffee and a sandwich.

"Maybe this will help you feel a little better."

"Thanks, Troy, I appreciate it."

Craig made his way to the Razor while the other two men went inside. When he reached the ATV he found the key and started the vehicle. It was extremely cold outside, but the Razor had a fresh new battery in it that was made for these conditions and it started with no problems. He let it sit and idle while he pulled the poncho out of the driver's seat and cleaned the snow from the others. Next he reached down and turned on the Maradyne heater he had installed on the machine. Most ATV's didn't come with any type of heaters built into them as a standard option package so Craig had an aftermarket heater installed. It came in handy on many occasions, especially up north. The heater only put out about 26,000 BTU's, but it kept their feet and legs warm inside. The Razor had a half windshield and full doors. They could pull down the plastic door side windows to keep some of the cold air out. They would be quite comfortable.

He walked around and checked all of the tires and made sure he hadn't cut any of them down. He was checking the rear passenger tire when he suddenly heard a blood curdling scream from the mountain that made the hair on his neck stand straight up. He stood up and looked around while at the same time he knew he couldn't see anything in the dark. The scream lasted about five seconds and the longer it did, the more uncomfortable he became. He figured it must be a mountain lion. He had heard them before, but this one seemed different though he couldn't quite figure out why.

Craig jumped in the driver's seat, drove up to the porch of the cabin and revved the engine up to let the others know he was ready. A few minutes later Troy and Phil showed up at the door with two thermoses of coffee and a handful of sandwiches. Troy climbed in the front passenger seat and Phil in the back.

"Thought you might like something to eat," Troy said as he handed Craig a ham and cheese sandwich on rye.

"Damn, I didn't know how hungry I was until you pointed it out," Craig said. "Let's get going, fellas. It's getting late and I aim to hunt first thing in the morning."

Craig took a bite of the sandwich and gunned the Razor to life, throwing snow behind them as they flew out of the driveway. They got to the trail turn off and headed up the mountain side.

"Did you fellas hear that mountain lion scream earlier?" Craig asked over the baffled engine pipes of the Razor.

"No, I didn't hear it. I doubt you could hear much of anything inside that cabin. Those logs are solid," Phil replied.

"Nah, I didn't hear anything either," Troy said as they jostled around up the mountain trail. "Phil's right. You can't hear anything. You can't hear a horn honk inside if the doors are all closed."

"Well, it scared the hell out of me when I heard it. I was checking the tires when it screamed. It had to be a mountain lion. I've heard people say they scream like that. It probably high-tailed it out of there once it heard the Razor start up!"

The men drove up the dark mountain trail that led from the back of the barn to the ridge of the mountain. The snow was heavier now, but the temperature wasn't unbearable still in the low thirties. The ATV had no trouble negotiating the terrain with its knobby tread on the tires. They passed by the small pond where Troy had hunted earlier that morning and continued over the more rugged area of the trail which slowed them down a bit. About a half hour later Troy let out a muffled shout over the engine. "Hey I think that's our spot. Do you fellas want to walk in from here or drive to Phil's tree?"

They decided to drive into the woods until they reached the tree that Phil was hunting and then go on foot from there. Craig turned off the trail and followed the path where they had driven earlier that day. The trees weren't as thick in some areas so the going was quicker and in a short time they arrived at the tree where Phil's stand was still attached. It also still had the reflector buttons he used when he first scouted it. Craig and Troy got out of the Razor and started walking ahead and off to the side. It was equipped with bright halogen off-road lights and flooded the entire area nearby. Troy could hear the purr of the engine as he walked twenty yards to the right. Craig was about the same distance on the other side though Troy was unable to see him most of the time. He could see his stinger flashlight, however, as Craig moved around through the brush looking for the big rock.

After only a few minutes of searching Troy spotted a large rock off to his right and made his way over to check it out. Using his stinger he searched the trail for any sign of activity. Moving slowly and completely focused on the ground, Troy never noticed the huge hulking figure standing before him in the darkness.

+++

Troy moved his light back and forth, slowly searching the ground for signs of boot tracks, broken branches, dropped items or anything that would let him know that Phil had been there earlier tracking his buck. As he moved toward the rock he had spotted earlier, his light shined on something odd, something out of place. He stopped walking and shined his light up further up on a tree when suddenly the tree moved. Troy made eye contact with the creature and was suddenly paralyzed. He was screaming in terror, but the sound never left his throat! His body coursed with adrenaline and every muscle was flexed taut. He felt like he was having a heart attack, but could do nothing about it. His breathing stopped and his mind was in full panic mode making his vision go in and out as if a dark tunnel was closing in on him. He could no longer hear anything as the adrenaline flowed through his veins and his heart thumped rapidly in his chest.

The enormous creature stood at least eight feet tall with dark matted fur covering its body. A ferocious demonic face with red eyes and a large bulbous nose stared intently at Troy. It made a menacing gesture toward him and let out a fierce shriek that sent an unnerving chill throughout Troy's entire body. Unfrozen, his fingers unexpectedly let go of the flashlight in his attempt to flee. When the light hit the ground, Troy was finally able to move, but so panicked with fear that he was clumsy. He tripped reaching down for the flashlight and fell to his knees. He grasped for the light and heard the creature let out a deep low guttural growl as it moved toward him. Troy screamed, but this time out loud. His hand closed on the barrel of the light and he shined it in the direction of the beast. It was gone. He quickly shined the light all around him, but couldn't see the creature anywhere. He stumbled to his feet and ran.

+++

Craig was walking on the left side of the Razor when he heard the animal's scream. It echoed throughout the dark, snow covered woods and sent eerie chills down his spine. Was it a cougar? Then he heard Troy. He knew immediately that his shouts were filled with fear and panic and he turned in the direction he thought they were coming from. The screams sounded several yards away; he shined his light in their direction, but was too far away to make out any details. The Razor was too loud to hear anything in the woods. He yelled over at Phil to get his attention. He motioned for him to go fast! Phil had sat frozen, listening intently to the disturbance and then hit the gas once he figured out what it was. He cut a donut track in the terrain and threw snow in a rooster tail behind him. Phil could see Troy running back toward the ATV with his flashlight dancing crazily through the woods and steered to cut him off. He was about fifty yards away from Troy, but knew he could get there quickly. Craig started running as fast as he could. He thought for sure that a mountain lion had attacked Troy. None of the men had bothered to bring a rifle with them since they wouldn't be hunting as it was illegal at night. They didn't want to get in any major trouble for what the game wardens referred to as spot light hunting. The only weapons that any of the men had on them were their hunting knives. They knew those would be no match for a major predator like a mountain lion.

Phil brought the Razor incredibly fast up a small embankment and caught several feet of air. The engine revved hard and when he landed he lost control as it slid hard in the snow covered pine needles. Fortunately, the underbrush stopped the ATV's mad slide and helped Phil right the craft on top of the ridge near Troy. Troy grabbed for the top headache rail and flung himself in, yelling at Phil. "Get out of here now! God it's right behind us! You gotta get us out of here! Go! Go! Go!" he screamed.

Phil made a beeline for Craig and slowed just enough for Craig to fling himself in the back seat. Phil hollered, "Strap on those seat belts. It's going to be a hell of a ride, boys!"

He punched the gas and headed for the trail as fast as he could safely handle the ATV. The men scrambled to put their safety harnesses on, but it was easier said than done as the vehicle bounced around the rugged terrain.

"What is it Troy? Was it a mountain lion?" Craig yelled as Phil hit the gas and flew into a dip in the trail and then shot airborne coming up the other side.

"God no! It was... it was...it was huge! Oh my god! I can't believe it."

Troy was in a crazed panic and the others had a difficult time understanding what he was trying to tell them. They had never seen such a look of fear on their friend's face. They knew him well enough they trusted they should be moving away from it as quickly as possible if it had frightened him this much.

"What was huge?" Craig yelled. "What in the hell did you see, Troy?"

Just then Phil fish-tailed the Razor around a sharp curve in the trail and immediately slammed on the brakes, flinging the others forward in their seats. Directly in front of them on the trail was a downed elk. The bull was enormous and wasn't moving. The Razor's lights illuminated the huge beast and the men could see that it had several gaping holes on its hind quarters. The wounds were jagged like large claw marks had torn the hide and flesh. It was almost nauseating in its savagery. The bull didn't seem to notice the ATV sitting right in front of it, but the men could see the breath of the animal. They knew it was still alive, though not for long judging from the extent of the gashes.

"Damn!" Phil exclaimed as he sat back in his seat and looked intently at the animal. "Surely this isn't what we were running from? A damn elk? Seriously?"

Troy was in a serious panic mode pleading for Phil to hit the gas.

"No, no that's not what I saw. You've got to believe me. We're not safe here. Go around it. You gotta get us out of here and now!"

Phil released the brake and put his foot on the gas to move around the bull. The huge elk never moved as the ATV slowly drove around it.

"I have no idea what could have been large enough to have done that, but I do know that whatever it was, it's still out there and it's probably very close. I wonder if it was a Grizzly, Troy. Do you think that's what it was you saw?" Craig asked. He continued, "Either way, Troy, you may be right. We need to get the hell out of here right now and get back to the cabin before it tries to eat our asses next!"

Troy hunkered down in the passenger seat holding his arms and making himself as small as possible. He was visibly shaking and obviously terrified.

"You've got to believe me. It wasn't a bear or mountain lion. It was something I've never seen before. It was huge and standing on two legs like a man, but only bigger. It was completely covered in black fur. I swear it was no bear fellas. I swear it."

"I don't know what you saw, Troy, but something tore the hell out of an eight-hundred-pound elk.

Mountain lion or bear, it's not something that we need to be meeting up without here in these damn woods without a gun! Let's get home and get there now!"

Once Phil maneuvered past the dying elk and back on to the trail he punched the gas and let the Razor scream down the path. The exhaust had baffles on it to help quiet the motor when they were hunting, but when the throttle was opened up, the ATV was all performance and it could be heard. The men kept a wary eye out along the trail and Craig used his flashlight to watch behind them, especially when Phil had to slow in some areas to maneuver past obstacles. Finally, the men could see the lights from the cabin in the area below. The cabin was still some distance off, but the men felt some comfort in being able to see it as they fled the woods. The next part of the trail would hit a switch back and go along the top of the ridge before going down toward the lake and then finally to the cabin.

The men had to decide whether to cut through the woods and continue moving down toward the cabin or follow the trail that led back up in the direction they just fled; back to where the beast was that had terrified Troy and all, but fileted the elk?

"I don't care what it was that Troy saw. I just don't want to go back in that direction! If it was a bear or a cougar we don't have a thing in the world to defend ourselves with. A little hunting knife is all I have."

"My god, no!" Craig exclaimed. "I'm not feeling too good about going back up. I bet we can cut through and come out closer to the cabin. It's mostly pines in that area so maybe we can get lucky and go straight through. We'll blaze a new trail."

Troy was still huddled in the front seat watching the trail intently as if he could see into the darkness. In his mind he was reliving the moment when he encountered the creature. Could he have been mistaken? Could it have, indeed, been a bear? They do stand on their back legs, and when doing so can stand well over eight feet tall, but bears don't have manlike features in the face. They have long snouts with fangs designed to rip apart meat. It was not a bear. He just knew it was not a bear. The creature wasn't anything like he'd ever seen before. It resembled more of what he only thought were wild imaginings of campers all over North America. It looked like what everyone always called Sasquatch!

Chapter 10

Phil turned the Razor in the direction of the cabin. It was still quite some distance off, but with any luck the men could get there within an hour. Cutting through would be quicker than taking the trail back up to the ridge where it circled around by the lake. The underbrush and trees weren't too thick, but still the Razor wasn't as fast or nimble navigating the forest. Phil veered sharply to the left and the sudden movement flung the men hard against the doors.

"Sorry, fellas. Doing the best I can here. This stuff is thick."

"Why don't you pull up and let me take over, Phil?" Craig stated more than questioned.

"Alright, I'm feeling a little dizzy anyway," Phil replied as he brought the Razor to an abrupt halt. "Maybe you can get us out of here a lot faster than I can."

"Damn sure gonna try. Don't know what the hell it was that Troy saw up there, but I don't aim to stick around without a gun to find out!" Craig shouted over the engine of the Polaris. "Better buckle up back there, Phil. Gonna get this thing in a low altitude orbit."

Just as Craig hit the gas, a huge rock flew out of the darkness and smashed into the nose of the Razor with a loud explosive bang. The rock bounced off and landed on the trail by the driver's side. Craig instinctively hit the throttle and steered the Razor hard to the left just as another huge rock slammed into the ground beside the ATV.

"Get us out of here! Go! Go! Go!" Troy screamed.

The Razor rooster tailed snow, mud, and pine needles thirty feet in the air as Craig gunned it to escape the dangerous projectiles. The men were ducking tree limbs as best they could, but the snow flurries had turned to a near whiteout. The ATV lights reflected brightly off the snow, making it much harder to see.

"Where's it at?" Craig yelled out. "I can't see anything! That ain't any goddamn bear out there! Bears don't throw rocks!"

"Just get us out of here; go that way!" Phil yelled, pointing to his left as soon as he spotted an opening.

"I'm trying! I'm going to get us back to the trail so we can move faster."

Craig turned the ATV again, but this time headed back to where he thought the trail wound. He maneuvered the vehicle around larger trees, but anything smaller in diameter than a baseball, he drove straight over. The Polaris had a large metal skid plate beneath it to protect the engine and drive mechanisms from rocks or other dangerous objects. Snow flew from the knobby treads as he gunned the engine over the underbrush and rocky terrain, flying over dips and jarring the passengers with hard landings.

Craig knew he was headed back up the mountain side, but he also knew that whatever was below them wasn't friendly. His best option was to backtrack up the mountain slope then circle around before heading back down toward the cabin. With any luck, they would cross the main trail where they could go much faster. He suddenly came up on a large rock outcropping and veered around it. Just as he spun the wheel, the Razor's front tires hit a hole in the ground that jarred the steering wheel out of his hands. Panicked, Craig reached back and jerked the wheel. He hit the gas and the ATV slid sideways in the snow then careened up on two wheels. Craig did everything he could to bring the craft back down and steer out of the tip-over, but the bumpy terrain refused to allow it. He held it steady for a brief moment and then as if in slow motion, the machine tipped on to its side where it came to rest.

+++

The ATV lay on the driver's side with the sound of the engine gasping its last breath. The silence and the moment after were amazingly eerie. Craig reached up and turned off the ignition as Troy grasped frantically at his waist to unbuckle his seat belt. In doing so, he immediately fell over the center gear console and on top of Craig. The two men were wildly trying to untangle themselves when Phil unbuckled and scrambled out of the Razor. Phil reached down and pulled Troy up on his feet careful not to trample on Craig. Finally, Craig was able to reach his harness buckle, release it and stagger to his feet. The ATV weighed only about sixteen hundred pounds, but due to the incline where it came to rest, the men were not able to use their combined strength to lift it. The ground was simply too slippery with mud and snow.

"Dammit, fellas, let's get it pushed back over. We gotta hurry, that thing's not gonna be far behind!" Craig stated in a hushed, but agitated tone.

The three men reached out into the darkness to find a hand hold on the Razor in order to push it back on to all four wheels.

"All at once on three," Craig said. "One...Two... Three!" The men pushed hard, but struggled to raise the machine. Weighing over sixteen hundred pounds coupled with the slippery snow and mud they couldn't get it to budge enough to gain any leverage. They were standing on a downward slope from where the ATV had flipped on its side. Craig stood up and shook his head in disgust.

"I'm going to turn the lights back on so we can see what the hell we're doing here."

Just as he hit the lights Troy gasped and pointed. "It's already caught up to us," Troy whispered, with a look of shock and terror on his face. Phil quickly looked up and scanned the area where the lights were shining.

"Where is it? I don't see anything. Where'd it go?"

Troy just pointed into the woods. "It went behind that tree."

Craig reached down to his side and felt for his hunting knife.

"Look around, fellas, and see if you have any kind of weapon at all. I still have my hunting knife, but that's about it."

Troy snapped out of his distant stare and felt around on his side.

"Oh my god, I completely forgot about this!" He pulled his Colt 1911 out of its holster. "I grabbed it when we stopped at the cabin earlier. Guess I just forgot all about it when I saw that - that thing!"

"How many rounds do you have?" Craig asked.

"Seven in the clip, but it has one in the chamber. I don't have the extra clips though."

"Well that's better than a knife!" Craig stated intently. "Stay down behind the Razor. We'll keep the lights on so we can see a little anyways. Where are your flashlights?" he asked the men as he reached in to his own coat pocket and pulled out two flashlights. One was a handheld stinger, but the other one was attached to a band that he wrapped around his head and turned on.

"I have mine," Phil said, and reached for it in his pocket. He turned it on and shined the light into the trees all around the vehicle.

"I saw it up there in front of us when Craig turned on the lights. It moved behind that big tree going in that direction. I don't see anything now, but I swear I saw something moving and it was big!" Troy was pointing off to their left side, up the mountain slope and just out of reach of the Razor's lights. The falling snow was starting to come down much harder and faster making visibility even less now.

"I guess we can assume that whatever it is, it's out there watching us just out of the light. That tells me that whatever the goddamn thing is, it's intelligent and it's hunting us!" Phil exclaimed in a hushed, but intense voice as the men kneeled behind the overturned ATV.

"Then we need to move fast. We gotta find something to use for leverage and pry up on the Razor to flip it back up. There's got to be a tree around here close that we can cut down and use."

Craig reached into the back of the Razor and opened the toolbox. Upon doing so, all of the contents crashed out with loud metallic clanks rattling through the frame of the vehicle and falling to the ground. He quickly kneeled down and dug through the pile of tools. When he pulled his hand back, he was holding a limb-saw. Normally he used it for cutting small branches so he could get his stand up the tree unhindered.

"Phil, shine that light over this way," he demanded.

Phil turned the light toward the woods behind the ATV and shined it on several different trees before Craig saw the one he wanted

"There!"

The small tree was about six inches around with not many branches. It would make a perfect lever if the men could get it cut down and moved over to pry up the ATV.

"We need to get over there and cut that tree down fellas. Troy, are you good with that Colt?"

"Damn right. Let's go," Troy responded as he switched on his own flashlight. The men moved quickly together and got to the tree in a few seconds and began sawing at the base of it.

"Phil, you and Troy will have to watch every direction. I'm gonna work as quickly as I can, but it's going to take a few minutes with this limb saw," Craig told them. "If you see it, don't shoot until you know without a doubt you can hit it! Conserve that ammo. It's all we've got!"

Phil and Troy used their flashlights and kept scanning the area all around them. No more rocks were thrown in their direction and the men had not heard anything in the woods. The snowfall was heavy and the only sound that could be heard was the hissing as it hit the air and collided with the ground.

After about ten minutes of sawing, the tree finally fell. Craig moved to trim the top and the small branches along the length of the small tree. He could see well enough with the headlamp he wore around his forehead. It wasn't as bright as the stinger, but he needed to be able to use both hands. He trusted that the others would keep a watch out and alert him to anything that moved.

"If you see it, don't miss!" Craig said, as he sawed off the top of the tree. The tree slipped in his grasped when the top section fell off with his sawing. He instinctively reached down to grab it, but it was too heavy to hold. He yanked his hand back in pain as a splintered limb slashed a huge gash through his gloves. Muttering under his breath, he quickly picked the hand cut lever up and began sawing off the small limbs again, not paying any attention to the nasty wound. Once he had the tree cut and trimmed to the length that he wanted, he asked for help to move it over to the ATV. It was about twelve feet in length now, yet still quite green and heavy. Troy walked in front with the pistol in one hand and his flashlight in the other keeping a watchful eye out for the creature.

The wind was blowing harder now stinging the men's faces as they trudged back over to the overturned vehicle. It was extremely cold and now the men could really feel it on the exposed skin around their eyes.

"We've got to move fast, fellas. It's way too cold to be out here," Craig said as he bent down to drop his end of the log. Phil dropped his end and stood to lock around.

"What's the plan?"

"We don't really have anything big and solid enough to use as a fulcrum but I think we may be able to pile up a few of these rocks scattered around here. Let me dig some of this snow and mud out from under the roll cage and then we can slide the log in place. Phil, you find a couple of the biggest rocks you can. And look for flat ones."

"I'll see what I can find, but Troy, you keep that gun handy and whatever you do, don't shoot me!" With that statement, Phil used his flash light and started searching around the ATV for some rocks. After a brief moment he found a large fairly flat sided rock he thought would work. He reached down with his empty hand and tried to nudge the rock up, but it was frozen to the ground in the snow. Phil stood back up and shined his light all around the ground looking for something to help pry the rock up with when a quick flutter of movement caught the corner of his eye. He wasn't sure what it was, but he knew he saw something move for just a split second. He quickly moved his flashlight beam back and forth scanning the area deliberately and carefully, but could see nothing further. He heard no other sounds, but the snow, wind, and trees. He turned to tell Troy and Craig that he thought he saw something when he heard the first shot!

+++

Troy was covering Craig as he worked to dig out around the ATV so that they would be able to get the log under it and gain some leverage. He stood just behind the Razor where he could keep an eye on Phil as he searched for a rock. Phil had gone about fifteen yards away from the overturned ATV, but Troy could still see his flashlight moving through the darkness.

"Ugh, this damn snow and mud is slippery as hell, but it's also hard as a rock just underneath it. I have a small camp shovel in the back here if I can get it out." Craig grunted. He moved over to rummage through the back of the ATV and after a few minutes exclaimed, "Found it!"

Troy was turning to look back at Craig when his light shined directly into the face of the creature. It was standing not more than twenty yards away. Troy pulled the Colt up instinctively across his other hand and with the light still aimed at the beast, squeezed the trigger. BOOM! BOOM!

The report of the .45 caliber pistol was deafening. As soon as he pulled the trigger Troy's ears popped and a loud ringing caused him to wince in pain. The creature moved incredibly fast for its size and Troy could not keep his flashlight on it. The huge, hairy beast darted into the trees swiftly and silently. Troy was searching the woods so intently that he never heard Craig shouting at him.

"Troy, where is it? What are you shooting at?"

"It was right there coming up behind us! Oh my God, it's huge! Oh my God, Oh my God!" Troy stammered rapid fire like a machine gun. "I think I hit it. I know I hit it. There's no way I could've missed at that range! No way! And it didn't even flinch!"

"Calm down Troy, I don't see anything now and I don't hear anything. Maybe you killed it. If not, maybe you scared it off," Craig said. "Just calm down and be ready if it comes back around. Phil, you find a rock yet? Let's get this damn thing rubber side down!"

Phil hurried back carrying a large flat rock. He walked around to the low side, and together with Craig's help, set the rock near the roll cage of the ATV. In this position they would be able to get the log under the bars and lift the ATV up on its wheels again. Craig cleared away a little more of the frozen earth so they could get the log further under it to get the largest lift potential. Once the log was lowered into position Craig called for all the men to get on the end of the log and start prying up the machine. He would stay on the front of the crew so that once the ATV started coming up he could move in closer and use all of his strength to push it onto its wheels. Phil took up a position on one side of the log and Troy the opposite so that together they could keep it from sliding back and forth.

"On three," Craig said. "One, Two, Three!" And with a big heave, the men began to slowly lift the Razor up. Once it got about three feet off the ground, Craig moved closer to the craft and lifted on it with his hands. Using the combined weight and strength of all three men, the ATV finally came up and bounced back down on the wheels.

"Damn right!" Craig exclaimed. "Let's get going."

The men scrambled to get in the ATV with Craig at the wheel. Troy ran around to the passenger seat.

"I hope this thing starts up," Craig said as he reached down and turned the key. The engine roared to life immediately and Craig feathered the throttle a few times to rev the engine. The pipes gave off a loud bleating and popping sound and the Razor started running smoothly.

"I'd have bet a dollar this thing wouldn't have started up with the way our luck is going," Phil said, as he began to climb up into the back passenger seat. He reached for the grab bar and put a foot on the side rail to climb up just as he felt something grab his shoulder. He was slung several feet backwards onto the ground, landing with such force that he completely lost consciousness.

"Hurry up, Phil, let's get moving!" Craig hollered over the loud blat of the engine. Craig suddenly felt the ATV start shaking and he looked back to see a huge dark mass grab Phil by the shoulder and throw him like a rag doll yards away from the Razor. He couldn't make out the beast's face, but he could tell that it was a much taller than the ATV and apparently incredibly strong as it began shaking it like it was a toy!

Chapter 11

Instinctively, Craig hit the gas causing it to lurch forward, screaming like a banshee into the night and sending snow, mud, and rocks high into the air. The creature let out an enormous scream that was guttural and low pitched followed by a short series of what could be described as loud grunts or coughs. It began chasing the ATV and followed them for quite a long distance before stopping. Craig was driving as fast as the Razor could navigate the treacherous mountain, hitting low branches, trees, and rocks in a harrowing attempt to evade the creature. Troy, with his Colt in hand, fired at the animal until he ran out of ammo.

"That's all I have, Craig, I'm empty! We've got to go back and get Phil. He's back there somewhere and whatever that thing is, it knows where he is!"

+++

Phil picked himself up off the ground. His chest was hurt and he was trying desperately to catch his breath while watching the Razor rocket out of reach. He had reached up to grab hold of the ATV and jump in when he felt a clamp around his shoulders. In the next instant, the beast had gripped him so incredibly tight and threw him to the ground with the force of a freight train! He strained his senses to listen for any sign of the giant predator. He couldn't see anything in the pitch black other than the lights on the Razor as it bounced its way through the woods, but he could tell that the beast was giving chase. He never really saw it, but he could hear the report of the pistol shots being fired so he knew it must be chasing them. At least that would give him a few minutes to try and get away. He assumed it was a bear by the sheer size of it, but why was it not hibernating? What could have driven the beast out? Within a few minutes the ATV was out of site and he could no longer hear it. He knew that Craig and Troy wouldn't simply leave him there, but he also knew that they would have to shake the beast first before they could return to pick him up. He had to think it was a bear and that it couldn't possibly be what Troy insisted it was. It was NOT a Bigfoot, Sasquatch, Yeti or whatever else all those crazy people often reported seeing. He simply did not believe in it. It had to be a bear. No other explanation.

That didn't negate the dangerous position he was in right now however. He had two choices. Stay and hide with hopes not to be found by the creature or run and pray that he could find his way to the cabin before the beast found him! He hoped that Craig and Troy would return for him just as soon as they could shake the beast, but he also knew the bear could come back and that it would be able to smell him and locate him easily. He was at a huge disadvantage. This was the bear's backyard and he knew the area well. Phil was a stranger to the area and certainly did not have the astute senses that an animal would have. He was also blind in the dark and he dare not turn on his flashlight yet. Should he climb a tree he wondered? Bears can climb trees, he whispered to himself. He thought. A bear that big though, maybe the bigger they got the less likely it was for them to climb trees. I need to do something though. He knew it was the beast that caught him and knocked him back. His chest was feeling the blow and he was sore. He knew he would have a very nasty bruise on his back and he also knew he didn't have much time before it came back!

+++

The beast seemed to have stopped chasing the ATV after a few minutes, but the men had no intention of stopping to look around. They were intent on getting back to their friend as fast as possible. Unfortunately, they needed weapons first and they prayed that Phil would be able to hide long enough for them to retrieve weapons before they came back.

"I hope Phil can find somewhere to hide!"

"Me too, I didn't get a good look at that thing, but whether it's a bear, Bigfoot, or Sasquatch, it's pissed off!" Craig shouted.

Troy had just finished helping Craig get his harness on when Craig mentioned the Sasquatch and he reached down to buckle his own harness.

"Craig, I'm here to tell you, that's no damn bear! I saw it face to face and it looked straight at me with some kind of human like intelligence. It weirded me out big time. I've never believed in a Sasquatch or Bigfoot or whatever you want to call it until now. I know you think I'm crazy, but that damn thing looked me straight in the eye. It wasn't a bear!"

The cabin lights came into view as the men sped crazily down the mountain side dodging in and out of trees barely missing huge boulders and laydowns.

"There's the cabin, Craig. Make your way over to that tall stand of pines. We can pick up the trail there and then the road is just past that."

"You got it!"

Craig guided the Razor down the mountain slope and found the trail just where Troy said they would. The wind had lain down a little though the snow was still falling hard and fast. The valley where the cabin rested now lay peaceful and quite. It was a huge contrast to the wild chase and cacophony of terror that had taken place only a few minutes earlier. The night was still very cold, but tolerable. After a few minutes they came to the road that wound straight to the bridge over the lake and the cabin just beyond. Craig bounced the ATV over the bridge as fast he could push the 4-wheeler and headed straight for the cabin; where the road was didn't really matter at this point. He steered a fast, straight line for the front porch. Troy had already unbuckled his seat harness when Craig slammed on the brakes and slid to a stop inches from the front steps.

"Get that door open and turn on every light in the house you have. I'm going to grab a gun out of my truck and get to the barn. We have to refuel the Razor if we're going back to find Phil!"

"Roger that!"

Troy made his way up the cabin steps. He reached under one of the chairs that sat on the porch, found the hidden spare key, and unlocked the front door. Once inside, he turned on all of the outside lights, made sure to turn on all the lights in the cabin, and opened the window blinds. If Phil was trying to get back to the cabin in the dark, he could possibly see the lights from the mountain to help navigate by. Once he had completed that task, he went to the den where he kept his guns and ammunition. He reached for the 45/70 and found a full box of ammo. He loaded the rifle and then reloaded the 1911 pistol and grabbed the extra clip he kept for it upstairs. He could hear Craig outside and stepped out onto the top deck to check on him.

"Hey, Craig, did you get it fueled up already?" he asked.

"Yeah, she's full. I got my pistol out of the truck but I only have the two clips for it. Do you have any more forty-five rounds?"

"I have a few boxes. I also have my forty-five seventy Henry with fifty rounds and a shotgun."

"Good, I'll run in to grab my gear and meet you downstairs."

Craig finished getting the 4 wheeler ready, ran up the cabin steps, and met Troy in the living room where Troy had lain out his guns and ammunition.

"I'll grab my other guns out of my room. We need something to carry them in when we go back out...something to strap them down to keep 'em from bouncing all over the place and losing 'em! There are only two scabbards on board the Razor."

"I have some bungee straps in the top kitchen drawer. Maybe we can use them to secure the rifles." Troy said, as he turned and just as quickly, stopped. "Hey, man, you're bleeding all over the place!"

Craig held his hands up and sure enough, blood was dripping from his hand. He had not noticed because of the adrenaline pumping through his body. The tree had cut his hand pretty badly and now that he had pulled his gloves off in the house, the blood was dripping freely, puddling on the wooden floor. He looked where he had just been and there was blood on the bedroom door frame and the kitchen counter. They both had walked in it too.

"We don't have time to clean it up right now. The blood is all on wood so it'll be fine. Just get me something to put on it and let's get out there and find Phil."

"Let me take a look at it first," Troy said as he walked Craig over to the kitchen sink and helped him wash the wound. The tree had torn through his palm and ripped a gouge into his wrist. It was a pretty ugly wound and one that would require a real doctor and several stitches, but they would have to make do with what they had until they found Phil and got to the doctor. Troy patched him up and they were ready to move in just a few minutes. "That'll work, best I can do right now anyway," Troy said once he had completed his triage.

"Hurts like hell, but it'll do!" Craig said as he quickly moved to the front room. "I have my AR15 and at least two-hundred rounds of ammo. That beast has an Osprey 10X on it, I don't care what the hell that thing is, it's going down! I just remembered that Phil has his SKS in the truck too so you might grab it and the ammo case. It's got at least a few hundred rounds. Leave it here for him in case he makes it back before we do."

"Let's get to it!" Troy exclaimed and he headed back out to the truck.

"Hey, Troy! Wait a minute. Maybe we should give the sheriff a call first?" Craig said.

"Good idea, Craig. If you'll get that SKS and ammo, I'll find the phone and make the call." Troy headed back into the house and found the phone laying on the coffee table and tried it; no signal! "Damn it," he muttered as he walked into the kitchen and checked the wireless internet router. The top light was lit up solid, but unfortunately the connection light was flashing rapidly meaning that there was no connection. "Bad news, Craig!" he shouted. "Internet's out! No way to call out."

"Oh good god, man!" Craig exclaimed as he came back into the living room. "Is that the only way to make a call?"

"Yeah, 'fraid so. Sometimes you can send or receive texts, but only under the best of circumstances, when there's a weak signal. Right now there's no signal at all. Must be the snow blocking the receiver on the roof," Troy responded.

The two men hurried out the front door of the cabin. Troy turned on his flashlight and shined it up on the roof. Sure enough, snow had piled up around the dish blocking the signal. The dish was close to the cabin's chimney which helped to keep it warm enough to keep ice from freezing it up, but that didn't stop the snow from piling up on it.

"Damn, do you have a ladder to get up there?" Craig asked.

"Yeah, it's in the shed. I'll need your help to get it down."

The men made their way over to the shed and with Craig's help, Troy was able to find the ladder and get it out the door. They stood it next to the cabin and Troy began to ascend. "Hold this thing steady. My boots have mud and snow all over 'em."

"You got it. Just hurry, buddy! Hopefully that thing hasn't followed us here. I sure have a funny feeling right now!"

Troy made his way up the ladder. Once he reached the roof he realized that he had an even bigger problem. How was he going to navigate his way up the slope of the roof with it covered in wet, slippery snow and ice?

"Craig, throw me the broom from the kitchen. I may be able to reach it with that. I can't make it any further up the roof. It's too slick."

Craig returned and tossed the broom up to Troy. Troy missed the first few attempts, but finally snagged it. Even with the broom he was still just a little too short to reach it. He decided to go one more rung up the ladder, but that left him with no hand hold and no way to support himself if he lost his balance. With his feet perched vicariously on the top rung, he lay down on the roof and stretched the broom out to the dish. He could reach it, but he didn't have much balance or control. He swatted at the dish and was making slow progress.

"How's it coming, Troy?" Craig asked from below.

"Slow, real slow," Troy grunted. He reached out with the broom again and this time he hit the lens square on and was able to knock most of the snow off of it. "Hey, that may have done the trick. I'm coming down. Hold me steady."

He tossed the broom harmlessly to the ground and began his descent. Breathing a sigh of relief when his foot found the rung just below him, he reached for the next one. This time, he was not so lucky and his foot slipped. Desperately clawing for the ladder in the darkness he misjudged the top of the rails and found only empty air. His shoulder hit the side of the roof as he fell off balance and his feet actually pushed the ladder to the side. Troy's fall was straight down. Craig tried his best to maintain a grip on the ladder, but once he knew Troy was no longer on it, he let it go and tried to get out of the way.

Troy landed heavily on his left shoulder and back. The blow knocked his breathe out and he was struggling to breathe. Craig was by his side quickly. "Hey man! Are you okay?"

Finally, Troy was able to breathe again and rolled onto his back. When he moved, a sharp, piercing pain was stabbing him in his side. He immediately knew that he had broken a rib, maybe two.

"I think I broke a rib. It sure feels like it!" Troy gasped.

"Just freaking fantastic! Let me help you inside and we can check it out. Anything else hurting? Test your legs and feet."

"Nah, I think that's it. Help me up."

Craig reached down and grabbed Troy's arm and hoisted him up to his feet. Troy was in obvious pain, but he knew there wasn't much they could do about it here. They made their way inside the cabin and Craig helped him to the sofa.

"Better lie down right here for a minute. I'll stoke the fire back up and put some more wood on."

"Craig, check the wireless router first! See if it has a connection now."

Troy reached for the television remote laying on the coffee table in front of the sofa. He turned it on and waited a moment for the TV to power up. If the satellite receiver had reception enough for the television, then the chances were good that the phone would also work.

"All the lights are solid green except the one on the bottom. It's blinking slowly. Is that good?" Craig asked.

"That means that it's on but it's not a stable connection. It may still work enough to get a phone call out though. Let's give it a shot anyway." Troy's phone lay beside him on the coffee table. He winced sharply from his broken rib as he reached over to pick up the cell. Only one bar showed up. At least that was something. With any luck at all the call would go through, so he quickly dialed. After a few seconds, he heard the familiar ring tone on the other end. Just as the dispatcher answered, the cell lost reception and the call ended. He quickly hit redial. The cell lost signal two more times just as the dispatcher answered the call.

"No luck, Craig. It just doesn't have a good enough signal to make a call."

"What about an email?" Craig asked. "Maybe you can get word out that way!"

Troy asked Craig to grab his lap top from the upstairs bedroom. Craig hurried up the stairs, retrieved the laptop and brought it quickly back down to Troy. A few minutes later an email was sent to the sheriff's department in hopes that someone would come.

"That's about all we can do right now. No idea if it actually went through or not, but I gotta hope!"

"Keep a close eye on it and see if anyone responds," Craig said. "I need to get out there and find Phil. He's in serious trouble and a long ways from here and you're in no shape to come with me."

"I'm not staying here!" Troy announced. "I've got to do something to help."

The men decided on a plan of action. Craig would take the ATV back out to find Phil. The nights were very cold up in the mountains and he could die of hypothermia even if the creature never found him. They weren't sure what was out there, but Troy was certain that it wasn't a bear. Whatever it was, it was incredibly large and powerful! Phil was no match for that and they knew he had little chance of surviving the night if they didn't find him. When Craig left, Troy would also leave in the Jeep and try to get to town for help.

Craig left the SKS rifle and an ammo box full of rounds in the living room just in case Phil made his way back and needed it. Next, he took a Springfield .45 pistol from his truck, a bushmaster with extra clips and a Hart 300 Ultra Mag sport rifle. He helped Troy up off the sofa and led him to the Jeep. "Keep it hammered and get there as fast as you can, Troy. Phil's out there somewhere and we need all the help we can get. Just be careful! If you see that thing, shoot to kill!"

"I will, believe me!" Troy said. "I have my .45 and the Henry. If I see it, it's not going far! Not without a fight!"

Craig loaded his rifles into the ATV and strapped them down using the bungee cords Troy found earlier. He assisted Troy into the Jeep and wished him good luck, then turned to look around one more time to make sure nothing was nearby. A couple of the off-road lights were broken, but the ATV still had plenty that weren't. Craig would be able to see for several meters in front of him and if he stopped long enough, he could also use the spot light near the driver's left hand. He jumped in the Razor, fired it up and hit the gas.

Chapter 12

Troy watched Craig leave on the ATV. The lights were shining brightly across the snow covered landscape all the way down to the boat dock. His ribs were hurting terribly, but he was able to buckle his seatbelt and start the Jeep. He checked his pistol in the seat beside him along with the Henry rifle. He wanted to make certain that if he were to see the creature, he would have ready access to the weapons.

Shifting into drive, he reached down to engage the four-wheel drive low. A stabbing pain jolted him back upright immediately. Thoughts ran through his mind that he should have asked Craig to assist him before he took off on the Razor. The 4-wheel drive shifter was in the floor board and very stiff. The act of bending down and reaching for it alone was bad enough, but as soon as Troy put effort into shifting the lever, the pain in his ribs was unbearable. He would have to attempt the drive out in 2-wheel high.

The dirt road into town was several miles of mud and snow. He pulled out and looked in the rear view mirror at the cabin shining from all of the lights reflecting off the snow on the ground. The men made sure that the door to the cabin was unlocked in case Phil made his way back. They also made sure that there were other guns and weapons in the house. If by chance Phil did indeed make it back, he would need something for protection.

The 4X4 bounced along the driveway as Troy made his way toward town. He began shaking from the bitter cold and could see his breath start to fog up the windshield. Troy's adrenaline had kept the cold at bay, but now that he was rested a little and was calmer, he could really feel the cold. He reached over and turned the heater on low. Once the Jeep warmed up a little, the heat would feel good. If he was this cold, his buddy stranded out in the middle of the woods had to be miserable. Troy hoped that Craig would get to him quickly.

Snow started falling again. Lightly at first, but as Troy continued along the road the flakes became larger and denser. The windshield wipers were struggling to keep the snow off of the windshield and the visibility was going from bad to worse. He wasn't aware of any major storms that were supposed to be moving in, but he had to admit, he hadn't given much attention to the news in a few days. Things can change rapidly in the mountains and he knew that they had to get help out here as quickly as possible. Phil would be struggling to stay warm. He was more worried about staying alive! Whatever that thing was, it was terrifying.

Troy turned the heat up to high and made sure the defroster was on. The windshield was fogging up badly from his breathing which just made the visibility even worse. He drove as quickly as he could, but the road was slick and getting worse from the snowfall. He knew if it got much worse, there would be no getting in or out.

He finally made it to the bridge that crossed the lake and began up the slope. The Jeep slid sideways as the front wheels lost traction. The snow was deep here and the wet ground was frozen solid underneath. He struggled with the wheel, but got the Jeep to right itself and began back up the slope. The ground was simply too slick for the Jeep to get any traction without the 4-wheel drive engaged. Troy shifted into reverse and carefully backed down the hill in order to get a better run at it. If he could just get some momentum, he could probably make it up onto the bridge. Then, he should be able to cross with no issues. Troy backed down the hill and allowed another twenty or thirty feet more before he stopped and shifted back into drive. He leaned over and reached for the 4-wheel drive lever. If he could just get it shifted, he wouldn't have any trouble at all navigating the slope. As he leaned down the sharp pain in his side throbbed so hard that he nearly passed out. He sat up in the seat, his back straight, and held pressure on his side. His breathing came in short gasps. He would have to go at it without the 4-wheel drive.

Once he regained his composure, he stepped on the gas and slowly picked up speed as he approached the slope up to the bridge. It wasn't incredibly steep, but the transition from the level road to the top of the bridge was only about twelve feet which made it difficult to ascend under these conditions. The Jeep hit the bottom of the slope and he immediately felt the pain in his ribs and almost blacked out. The front wheels lost traction, but the momentum carried the Jeep straight and the back wheels were pushing the vehicle up. With a huge sigh of relief, he crested over the slope onto the level platform of the bridge and began crossing. The snow was piled about a foot high, but the Jeep had no trouble moving across. When he reached the middle of the bridge he glanced over toward the cabin. At a mile away, the cabin lights could be seen even through the snow storm. He couldn't make out much more than that and he turned back to the road. Crossing the bridge is hopefully the hardest part of this trip, he thought. He reached the other end and started down the slope. He drove down with no trouble and turned onto the main road. From here, he knew, should be an easier drive. Unfortunately, it was going to be very slow due to the limited visibility and the slick roads.

The road stretched along the lake shore for quite a ways before descending for several miles to reach the main highway into town. It wasn't a well-kept road and Troy's house was the only one out this way. Technically, it was a county road, but it felt more like a very long private drive. The county would send a road grader out this way sometimes, but for the most part, there was very little traffic for them to worry about. Troy's ribs were hurting terribly now and the constant bumping of the road wasn't helping. He tried adjusting his seat to lean back a little more. That seemed to help a little. He held pressure against his side with one hand making it difficult to drive with only one on the wheel. As the jeep rounded a curve, Troy had to quickly turn the wheel to navigate around a huge, old, and very dead aspen that must have fallen within the last few hours. It blocked the dirt road entirely. The left front wheel slammed into a pot hole jolting him forward in the seat. His seatbelt held him in place, but the force of the blow on his ribs was enough to make him pass out. Troy's foot hit the gas pedal as he crumpled back in his seat and lost his grip on the wheel. The jeep careened off the road, down the embankment and smashed head-on into a large pine tree.

Chapter 13

Craig threw a glance over his shoulder at Troy driving away in his Jeep. He was now racing the ATV back toward the mountain. He had to get to Phil as quickly as possible. It was getting dangerously cold outside and that thing was still out there. Wind chill alone would be well below freezing. Craig was a tough outdoorsman type and respected the power and size of bears, but he wasn't afraid. Not as long as he was properly armed! He had no problem heading straight back to where it first attacked them. He was determined to find his buddy and bring him home.

The ATV had no trouble negotiating the treacherous mountain. It was a four-wheel drive and very powerful and nimble. The downfall of snow became much heavier, however, and Craig had a difficult time seeing very far ahead. He made it to the trail where it started up the mountain and gunned the Razor into the trees. The trail wound up and over the rocky, snow covered mountainside with blind corners and hair-pin turns. Craig kept his handgun in his coat for easy reach just in case he needed it.

Just ahead, Craig could make out a rocky overhang and the trail wound just below it. He pulled up under it and cut the engine leaving the lights on. He listened intently in case Phil had seen him and was yelling for him. It would be very difficult to hear over the sound of the engine. He shined the spotlight all around, but could see nothing except the snow falling through the pines. The constant hissing sound of the snow falling so rapidly and dense was the only thing that could be heard. Knowing that a bear, a pissed off psycho killer bear, was on a rampage made the expansive woodland scene very eerie.

Craig reached for the familiar butt of his pistol for reassurance. It was easily accessible even through his gloved fingers. Once he felt confident that it was where he could get to it quickly, he reached down, fired the Razor back up and hit the gas. He needed to locate the area where they were attacked in hopes of finding Phil nearby. He knew he would be coming up to the spot soon where they first left the trail, but he wasn't sure if he would be able to spot any sign of it now due to all the snow. Even the forest floor was becoming thicker with the white powder. He would have to hurry.

He pushed the ATV hard for the next few hundred yards before slowing in a wide open spot on the trail. He stopped the Razor and, once again, killed the engine and listened intently for any sign from Phil. He didn't see anything with the spotlight as he shined it around the forest. He was reaching down to fire up the engine and move on when he heard a thump on the ground near the ATV. A large rock about the size of a softball landed hard on the trail and rolled up close. Too close! This time, he saw the general direction it came from and he turned the powerful spotlight that way. He saw something moving off deeper into the woods, but he couldn't be certain as to what it was due to the reduced visibility of the snow. The forest was open enough for him to get the ATV through quickly and he felt he could rely on his driving skills to get in and out without issue. He hit the gas and turned the wheel hard. He was in pursuit and not backing down. If it was the creature, then it would have a fight on its hands.

+++

Troy awoke to the sound of static on the radio of the Jeep. His head hurt and his vision was blurry. When he reached up to touch his temple he felt the intense pain in his side as his ribs reminded him of his injury. He winced sharply and his breath caught in his throat. He decided if he didn't move carefully, he may pass out again and that's the last thing he needed. When he pulled his hand away from his head he knew the reason for the blurry vision. He had a cut on his right temple that had bled quite profusely. His nose felt numb and when he touched it, he knew it was broken. The airbag had blown out and was to be thanked for most of the damage. His whole face felt sticky from the blood. *That explains why my head is pounding*, he thought.

Fortunately for him, the windshield was still intact and it was still warmer inside than it was out. *I must've only been out for a few minutes*, he thought. He could see that he had struck a tree when he crashed the Jeep. The driver's side headlight had busted on impact, but the fog lights were still on as well as the passenger headlight. He reached over, hit the power button, and turned the radio off. He could see that the gear shift had been knocked into park somehow; maybe he did it before he blacked out completely. He reached up to the steering wheel and tried to rip the airbag off. It was too tough so he just stuffed it back around the wheel and hoped that the Jeep would start and run. He turned the key and the engine roared to life. He slipped it down to reverse and sluggishly sat back upright in his seat. He stepped on the gas pedal gently at first, but the Jeep's back wheels simply spun. He gave it more gas and it began to move ever so slightly, but then the wheels could be heard slipping in the mud and snow and only digging deeper. The Jeep wouldn't budge another inch. Troy slipped the gear shift into neutral.

He let his arm fall off the main shifter over to the four-wheel drive selector and rest on the console. The only way possible of getting out of this alive was for someone to come along and rescue him or he had to get the Jeep shifted into four-wheel low. He knew it wasn't likely anyone would come along anytime in the next several days, maybe even weeks. No matter how badly it hurt, he had to get out of that ditch! The shifter on the Jeep was extremely stiff especially when the vehicle was sitting idle. It worked best when the Jeep was moving slowly, but that was not an option. He leaned down and tucked his right arm close to his ribs and used his left arm across his body to keep it there tightly. Using his forearm more than the rest of his body he pulled on the shifter. At first, it wouldn't budge, but as he concentrated harder he finally managed to get it to move into the first notch, neutral. He needed to go one more notch to engage the Jeep into four-wheel low. He took a slow and deliberate breath and began pulling on the lever.

+++

Phil made a quick check of his personal belongings by searching through his pockets. He found his small flashlight, his hunting knife with a seven-inch blade, a small pocket sized, water-proof first aid kit complete with matches, antibiotic ointment and Band-Aids, wallet, and as luck would have it, his cell phone. He knew he had no reception up here on the mountain; there wasn't a cell tower for miles. He could possibly make it to higher elevation where it might be possible to get a clear signal, at least strong enough to get out a text message. That was one option albeit a dangerous one. He certainly didn't want to get stuck up here on this mountain much longer. This kind of weather is extremely dangerous. He could die from hypothermia. His next option was his best option and the safest, straight down. He could feel the slope with his feet even in the darkness.

He knew that he didn't have much time before the creature came back so began walking away from the direction the others went. He knew it was too cold to try to wait it out and stay idle. He had to get moving. He thought if he could make his way down he would eventually run into the road that led to the cabin. Alone in the dark on an unfamiliar mountain, he had no way of knowing which direction he was going so it was a huge gamble and he knew it. He had no choice. He couldn't stay here.

Using his flashlight sparingly he began at a quick pace only to stop and listen at intervals for any sound that something may be close by. The snow was falling heavily and he only used the flashlight pointing down at his feet. If he shined the light ahead, he couldn't see beyond a few feet as the snow was too heavy. He had to rely mostly on his sense of hearing for signs of danger.

He was beginning to feel the effects of the cold weather as the temperature dropped to what he figured to be hovering around twenty degrees, but the wind chill made it seem much colder. He had to keep pushing forward.

When Phil was a young boy he had gone deer hunting with his uncle many times in a remote area in Oklahoma. Armed only with a handmade bois d 'arc bow and a hunting knife he was taught how to navigate the forest and survive off the land. He spent many days and nights alone in the woods. He became a seasoned hunter and very tough. He learned to respect the land and to give thanks for the great creator's gifts of life.

He was familiar with the climate and weather patterns in his home area, but not much with that of these mountains. He knew that in the fall the weather could be clear with crisp blue skies and generally dry, but snowstorms like this one were very common. The aspens had already begun changing colors and the elk mating season had come to an end. Many of the mountain roads were closed for the season in preparation for the treacherous overpasses.

Walking became more and more labor intensive as the snow on the ground grew deeper. He was struggling intensely and he knew he was sweating too much. The sweat would get his clothing wet increasing his chances of lowering his body temperature and possibly frostbite. It was getting more difficult to trudge on each time he stopped to listen for pursuit. It was also harder to hear anything over the pounding of his chest and the heavy breathing. He was dizzy and he knew it was from the concussion, but there was little he could do about it. Once, he thought he heard the sound of shouting. He strained hard to listen, but heard nothing else; probably just the wind.

Phil was pushing ahead in the ankle deep snow when he recalled a time he had gotten lost as a little boy. He had been out playing with several other kids in the woods near his grandfather's home in Oklahoma. They had been swimming in the river when he saw a rabbit nearby on the bank. He became curious about it and began watching it closely. Soon, the rabbit hopped away, and Phil decided to follow it. The rabbit didn't seem to mind that he was behind him and it even seemed as if he wanted Phil to follow him. The other boys never noticed him wonder off. The rabbit would stop and nibble on some grass here and there, but it never ran away or tried to hide. It allowed Phil to get very close before hopping, slowly away.

'Where are you taking me, mister rabbit?" Phil would ask it, but the rabbit never spoke. Before long, Phil noticed that it was starting to get dark. He realized that he must have been gone for hours now and he didn't know where he was. He looked around, but could not find any familiar land marks.

"Mister Rabbit, I think we are lost."

The rabbit just sat there quietly munching on clover and never said a word.

"That was a very mean trick you played on me," Phil scolded the rabbit. "How am I going to find my way home now?"

The rabbit, still, would not speak to him. He simply sat there munching on clover with his small nose twitching and staring up at the boy.

Snapping out of his memory fog, Phil became aware of a new sound. At first, he couldn't imagine what it could be. He was used to hearing the sound of the snowflakes falling to the ground like very light drops of rain. He stopped in his tracks and listened intently. It sounded like running water and he was very near it. He would have to be very careful in the dark. His flashlight was small, but powerfully bright. He had been careful to keep the beam pointed down and his fingers covering all but a small pin sized beam of light to see a few feet ahead. He dared not shine it ahead of himself very far because the light may give away his position to the creature who he hoped had given up on finding him. He hadn't remembered seeing any streams during the daylight hours, but that didn't mean much. There must be a hundred streams that came down out of these mountains and filled the lake and the rivers below. He was still descending, however, and his hopes of picking up the road soon were brightened by the stream gurgling. He could follow it down to the lake and from there he knew how to get back to the cabin and how to get back to safety!

+++

Craig had every light on the ATV turned on as he hammered the throttle down. He spun the wheel and the Razor cut through the snow like a plow through very fine sandy loam. He reached up to his chest and felt the reassurance of his .45 snuggly in its holster and then reached down and patted the SKS he had bungeed to the passenger seat. Giant grizzly or Sasquatch, he wasn't afraid as long as he had his weapons to even the playing field.

Up ahead he caught a glance of movement off to his right and he hit the gas cutting hard right. He flew between two large trees running over a few small saplings that slapped back up behind him. Once through the large natural gateway the ATV hit a small incline and went air-born straight up. The ATV landed with a huge crash as Craig turned the wheel sharply and hit the brakes, sliding sideways to a halt. He already had one hand going for the spotlight handle and the other drawing his .45. He saw the creature where he anticipated it would be and let go with several rounds. The report of the weapon was deafening. The creature roared loudly, out of being hit from the discharge or from anger Craig couldn't tell. It had quickly disappeared behind a large stand of trees. He could see that it was huge, though he couldn't make out anything more than it being bipedal and extremely large with black matted fur. He quickly reached for the SKS and brought it up ready to fire in case the beast charged. He shined the spotlight all over the area while keeping an eye out for possible escape routes through the trees. If he had to make a run, he would be ready!

The Razor was suddenly jolted hard and Craig turned his head to look behind him while at the same time hitting the gas. The four-wheeler lurched forward and he turned the wheel sharply. The craft rocketed into a one-eighty spin. Somehow the beast had gotten behind him and had rammed the Razor. Craig had the SKS rifle across his chest with one hand on the wheel and one on the rifle grip. He quickly brought the rifle up to bear at the beast and let go with several rounds. This time Craig knew he hit it. The creature screamed in one of the most blood curdling rages Craig had ever heard. It literally shook him to his core. It was terrifying. The ATV lights were aimed directly at the beast and Craig could see it fully as the rage filled eyes stared straight at him before it bounded off into the woods. Craig triggered off several more rounds, but lost sight of it quickly.

If a deer or other animal was wounded by a hunter, it was always best to be patient and not pressure the game. Often times a deer could run for miles after a mortal wound from a rifle or arrow only because the hunter pushed it to flee and allowed the animal's adrenaline to keep it going. If left alone, the animal would usually expire within a few yards and tracking would be unnecessary. Under normal conditions, he would have waited a bit. This was not a normal situation.

Once he made a quick study of the area he hit the gas and gave pursuit. He couldn't let this thing catch him off guard again. There was nothing more ferocious than a wounded animal or one cornered.

+++

Troy suddenly sat bolt right up in the seat. Adrenaline kicked in when he heard the report of the heavy caliber pistol. He knew the sound very well. The report from a .45 was distinctive, especially out in the middle of nowhere with no other sounds around except the falling of the snow. The pistol sounded quite some distance away, and it gave Troy hope, but at the same time trepidation. He knew that it had to be Craig and he felt good that he had a weapon with him. Craig was a big man and didn't scare easily. Matter of fact, Troy never knew him to ever back down from anything. Craig wasn't a bully though he was bull headed. He wouldn't run from a fight, but Troy saw the beast with his own eyes. It wasn't a bear! He knew exactly what it was though nobody would ever believe it if they didn't see it for themselves.

Troy's mind reverted back to his ribs. He was in serious pain, and when he rose up suddenly from hearing the gun shots it sent more stabs of pain straight through him. He looked down at the shifter. Apparently, his quick reaction to the sound resulted in his subconscious effort to pull the shifter into four-wheel low. He gingerly reached over and gripped the regular shifter and notched it in reverse. Sitting back up, he put both hands on the wheel, straightened up, and leaned back into the seat.

The snow was coming down heavy, but he knew the basic terrain here. He slowly pressed on the gas pedal and the Jeep began moving backward and then hung up. He tried to give it more gas, but it was stuck on something. He unbuckled his seatbelt, and opened the door. Holding onto his ribs with one arm he pushed the door open and crawled out into the gusting snow. He saw what he was stuck on right away. One of the branches from the tree had broken off and was stuck in the wheel well. Grimacing from the pain, he made his way around the door and reached down to pull the limb free. He was in serious pain and he was careful not to injure himself further. His hands were so cold that they felt like the skin was paper thin. As he pulled on the limb, his hands slid on the bark of the tree and the abrasions stung fiercely in the freezing weather. He was finally able to pull the limb free and returned back to the driver's seat.

With the limb freed from the wheel well he had no problems backing up away from the tree and there he stopped, reached back to the shifter and started to put it in drive when he heard more reports of more gun fire. This was a different sound, more rapid fire and several of them. After a few seconds, there were more shots echoing over the mountain. There was no way of knowing exactly where the shots were coming from, but he knew it could be quite some distance away. Whatever he was shooting at, Troy certainly hoped Craig hit it and stopped it!

+++

Phil heard the first shots. They were close, but how close he couldn't tell. The sounds up here on the mountain tended to swirl with the wind. He stood completely still and quiet. He turned off the flashlight and listened intently. He couldn't hear anything else except the hissing of the falling snow. If he were to guess, the sounds came from somewhere above his current position. He was getting very tired and dizzy, not to mention colder. He had cold weather gear on, but the exposure while on foot wasn't in his favor. He couldn't move quickly. The snow was piling up making his progress even more difficult.

Different scenarios played out in his mind. It could be Troy and Craig coming for him and running into the beast. They may have killed it and now are looking for him. If that's the case, then he could turn his flashlight back on and make himself more visible in the woods so that they would spot him. On the other hand, if they only scared the creature away, it could be running from the gun shots and could run directly at him! He needed to keep moving in order to keep the warmth in his body. If he stayed still too long, it would prove to be much more difficult to get started again. The cold would certainly begin sitting in on his aching limbs. He decided to stay on his current path of descent as it would be much easier on him than trying to climb up the mountain.

He flipped his flashlight back on and placed it in his hand where his fingers could cover the majority of the beam leaving just enough light to see where he was stepping. He took a few steps and heard more shots that stopped him in his tracks. Those were different than the first one. Those he knew very well. That distinctive sound was the rat-tat-tat of an SKS rifle, and that certainly had to be Craig and Troy. They must've been able to get away and get back to the cabin for weapons. He knew they were out looking for him now and the fear of being caught alone by the beast was dissipating somewhat. He picked up his steps and began moving quicker. The adrenaline coursed through his veins like electricity through copper wires in a house, extending to every limb and giving him a boost of strength. Unfortunately, it also increased his heart rate and hearing impairing his vision. He never noticed he was standing too close to the stream until the ground gave way beneath his feet.

Chapter 14

The Jeep had no trouble gaining traction, and Troy was able to climb back up on to the road with little effort. He knew it would take a good hour to get to town even if he was in good shape and the roads were clear. His first priority would be to find the sheriff and send help out here, and then he would have to get to the emergency room and see the doctor. The heat felt good on his legs so he turned it up another notch. He could only drive about twenty-five miles per hour at best and with the snow coming down as hard as it was, it would only become more difficult slowing his progress. That was very worrisome. If he was having a difficult time traversing the roads, then obviously it would be just as difficult for any rescue vehicles. All of the sheriff's deputies in town drove four-wheel drive vehicles, but they were no better off than the Jeep. When it came to rugged terrain, there weren't many vehicles better suited than the Jeep Wrangler. This wasn't simply a matter of rugged terrain. It was a matter of clear passes through this winter storm.

The vehicle bounced in and out of potholes hidden in the road by the snowfall. Troy felt every last one of them and the pain to go along with them. The heat felt great on his legs, but it was also making him a little drowsy. Falling asleep at the wheel was the last thing he needed so he cracked the window to get fresh, cold air on his face.

Finally, Troy made it to the main highway into town and turned on to it. The dirt road sloped up onto the highway and the transition was deep with snow, but it gave the Jeep no trouble. Road signs marked the edges of the highway route with passing lanes and caution signs. He had spent the better part of an hour on the dirt road and was about half-way to town at this point. He wasn't able to make any better time and in fact, the highway wasn't nearly as passable as the dirt road had been. A million thoughts kept running through his head. What would the sheriff think of the story? Have Craig and Phil shot and killed the beast? Are they safe? Should he even mention the fact that it was a nine-foot tall creature that walked upright like a man? Would the sheriff believe him at all or should he simply say that it was a bear that attacked them and leave it at that?

He reached over and turned on the radio. Maybe he could hear something about the weather. He toggled through the stations until he found the one he wanted and left it there. This was a local radio station that gave weather reports often, as well as information about any roads that had been declared unpassable. The thought just occurred to him that the road that he was on currently could be closed if the weather got much worse. He struggled to tell where the road was and tried gauging it by the flatness of the terrain. The headlights against the brightness of the falling snow weren't much help in seeing more than a few feet at a time. Unfortunately, the radio station was already set to automated playback and there were no live updates - just country music playing with commercials sandwiched in between.

As the air in the Jeep warmed, Troy began coughing which caused his rib cage to tighten. The pain was agonizing and a few times he thought he would pass out. He was sweating profusely and he was extremely weakened. He slowed down until he could refocus and get past the nausea that the pain and the coughing were causing. He knew he had to get to the doctor quickly. The deserted stretch of highway was undulating and twisting, but at the pace Troy was forced to drive, it wasn't difficult. There were a few areas of the highway that had fairly steep descending grades and Troy handled those by slowing down to a crawl and simply allowing the Jeep's engine brake to keep the wheels slow and steady.

The snow was falling just as hard as ever when he reached the edge of town. He noticed the clock on the radio was 3:47am which meant that he had been driving for over two hours and he had seen no other vehicles along the way. Why would he? Not only was it early in the morning, but when storms like this hit, no one came out in it unless it was absolutely necessary. He was struggling to stay conscious, but his injuries were taking their toll on his body. Each time he coughed, he felt the intense pain from his broken ribs pierce through his body. He was now sweating and shaking uncontrollably and his hands could barely stay on the steering wheel. The Jeep rolled through the traffic light at the east end of town, never stopping for the bright, red light. The vehicle suddenly careened into a snow drift on the side of the road coming to a stop and remained motionless in the powdery embankment. The one good headlight of the Jeep buried in the snow as if it was the flame of a candle snuffed out by the wind. The soft yellow glow of the street lights was the only witness to the incident.

+++

The Razor tore through the woods in pursuit of the creature. Craig holstered his .45 and made sure that the SKS was secure before moving too far. He had plenty of ammo and still had a few other guns strapped down in the back seat. He thought he saw the beast in the headlights for a quick moment and he hit the gas harder. It wasn't far away, but he needed to be closer to it if he wanted to get a good shot at it. The ATV bounced over rocks and small trees with little effort. The snow coming down was his only hindrance and he wasn't able to see as far as he would've liked. When he came over a small incline, he saw the trail that ran perpendicular to his current direction and he turned the wheel sharply. He knew the direction the creature was running and he knew that at this point in the trail he could circle back around and intersect the beast's path only a few hundred yards away. He could cut it off and end this thing!

Craig hit the gas and the Razor ripped through the deepening snow down the trail. It was getting extremely cold, but Craig never noticed as the adrenaline was still coursing through his veins. He had a great sense of direction and knew when the trail had turned the way he wanted it to. He came to a sliding halt, grabbed the pistol out of its shoulder holster and aimed the spotlight beam through the woods.

"There you are!" he shouted when he finally saw movement.

It looked as if the creature was trying to slide around behind him now. Craig let go of the spotlight handle, hit the gas and shot off toward the creature. The right wheel of the ATV unexpectedly hit a rock hidden by the snow and jolted the vehicle harshly. Craig lost sight of the creature for a split second and when he looked back up, it was gone. He nervously looked around the area with the search light in one hand and his pistol in the other. He knew there was nothing worse than a wounded animal. The beast would either put up a ferocious fight or flee. So far, it showed signs of doing both! It was completely unpredictable. He thought he heard something and he spun the light back around to the side, but it was too late. The beast had somehow gotten around to the side of the ATV and slammed its huge arms down on top of it with a crazed ferocity. The screaming and growling was deafening as the beast rained its fury down on the ATV, trying to destroy it and the man inside!

Craig tried aiming his pistol at the creature, but the gun slipped from his grasp due to the bombardment the huge brute was doing to the machine. He bent down, reaching for the gun, but the seat belt harness kept him from it. In a panic, he unlatched the harness and jumped across the console away from the beast. He was able to retrieve his pistol as he scrambled into the floor-board of the ATV. In his attempt to clear the console, his knee hit the switch and killed the engine. His arms were pinned beneath him, but he managed to roll onto his side just enough to bring the pistol to bear on the beast and empty the clip. The creature fell back away from the Razor into the darkness allowing Craig time to scramble up out of the awkward position he was in. He was such a large man, this was no easy task, but the adrenaline allowed him to move remarkably fast. The metal covering the roll cage bars above his head were caved in so he was unable to sit up completely. The spotlight on the side of the vehicle and the driving lights on top had been ripped completely off so he couldn't see much on the side where the creature had fallen. Only one light on top and one or two on the front of the ATV were still working.

He reached down and tried the switch. The Razor roared to life! Craig slammed it in gear and hit the gas, spinning mud and snow behind him as he jetted forward and cut the wheel hard left. The Razor spun into a ninety degree turn and rocked to a halt when he hit the brakes. He knew he hit the beast, but it was nowhere to be seen!

The snow was still coming down hard, but he could see directly in front of the ATV where the few remaining lights were aimed. He quickly dropped the empty clip and slid another one in and slammed the .45 closed. Pulling out his flashlight from his inside pocket, he shined the light all around the vehicle. He hit the gas and sped forward for about twenty-five yards before he spun around in a one-eighty again. He was leery about the beast being able to circle around behind him and he wasn't going to let it happen again. This time when he stopped, he thought he saw some movement just out of range of the headlights back from where he first shot the thing. He hit the gas hard and the ATV lurched forward and was met immediately with a huge tree limb exploding with tremendous force on the passenger side. The blow caved in the front roll cage and shattered the remaining lights on top. Only one headlight and two small pin lights underneath remained. Craig flinched away from the flying debris, hit the gas hard and turned the Razor. Snow and mud flew everywhere and the engine screamed. Craig never saw the huge pine until it was too late. He collided head-on with a massive tree only thirty feet away from the creature.

Stunned by the impact, Craig was unable to move for a few seconds. That's all the time the beast needed. A huge, hairy arm reached into the Razor, grabbed Craig by the head and shoulders and pulled him out like a rag doll kicking and screaming. Once the monster had him out of the ATV, he lifted him high over his head and slammed the big man to the ground. Craig hit the ground with a hard 'THUD' and immediately reached for his holster, but his gun wasn't there. He felt the beast grab his ankle and he tried kicking at the giant hands as hard as he could. He desperately tried to crawl away from it back toward the Razor, but its grip was too strong. As the beast dragged him, his hands found a tree branch in the darkness. He grabbed it and swung it as hard as he could. He swung repeatedly at the giant hands that held his ankle in a viselike grip. The beast dropped his leg and ripped the limb out of his hands. The monster screamed in a fit of rage that sent shock waves through Craig's body. It brought the tree branch down hard on Craig again and again in a brutal attack that left the man lying on the ground in an unrecognizable heap.

+++

Phil suddenly felt himself suspended in mid-air. He was falling down the icy embankment toward the running water below. He grabbed frantically at anything he could, clawing madly at the snow covered slope. His gloves weren't much help on the slick surface of the snow and ice, but he managed to arrest his descent. His body lay prone against the slanted embankment; he slowly began to crawl his way back up. His boots dug into the fresh snow while his shoulders and arms ached trying to pull his weight up. Finally, he was able to move up and over the edge and lay there on the solid, flat surface catching his breath. His mind was racing as his lungs screamed for air. As he lay there, he could have sworn that he heard more gun shots in his frantic struggles, but could not be certain. Then suddenly, he heard the scream of an animal so incredibly terrifying he bolted straight up on his feet in a sheer panic!

He could see his flashlight lying on the ground where he dropped it when he began falling. He made his way over to it and retrieved it. His body ached from the cold and he longed for the warmth of a hot fire. He couldn't afford to stop and try to build one, not yet anyway. He listened intently for any more sounds, but hearing nothing, he began moving down the mountain away from that confrontation. He had no idea if his buddies killed it or just angered it. He needed to put as much distance between him and the nightmare on this mountain as he could. He had no weapons and no way to fend off an attack.

Putting one foot in front of the other proved to be extremely difficult being half frozen, but he managed. He had a warm hunting cap with a neoprene face mask that kept the elements at bay somewhat, but he was still losing a lot of body heat. He knew he had to get off the mountain quickly and get back to the cabin! There he should be able to get warmed back up and find help!

Using the flashlight sparingly, Phil made his way down, following the stream. About halfway down, he came across an obvious trail wide enough for an ATV or tractor. He remembered Troy telling him about the trails that the previous owners had made through the mountain. He also remembered that all of the trails that led down also led back to the road to the cabin.

Elated, he followed the trail down through a series of twists and turns until he eventually found the road. The only problem he had now was figuring out which direction led back to the cabin as he was more than a little disoriented in the darkness. He was also feeling the effects of the concussion which wasn't helping. The point where the trail met the road was on a curve. Both seemed to lead in the direction he thought the cabin should be. He had a fifty-fifty shot at choosing the correct one. He made a decision and began trudging through the snow.

Chapter 15

Sheriff Blaine sipped his coffee while he read through his stack of reports. It was only five a.m., but he was an early riser and during winter storms like this, he often stayed at the office. A few of his deputies were also there, but they had worked a late shift. They had cots in their offices and they could shower in the jail. They rarely kept anyone in their jail more than overnight; usually those were public intoxication violators just sleeping it off. They would pay their fines and leave the next day once they sobered up. The town of Hawthorn was filled with a lot of good, hard working families and was very tight knit, but there just wasn't a lot to do up in the mountains sometimes. They welcomed outside visitors and went out of their way to be warm and inviting.

Nick nearly jumped straight out of his chair when the solitude of the early morning silence was suddenly disturbed by the ringing of the telephone. Startled, the Sheriff hurriedly picked up.

"Hello. Sheriff's office."

"Sheriff?" The caller asked.

"Yes, this is Sheriff Blaine. How can I help you?" It was Ray Horn at the fire department.

"Hey Nick, we received a call about twenty minutes ago. Burt, the snow plow driver, apparently found a man that wrecked his car over on 4th street. He called EMS and got him to the emergency room. They locked the vehicle up and took the keys so we'll leave that up to you to check out. Burt's back on the plow, but if you need him, he's not hard to find."

"Thanks, Ray. I'll send a deputy over to check it out."

A few minutes later the phone rang again. This time it was the doctor on the other end.

"Sheriff, this is Doctor Jenkins. I'm at the ER. Got a new patient this morning and thought you might be interested."

"Is that right? Who is it?" The Sheriff asked as he noticed Deputy Larson make his way into the room half asleep and headed straight over to the coffee pot.

After a few minutes of conversation the Sheriff hung up the phone.

"Well, what kind of blood-thirsty criminal activity is going on at this God forsaken hour of the night?" The deputy asked.

"Well, good morning sunshine!" The Sheriff laughed. "It seems that the Turner fellow showed up at the ER just a bit ago with broken ribs and banged up pretty badly. Doc says he's in and out of consciousness. Can't get anything out of him; nothing that makes sense anyway. Burt was on the snow plow when he found 'im slumped over in his car and brought him in. Apparently, he wrecked in town and was knocked unconscious. Has 'im checked in a room now. Not sure what to make of it really."

"Sounds like he's had a bad time of it! I wonder what happened to his two buddies," the deputy asked. "Maybe they pulled out before this storm hit and headed back home. Didn't want to get caught in it."

"Maybe. I had planned on making a trip out there today about noon, but it looks like I just need to drive across town to the hospital now," the Sheriff replied.

"Doc said Turner had been muttering crazy stuff when Burt brought him in. I'll grab one of the sleds in a bit and go check on him and see if I can get the story. Why don't you see if you can raise Burt on the radio and meet up with him somewhere and get a statement from him...find out where his car is and get it towed."

The sheriff could hear Larson on the phone calling for the snow plow driver. After a few minutes Burt answered him back and the two arranged to meet up at a local coffee shop. With that, the deputy turned to his office to get his things together for the ride over. Burt would be out on the city streets trying to keep them as clear as possible in this storm. Emergencies happened and first responders would still need to be able to get around though most people knew to stay indoors during these conditions. Storms like this could hit suddenly and could be brutal. The weather reports warned them a few days ago that it could be a sizable storm and dump quite a bit of snow.

Finally suited up in cold weather gear, Deputy Larson made his way to the garage where the vehicles were kept. He opened one of the garage bay doors and climbed on a snow mobile. He started the sled, let it idle until it warmed up and then started out into the snow storm to meet Burt. Most folks living in the mountains owned four-wheel drive vehicles and it wasn't uncommon to see many of them with snow plows on them in the winter. Many people also owned snow mobiles which often was the only way around. Every able bodied person did all they could to make sure that the community was taken care of and could travel. Most of the local businesses stayed open during normal hours. Things slowed down, but by no means would snow storms stop the town completely. They were used to these kinds of living conditions.

The front door of the Sheriff's office suddenly opened and Lindsey Watney walked in along with a brutal gust of cold wind and snow. She was the dispatcher and worked the day shift. After she closed the door and stamped her boots off she headed straight over to the coffee pot.

"Good morning Nick!" she said in a gruff morning voice.

"Morning Linds," the Sheriff responded. "How was your ride over?"

"Cold, very cold! I have no idea what makes me stay in this place. I could be living in California or Florida where it's warm all the time," She said.

Lindsey was an attractive single lady in her early forties with long red hair, emerald green eyes and a very curvy figure. She could certainly turn heads no matter how she was dressed though she filled out her uniform quite well. She liked to go out in the evenings to the local Three Frogs Tavern. She played just as hard as she worked, but she wasn't getting any younger and it took a little longer in the mornings to recover than it did in her younger days. After pouring a cup of coffee she made her way over to her desk.

"Any calls come in Sheriff?"

"Interestingly enough, yes."

The sheriff relayed all that he knew about the Turner case and that he had sent Larson over to meet with Burt. The older man walked over and poured another cup of coffee and then switched on the radio. Soon, the air was filled with classic country music that the sheriff preferred. The others didn't mind as it was mostly just a little background filler as they went about their daily duties. A few of the other deputies would be getting up and getting ready for their shifts. They would take four wheel drive pickups or sleds out on patrol as the weather could make navigating a little treacherous in certain places on the mountain.

+++

The snow was falling steadily, though not nearly as heavy as it was the day before. The wind was gusting and bringing in a frozen arctic blast with it. The wind chill alone dropped below freezing. Deputy Larson soon found the small coffee shop on the main street of town and parked his snow-mobile in front. Walking inside, he felt the heat from the pot-bellied stove in the corner and it felt good. He was soon greeted by an older lady with soft brown eyes and short graying hair.

"Good morning, didn't expect anyone this early, but I have coffee on. Have a seat deputy."

Mrs. Townsend was a sweet lady who was raising her grandchildren. One of which, a cute little five year old girl, watched the deputy with the flickering flames of the firelight shining off her chubby little cheeks. She shrank down on her knees as she peered over the back of the chair.

"Thanks Mrs. Townsend, how are you doing this morning?" Larson asked. "I'm sure glad you're always open. I've been dying for one of your cream cheese Danishes."

She laughed politely as she poured him a cup of hot coffee. "You know me Billy, I have to be busy doing something or I'll simply do nothing at all. Besides, I have to fix breakfast for these kids anyway so I might as well fix breakfast for any brave soul that feels like getting out in this winter storm. Can I get you something besides the coffee and Danish Billy? "

+++

The snow fall was just as heavy as ever if not thicker. Phil had seen a lot of snow before, but this storm was seriously monumental to him. The wind chill alone was excruciating. He had no idea how human beings could possibly live like this for several months out of the year. He needed sunshine and warmth on his face and his thoughts lingered to his home in Oklahoma. He worked at a local factory as a welder and he was used to the extreme temperature. The snow, ice and constant freezing wind-chill were something that he could handle on short excursions, but this was not what he bargained for. He had been slogging away now for what felt like hours, but in reality was only about a half an hour since he had found the road. He hadn't heard anymore gun shots and thankfully, no more of those terrifying screams from that creature. He had been trying to believe that Craig and Troy had killed the beast and would be along any moment now though he hadn't heard the familiar sound of the ATV.

It was beginning to get lighter outside though there was no sunrise that he could see. Probably wouldn't see the sun again for weeks. He could just make out silhouettes of the trees that lined the edges of the road. He clicked his flashlight off and put it away in his coat pocket. He kept his hands tucked away under his arms and huddled as tightly as he could, attempting to retain as much of his body warmth as possible. His cold weather gear was well insulated, but was no match for this extended period. He was frozen to the bone and his legs screamed at him to just stop, but he had to keep moving for fear of dying out here. Every step was harder and harder. *Just stop and rest*, he thought, *it would be okay to just rest for a few minutes. Catch your breath and then, move on.* No. He knew he shouldn't, he had to keep moving and get out of the weather. It wouldn't be long now and he could enjoy the warmth of the fireplace and maybe something hot to eat. The thought of the smell of bacon sizzling in the frying pan and coffee on the stove was tantalizing. Soon, he thought, soon.

Phil suddenly stopped short in his tracks as an ear piercing shriek split the cold morning air near him and made the hair on the back of his neck stand straight up. It sounded mournful, deep, and as if in agonizing pain yet terrifying at the same time. It froze him in place, shrinking down inside himself trying to become invisible yet knowing he was standing out in the open roadway. There was no way of knowing what that sound was or where it came from as it seemed omnipresent on the mountain. He had never heard anything like it in all his years…with the exception of earlier when he had heard the gun shots too. This time, there were no accompanying gun shots. No other sounds at all; just the falling snow.

Phil's mind was racing as his eyes scanned the area quickly, looking for any movement. Next to the road near him was a stand of cedar trees. He leaped over to them and scrambled underneath the bushy canopy and curled up to hide. As he lay there shivering both from the cold and pure fear, he heard the despondent scream of the creature again. This time, it seemed even closer. It actually sounded lower in pitch and had more of a deep, resonating growl similar to that of a lion. Confused, Phil carefully pushed himself up to a sitting position against the trunk of the tree, careful not to make any sound that would give his position away. He couldn't see much through the snow covered branches of the cedar trees though he could hear something moving through the woods coming toward him.

He frantically felt around in his pockets for anything at all that could be used as a weapon. His hands were trembling with fear and cold as he came up empty. Not even a nearby branch that he could use as a spear point or club. He had to hope and pray that whatever it was that was coming his way did not sense his presence. Again, he heard the creature give out a low mournful growl. Then, he heard an answering growl from further up. 'Oh God', he thought, 'there's not just one. There's more!'

+++

Burt stopped the snow plow in the parking lot across from the small café and made his way across the street. The snow was still coming down and not many vehicles were out and about though a few could be seen in the city streets. As he walked in Mrs. Townsend greeted him.

"Good morning."

"Good morning Mrs. Townsend," Burt began, "could you bring me a cup of coffee please? black."

"Coming right up Burt." She replied.

The deputy waved Burt over as he finished eating his pastry.

"Hey Burt, thanks for meeting me, appreciate it."

"No problem Billy, about time for a break anyway. Been out since 4am when I took over for Randy. He worked a ten hour shift and it looks like I'll be doing about the same. Storm's gonna last a few days and really cover things up, but we'll have several plows going to keep the streets as clear as possible," Burt replied.

"Yeah it's nasty out there. The ski slopes will be great with this much natural powder. I stayed at the office last night. No matter how used to it everyone is, when one of these storms comes through it really slows things down." The deputy said. "So what can you tell me about that accident this morning?"

"Well, I can tell you this. That Jeep took a real beating long before he got to where I found it over on 4th street! The airbags had been deployed and the front end caved it. From the looks of it, I'd say he hit a tree head on."

Burt reached into his pocket and withdrew a set of keys and handed them to the deputy.

"These are the keys to it. I didn't try to move it in case you needed to check it out first. Looks like he passed out at the wheel and just drifted off the road and the snow drift stopped him. I haven't a clue how it was even drivable with that airbag blown out like that."

"Hmmm," the deputy responded. "It sounds like he was trying to get to the hospital on his own after he wrecked it. He had a couple of friends that were staying with him though. Apparently he had invited them up to stay with him and go hunting. Wonder why they weren't with him? Did you see any signs that they may have been around?"

"No. There wasn't anyone else there," Burt replied. "But hey, he did have a Colt .45 on him when I found him. It was lying in the passenger floor board. I left it locked up in his Jeep. There's also a rifle in there too. Told the paramedics when they got there though. Not that there's anything wrong with that. I just don't want it to go missing or anything ya know."

The snow plow driver told him that he had been clearing the streets when he spotted the Jeep. The lights were on and it was still running. Normally he wouldn't have paid much attention to it, but the Jeep was nosed into the snow drift perpendicular to the curb so he stopped his truck and walked over to see if anyone was in it. That's when he found Troy slumped over the wheel.

Burt immediately called 911 and then called his dispatcher to let him know. Burt had to reach in and put the vehicle's transmission into park. The heater was still on full so he left the engine running for that reason until the paramedics got him safely out. The ambulance arrived within a few minutes and carefully extracted Troy and took him to the hospital. Afterwards, Burt turned the engine off, locked the Jeep up, and put the keys in his pocket.

Deputy Larson and Burt sat and talked for about half an hour as Mrs. Townsend scurried around the kitchen. The little girl watched cartoons on the television, paying no attention to the grownups talking. A couple of people came into the café and ordered breakfast and lingered near the warm stove in the back.

After Larson got the necessary information he needed, he thanked Burt for meeting him, paid for his coffee and headed for the door. Before stepping out, he put on his coat, gloves, and helmet. His cold weather gear protected him from the elements as long as he wore it properly. Once geared up, he stepped out, started the sled and drove off in the direction of where Burt told him the Jeep was.

The town of Hawthorn was more of a mural on a dreary, gray canvas of winter skies. The artist, in this case, Mother Nature, was painting with only one color, white. The fluffy, white discs of snow were falling while the brush stroke of the wind carried it in the perfect pattern outlining buildings, cars, trees and the entire landscape. The artist used the wind as a brush with wispy and carefree strokes leaving nothing untouched.

The deputy traveled down Main Street and turned west when he reached fourth. He made great time on the machine and soon found the Jeep just as Burt described. It was nosed against the curb stuck in a deep snow drift. No businesses were open at that particular location as it was mostly a warehouse district. He stopped next to the Jeep and took a look around. The snow fall had long covered any possible tracks of other vehicles or people. He walked around to the front of the Jeep and gave out a soft whistle when he saw the damage. Indeed, it looked like Troy had smacked head-on into a very large tree. He knew it was a tree from all of the bark still embedded in the grill. He took out his cell phone and snapped some photos before taking a look inside.

The airbags had deployed and apparently Troy couldn't remove it so he had wrapped it around the steering wheel so that he could drive it. There was some blood on the white canvas airbag and on the steering wheel, gear shifter and radio. Not a lot, but enough to be concerned about. The deputy snapped some more photos and then called the sheriff.

"Hey sheriff, I talked to Burt and I'm at the Jeep now. Took some photos and I'll call the wrecker to come pick it up. It's stuck in the snow out in front of the old Thompson warehouse on fourth."

"Okay, Billy," The sheriff responded. "Sounds good. I'm going to run over to the hospital now and check on our boy. See if I can get some answers."

The sheriff hung up the phone and turned his attention to the weather report that was on the television.

"Turn that up Linds," Nick asked, as he switched off the radio.

"It looks like this storm is sitting in for a long spell. I'd better get over to the hospital and check on that Turner fellow. I'll take my truck. If you need me..." The Sheriff trailed off as he pulled on his coat and gloves.

"Yup, I know how to reach ya!" Lindsey said as she gave a nod at the sheriff.

Chapter 16

Blaine walked out of his office, got in his truck and headed for the hospital. There were only a handful of vehicles out on the road at this time of the morning. Most folks were headed to work; others were out getting groceries and running errands. The town relied mostly on the tourist trade of sportsmen from hunting and fishing to skiing. The small resort town was bundled up fairly well for this winter storm. Like the many other storms before this one, it too would pass. The residents were very well adept to the environment.

The sheriff made his way across town stopping at the occasional red light. There were more snow mobiles than automobiles at the moment. It was simply a way of life up here. There were at least a dozen places where visitors could rent them by the hour along with maps for trails that led all over the mountain to guide them. The trails were clearly marked with bright red flags. Even a few of the ski resorts rented them out to their guests as well. No matter how bad it snowed, one could almost certainly get around on a snow mobile.

Nick pulled into the hospital parking lot and found a spot near the front entrance. He called into dispatch to let them know he had arrived and would be on his mobile radio, turned off the ignition and headed towards the door. Once inside, he made his way over to the reception area and asked for Doctor Jenkins. After a few moments on the phone the young lady told the sheriff that the doctor was in his office now and he could go on back. She asked if he knew the way and after he told her yes, he walked down the hallway and made his way to the office.

"Come in Sheriff," Doctor Jenkins said when he noticed him start to knock on the open door frame.

"Thanks Doc. Thought I'd come by and check in on the Turner fella. Any news?"

"I was just getting ready to make my way back down there if you'd care to join me."

The two men left the doctor's office and headed for the patient floor where Troy was recovering. As they walked along, the doctor explained to the sheriff that troy had broken ribs, a broken nose, and multiple contusions that all seem to have been suffered from the crash.

"Sheriff, he's running a high fever which is my first priority. He's been out since he was brought in and quite honestly, he's not been resting peacefully at all. He's dehydrated so, of course, we've been giving him fluids and he's starting to really feel those busted ribs. He's been through some trauma and I'm not sure when he will be awake or even if he will be coherent when he is."

The doctor asked the sheriff if he knew if Troy had anyone listed as an emergency contact. Nick told him that as far as he knew, he lived alone. The two men entered the room where Troy was lying motionless. A nurse was just leaving and mentioned that his vitals were the same as earlier and answered a few more questions from the doctor. Afterwards, she excused herself and made her way out of the room scurrying to the next patient.

"One thing in his favor right now," the doctor started. "is the fact that physically, he's in very good shape and that will help him recover quicker, but those ribs are going to be painful for the next few weeks. He needs to stay right there in that bed until I release him. I expect he'll recover fully in no time though."

The sheriff asked the doctor a few more questions in hushed tones then began to leave. As they turned for the door they heard a sound behind them coming from Troy. Thinking he may be waking, the two men turned to the patient. Troy was slowly moving his head back and forth and his hands were slightly moving, trembling was the more correct term.

"What's happening Doc?" The sheriff asked.

The doctor went over to check on the patient and felt his forehead.

"Fever most likely. It could be from hypothermia. I'm just not sure how long he was out there or what all happened. Once that fever breaks though, he should be in much better shape. I think that's what has him so agitated and unable to rest well."

Troy's eyes suddenly flew wide open and he attempted to sit up.

"Help me hold him down! He'll do more damage to those ribs thrashing about like that."

Nick helped the doctor hold Troy back in the hospital bed by gently pushing on his shoulders. At the time a nurse passing by in the hallway heard the commotion and hurried into the room to assist; relieving the sheriff.

Troy was mumbling incoherently, but the sheriff could make out some of the words he was muttering.

"That thing is huge, help, oh God no!" After a moment, the delirium seemed to have passed and Troy once again was sleeping peacefully.

The sheriff asked the doctor, "What was all of that about?"

"I haven't a clue Sheriff, sounds to me like he's having a nightmare. Result of the fever I'm sure. We've got to get that down."

Nick backed up out of the way and let the medical staff check on their patient. Another nurse joined the group and after a few more minutes the doctor stepped away and allowed them to do their job. The sheriff talked with the doctor a few minutes longer and told him that if Troy's condition changed to let him know immediately. The doctor assured him that he would be the first to know.

As Sheriff Blaine walked out of the hospital into the cold, wind-driven snow, his thoughts were on the conversation he had with Troy's friends when he had brought the one fellow back into town. 'Didn't they say they were staying for a couple of weeks to go hunting? Why would they have left? They most likely wouldn't have any prior knowledge of how bad this winter storm would be so they had no reason to try and get ahead of it and go home.'

The engine roared to life when the sheriff turned the ignition key. He reached down for the radio and called his dispatcher to let her know that he was back in his truck and was heading out to check on Troy's cabin.

+++

The streets in town were easily traversed however the highway out to Troy's cabin wasn't as clear. The sheriff's truck was a large SUV four-wheel drive and Nick was a good driver in these conditions as most people in the mountains were. As long as people were careful and drove slowly they could usually get to where they needed to go. The county had snow plows running as well, but they had a lot more miles to cover than the city plows. If the roads or passes had been closed, the county commissioner would have let Nick know as soon as the call was made.

About twenty minutes later the sheriff spotted a large truck with a snow plow blade clearing the opposite side of the highway. As he approached he could see that it was Charlie Huffman, a local rancher in his late fifties who also worked for the county. Huffman had worked many years for the highway department. He was born and raised in this area and knew well the routes that needed clearing first. Nick knew Charlie and the other men that worked for the county commissioners. He often had lunch with them and at times dropped by the commissioner's equipment barns.

Nick waved to Charlie as he passed by. There were a few more vehicles that drove behind the snow plow most likely on their way into town. The snow had not let up and the truck was only capable of about thirty-five to forty miles per hour, but often slowing down to barely more than a crawl. Normally, it would take about an hour or so to get to Troy's cabin, but with this storm, that could easily double.

The sheriff had been around long enough to know that the weather patterns up at this altitude weren't nearly as predictable as he would like. *'Hopefully, this storm isn't a precursor to a really bad winter,'* he thought. It was early in the season for a snow storm like this one. Usually, they wouldn't get this much until December or later. The ski resorts were just now starting to open and were usually making their own snow at this time so this would be a welcome base for them.

The local businesses were built around the snow season so they were probably grateful for the snow. There were a couple of lakes that would freeze solid enough to support ice fishing and local resorts that rented out ice-fishing cabins that could be dragged out onto the lake. Many of the local folks had their own lake shanties they would drag out and leave each year, but it would still be a while before that would happen.

+++

Phil lay as quietly as he could under the protection of the cedar tree. He was frozen to the bone and shaking so hard that he had to bite down on a glove to keep his teeth from chattering. He had no idea what kind of animal these things were, but the last thing he wanted was for them to find him. He curled up as tightly as he could under the thick branches. The snow was coming down pretty hard and he hoped that helped to disguise his trail that led under the canopy. He silently prayed that they would pass him by!

The creatures were lumbering down out of the woods toward the road below where he lay hidden. Separated by only a few yards, they seemed to be coming to either side of his position. A smell crept into Phil's nostrils so putrid that he nearly gagged. It had to be coming from the animals. He buried his nose deeper into his chest and tried not to breathe deeply.

The first beast walked within a few feet of the cedar tree, but never stopped. Phil couldn't see much of the animal through the branches as they were thick with needles, but he could see the animal's feet and legs. It was as if a cold, dark aura exuded over the animal. His mind screamed, *'It's walking upright...on two legs!'* Though he could not make it out, he knew the beast was huge. He could hear its footsteps and feel how heavy it was with each stride. He felt relieved and started to breathe easier as it moved further away when he suddenly remembered. *'There are two of them!'*

The second beast followed its wounded mate down through the woods toward the lake at the bottom of the mountain. The snow was thick and the wind had picked up. The cold was not a worry for the bipedal creature with its dark black fur acting as a thick insulation. It was used to this type of weather as it ranged mostly in the snow cap regions of the mountains only coming down to lower elevations to hunt. Despite its enormous size, the creature was very quick and nimble as were the rest of its kind. They had to be stealthy to hunt and survive through the ages without being seen or captured. It was an ancient creature perhaps surviving from the last ice age in seclusion.

Dark crimson matted the fur in several places on the creature's body - the result of gunshot wounds. The blood dripped from the beast onto the soft, white down of the snow pack in a trail quickly being covered by the fresh falling powder and the blustery wind. The beast staggered along trying to keep pace with its mate, but falling behind. The other would pause long enough to look for danger and allow the other to catch up. They had a great sense for danger and were very good hunters. With incredible strength, the Sasquatch could easily break the neck of large mammals such as deer and sheep. A human stood no chance!

Phil could feel the presence of the adult Sasquatch nearby and attempted to keep his fear in check. He slowed his breathing and remained as still as possible in the current conditions and prayed the beasts wouldn't find him. The huge bipedal animal paused for a short moment very near Phil's location as if it had sensed something, but then continued on. Phil waited another few moments before breathing a sigh of relief. He was half frozen from the cold, but half frozen from fear. He had heard stories about creatures like these, but never dreamed in a million years that they could be true. He waited quietly for quite some time before he dared moved. In his nest under the tree he had a wind block and was actually starting to feel a little warmer. He slowly crawled out of his hiding spot and stood up looking around for the beasts that had hunted him and his friends.

He spotted their trail after a few moments. It seemed to be winding down the mountain side heading toward the lake. They were huge; easily standing eight feet tall or better and their strides in the snow were almost twice that of Phil's. They had crossed the road and as he stood up, he spotted the blood trail they were leaving behind. There was quite a bit of it and he knew that the creature had to be severely injured, most likely a result of Craig's and Troy's shooting. Phil wondered to himself what had become of them. He hoped his friends were still out looking for him, but he hadn't heard so much as another gunshot or the Razor's engine in a while now. *'Had they retreated back to the cabin? Had the creatures injured them or worse?'* He decided he should stay in the tree line next to the road and continue on to the cabin, hoping it wasn't far!

+++

Sheriff Blaine finally made it to the turnoff leading to Troy's cabin and exited the highway. The snow was blowing harder now and the visibility had worsened slowing him down even more. He wore ultraviolet coated lenses in his slightly tinted sunglasses which helped his vision in the bright, white snow. The dirt road was completely covered in over a foot of it and therefore difficult to make out. He had to be very careful not to venture off the road too much for fear of getting stuck in a bar ditch that was covered by the drifts.

The four-wheel drive crept along the desolate road. The man inside vigilant to his surroundings, looked for any sign of where the Jeep may have crashed or of the other two men. The wind was beginning to blow the snow much harder making visibility even worse. At one point he had to stop the vehicle altogether and wait for the snow to lighten up again.

After driving for about twenty minutes down the dirt road he came to an abrupt stop. A huge dead tree had fallen across the road blocking it entirely. There was no way around it in the truck. There wasn't enough room on either side to drive around and with the snow as deep as it was, he didn't want to take a chance of getting stuck. Even in four wheel drive, there was no way of knowing what was under the snow.

He stopped the vehicle and shifted it into park. He stepped out closing the door behind him and took a quick look around. He needed a chainsaw and about twenty minutes to cut the tree up, but he didn't have one with him. He knew he needed a snow mobile to get past this point and there was nothing more he could do other than turn around. He'd have to wait the storm out and bring a sled with him to get through the pass.

The sheriff turned to walk back to the truck. It sat there idling with the windshield wipers slowly waving back and forth, headlight beams shining into the snow filled air. He shivered from the cold air blowing snow into the collar of his coat. He pulled it up tight and continued on his way back to the truck never seeing the man standing in the middle of the road a few hundred yards ahead waving frantically for him!

+++

Phil could make out the headlights of the vehicle that was stopped in the mountain pass only a few hundred yards up the road. He took a chance that the creatures were gone now so he walked out into the middle of the road and tried to wave the vehicle down. He wasn't sure if they could see him or not because the snow was blowing so hard. Visibility was difficult, but he did his best to wave his arms overhead though he dared not yell at the vehicle in fear of alerting the beasts of his whereabouts.

The truck began moving, but it was backing up. Phil saw the taillights and then it was gone. Deflated and scared he turned back toward the direction of the cabin and pressed on. He had to make it soon. He was frozen, dizzy and weak from hunger. He suddenly realized he hadn't eaten anything in more than twenty-four hours nor had he had anything to drink. 'Hopefully the cabin is close. I don't think I can make it much further in this storm.' he thought to himself. If he could get there he would have a fighting chance. Out here in the open like this, he wouldn't survive.

He stayed in the tree line as best he could and followed the road. The going was very slow because of the deepening snow drifts. The storm was relentless and not letting up anytime soon. At least he could use it to his advantage and help cover his tracks. If he couldn't see very far, then the creatures couldn't either. That gave him hope as he trudged along. He kept a cautious eye out for the beasts, but saw no further sign of them.

Phil instinctively knew that the terrain was steadily on a down grade so he knew he was on the right track because he remembered the road from the bridge to the cabin was on a slight grade. He surmised he must be near the bridge. He started paying more attention to the terrain and eventually, he saw what he was looking for. The lake lay below!

Elated and confident he was near the cabin he took a chance that the creatures weren't nearby and moved onto the road where he felt he could make better time. He was frozen to the bone and he knew that if he didn't find shelter soon, he would die out here. Another twenty minutes and he saw the bridge crossing the lake. He must have come down much further away from the cabin than what he thought, but now he knew the cabin was only about another thirty to forty minute walk beyond the bridge. He was almost home!

+++

Doctor Jenkins was sitting at his desk dictating reports when a nurse hurried in.

"Doc, the Turner fellow just woke up and is asking for the sheriff. He's frantic and sounds half out of his mind."

The doctor quickly got up and followed the nurse to his patient's room. Troy was trying to get a nurse to understand how important it was for him to speak with the sheriff. He turned his attention to the doctor when he walked into the room.

"Doctor, you've got to get the sheriff over here. There's been an attack at the cabin. It was a huge grizzly that attacked us and he's got to get someone out there now. My friends are still out there and they need help. Phil was still out on the mountain lost somewhere and Craig went after him. I came to town to try and get help because I got hurt trying to fix the satellite dish on the house..." he trailed off as the doctor spoke up.

"Son I've already talked to the sheriff; he was here earlier. What I need for you to do is to lay back and rest. We'll get someone out there. I'm sure the sheriff can find your buddies. They'll be just fine."

Troy was exhausted and dehydrated. His injuries were taking a toll on him and he had no energy to argue. The pain medication that the doctor had prescribed kept him relaxed and groggy. He soon fell asleep again.

"Nurse Bradley, I'm heading back to my office to get in touch with the sheriff. Watch him and make sure he stays put. Don't let him hurt himself."

Doctor Jenkins hurriedly made his way back down the hospital hallway to his office, entered, and closed the door behind him. He sat down at his desk and picked up the phone. After a few moments, the dispatcher at the sheriff's office answered the call. The doctor explained that Mr. Turner had awakened long enough to talk to him and that he needed the sheriff to call him as soon as he could. He also relayed the information that Troy gave him as best he could. The dispatcher told him she would relay the message and that the sheriff was in the field now trying to get out to the cabin. He hadn't checked in for quite some time now so she would see if she could raise him.

After hanging up the phone, Lindsey keyed the microphone on the radio unit and called for the sheriff. After a few seconds, the speaker crackled with the sheriff's voice.

"Yeah, Linds, go ahead."

"Sheriff, ... kins just called. Said ..... woke up and .... about a .... attack. Said the other ......grizzly.... out there on the mountain some..... and was ......ed about them."

"Can you repeat that Linds, you're breaking up?"

She tried again, but this time she spoke in shorter bursts, hoping that the sheriff could get the main idea of what it was she was relaying.

"Try calling the cabin and see if you can get through to anyone out there."

I've already ..ied that She..ff, getting nothing."

"Damnit!" The Sheriff exclaimed. "I'm on Reed Road now. Tried getting to the cabin. Can't get through. Road blocked. I need a sled to make it through."

He wasn't sure if she could hear him or not. He couldn't take the chance and drive all the way back to town. He needed to stay put just in case the other two men were trying to get out of the valley.

".... for back-up?" He heard her say.

'Thank goodness,' he thought. 'Maybe she got it!'

"Yes, call Larson. Call Pete and Noland too. Bring snow mobiles."

After that the sheriff signed off. Hopefully, Lindsey got it all. Maybe she would even think to call Wayne over at the forestry office and let him know that they may have a bear prowling around scaring folks. She's been there long enough to know the routine.

Blaine turned his police lights on and continued up the road until he found a place to turn around safe enough not to get stuck. He slowly backed in, turned around and drove back toward the cabin once again. He knew he could only go so far, but he would wait there until his deputies arrived. Hopefully, it wouldn't be more than a couple of hours. Larson was very adept at his job and could get the others rounded up quickly and load the snow mobiles. That would be the only way in to the lake cabin of Troy Turners today.

Chapter 17

Phil Jackson's deep arctic camouflage coat wrapped snuggly about him with the hood pulled low and tight around his face. He kept a hole small enough that his dark brown eyes could peer out without exposing his skin. He leaned into the hard blowing wind and plodded heavily toward his goal. He couldn't see the road he was on, but he could tell that he was going in the right direction by keeping the lake on his right side. His mind was swimming with question after question.

'Where are Troy and Craig? Were they hurt? Were they still searching for him? Would they find him before the creatures did? What would he do if the creatures found him?' He wasn't able to run and he was much too tired even if he could.

It was still early in the day so at least he had the daylight to work with though he couldn't see anything, but trees and snow and a gray, blue sky. The snow had let up a little, but the cold and the wind seemed to have picked up in its place.

Phil's thoughts turned to home, wondering if he'd ever see it again. He was a Cherokee and lived traditional in many ways. He grew up in the woods around Tahlequah, Oklahoma and knew his way around them well. He hunted and fished for food, not simply for sport. His grandfather had taught him to revere the land and the gifts that the Creator bestowed upon them with the wild game. It was a way of life that he respected.

He was fluent in his first language just as he was at speaking English. He often said that when he dreamed at night, everyone spoke in Cherokee. Through the years after the three men became friends, he would teach them different words and their meanings. He often took them to powwows held during the holiday in September.

His uncle taught him to hunt and fish and how to be a responsible man. His mother worked for the tribe at the Nation's headquarters in Tahlequah and pushed Phil to go to school and learn as much as he could. She told him many times that an education is important. "You have and will always learn from life if you keep your eyes open and listen more than you speak." College was something they talked about often and when the time came, he was ready. He was always a good student and earned several scholarships along the way.

Phil remembered the first time he met Troy on campus. He had gone over to watch the team practice that afternoon. When they were done, he and Craig had planned on going over to the student union for dinner. Troy joined them in the dining hall. The three sat and laughed all evening telling jokes and stories about home. Later, they hung out after that every chance they got. The friendship was something that would last a lifetime.

He stopped suddenly and held as still as possible. He didn't know what it was, but he knew something was there. It may have been a slight movement he caught out of the corner of his eye or something that seemed out of place. He scanned the road ahead and the tree line all around. He couldn't see anything, but had the strange feeling of being watched. His senses were on high alert.

+++

Sheriff Blaine turned on the vehicle's emergency lights on top and continued down the road following the tracks he had just made. He remembered a spot just a little further up that was a little wider and he thought that may be a good place to park and wait on the others. It would take a couple of hours for them to reach him.

They would have to gather up all the snow mobiles and supplies for a search and rescue. Then, they would have to travel on the snow covered highway and this mountain road out to the cabin.

He found the wider spot in the road he was looking for and pulled as far as he could to one side. There he left the engine running, climbed out and rummaged through his tactical gear in the back. He found the black case he was looking for and returned to his seat in the front. The temp gauge showed that it was twenty-eight degrees outside, but the wind chill made it feel much lower. He opened the case and inspected the contents. Satisfied all was in order, he settled in for the wait. Nothing else he could do until his back up arrived.

The red and blue emergency lights from the vehicle reflected off of the stark white of the snow pack in a mesmerizing cascade of color. The windshield wipers made a hypnotizing woosh-thump sound every few seconds. Blaine was just about to doze off when he heard the crackle of the deputy come over the radio.

"Sheriff, this is Deputy Larson. Do you copy?"

"Yeah, I'm here Larson," the sheriff responded.

"Just turned off the highway on Reed Road. ETA should be about thirty to forty-five minutes to your position."

As the sheriff settled in to wait, his mind drifted to what Troy had said. The last thing the small town of Hawthorn needed was a bear attack. Nick Blaine had seen his share of wild animal attacks in these mountains and he knew the scare that it put into the locals, let alone tourists. Once rumors started going around about an attack, it would spread like wildfire and be embellished beyond the truth which was bad for business all the way around. His back-up would be here soon and they could begin a search for the other two hunters in question. With any luck at all, they were simply holed up at the cabin with no way to call out.

+++

Phil slowly tried raising his right foot. There it was; movement in the tree line just on the other side of the bridge. He wasn't sure if whoever or whatever it was spotted him, but he knew there was something there for certain now. It was just too far away in this wintery storm and he couldn't see it well enough. Was it the Sasquatch? Had they backtracked to lure him out? Whatever it was, it was between him and the safety of the cabin. He knew that once he made it to the bridge, the cabin was only a half a mile or so away. His heart began racing madly and his breath caught in his throat. It began moving out from the trees!

Phil didn't wait around to find out if the creature had seen him or not. He slowly lowered himself as close to the ground as possible and moved off the edge of the road and made his way into the trees. He knew that there was no way possible for him to go around the lake to the cabin. His only way in, and the fastest way in, was over that bridge!

Once he reached the tree line and he felt he was out of sight, he stood up and made a run for a better position. He wanted to try and maneuver close to this end of the bridge where he could keep an eye out for the beast. Maybe it didn't see him move off the road. It's possible that the creature never knew he was there at all. The snow was heavy and the wind was strong. Visibility wasn't very good and he was just lucky enough to have spotted the creature first.

The snow was deep and the moving was slow. The fact that he was half frozen and wrapped in arctic clothing also slowed him down considerably. If he had snow shoes, he may be able to move faster, but unfortunately, he didn't have any.

He spotted a group of cedar trees with thick, bushy branches and quickly made his way to them. He scurried under it and made a small hole where he could see under and out onto the road. There he waited. His hiding spot was only about twenty feet from the road, but the bridge was about fifty yards further away. The dark figure was just past the bridge on the other side, but in the tree line when it had moved forward. He would try to wait it out and see if he could sneak around behind it after it passed by.

Phil waited for what he thought was about fifteen minutes or so without seeing or hearing anything moving. Not that he would hear much in the soft powdery snow. He slowly crawled out of his hiding spot and moved toward the edge of the lake scanning everywhere he could for any sign of the creature. He was frozen stiff and exhausted, but the adrenaline rush helped to keep him moving forward. It took only a few minutes to get to the lake then he made his way along the edge toward the bridge. Once he got there he stopped and looked up at the bridge and all around the area closely. Seeing nothing further, he made the decision to cross.

He was about eight feet below the bottom of the bridge railings standing just on the edge of the lake. The steep incline would be difficult to climb, but it was either climb up here and cross or back-track and come down from the road to the bridge. The bridge was a trestle style and about a hundred feet across. The water looked fairly deep beneath it, but it was certainly too cold to try and swim across. He decided that he would try to climb up the snow covered bank and cross now. He didn't know what time of day it was, but he didn't want to be stuck on this side of the bridge when it got dark.

Moving cautiously, he leaned into the side of the incline and put both hands on the ground in front of him to get as much traction as he could. It would be slippery, but hopefully on all fours, it wouldn't present too much of a problem. He put one foot up and then reached up with the opposite hand inching his way up the slippery slope. For every foot he gained, he lost half of it sliding back down. It was exhausting and he had to lie flat every few minutes just to catch his breath. His lungs were screaming and his legs felt like frozen popsicles. He could barely bend them at his knees in order to climb up the slope. Finally reaching the crest of the eight foot hill, he peered over, scanning both the bridge and the road. Seeing nothing, he lurched for one of the metal railings to pull himself up, but it was frozen over with ice and snow causing him to lose his grip and fall backwards down the snowy embankment.

Tumbling over backwards and sliding down, Phil splashed into the edge of the water. He desperately grasped for anything to cling to, but came up empty handed. There was a ring of ice around the edge of the lake and he had nothing to pull himself up with. He tried kicking one of his legs up on the edge, but fell back into the water submerging briefly before popping back up. He was genuinely scared and began to panic as he struggled.

Gasping for air, he resurfaced and struggled to find a solid surface to cling to, but his gloves only found the slick surface of the snow covered bank. The edge of the lake wasn't particularly deep, but the muddy bottom below wouldn't allow for a solid foot hold. The water soaked his clothing rapidly making it heavier by the second. He was weakening and his struggle became sheer terror as he knew he would surely die. He tried leaping out onto the bank, but he didn't have enough strength or any hand holds. Clawing madly, he slipped back in again and went under.

He began to fade; his body was slowly succumbing to the frigid waters of the lake. His muscles screamed for oxygen and he continued to struggle to move, but his arms and legs had no more strength to give. He began to lose consciousness.

+++

Sheriff Blaine saw the headlights of the deputy's truck in his rear view mirror, took one last puff on his cigarette, rolled up his window and stepped out. He grabbed a black balaclava and slipped it on followed by his bright red parka with the word, Sheriff, emblazoned on the front and back. Before he closed up his parka completely, he opened the black case and pulled out the .454 Casull and strapped it into a shoulder holster underneath his coat. Grabbing a handful of extra rounds and dropping them in his pocket he turned to meet his deputies.

Larson's truck stopped next to the sheriff and three doors opened almost simultaneously. Nick knew that his dispatcher understood what he was trying to tell her about the situation. He didn't want any more than what he offered over the radio to go out publicly; not until he knew for sure what he was actually dealing with. He wasn't certain if the other two men were truly missing or not. If they were, then they would do a preliminary search while calling in for more emergency personnel. With any luck, the two men would be found sitting in front of the fireplace back at Troy's cabin. Better safe than sorry.

"I guess the roads are getting even worse?" The sheriff asked as a way of greeting.

"Yeah, I think we made pretty good time though. No way can the road crews keep up with this storm. I take it we're headed to Turner's cabin to look for his two hunting buddies?" Larson replied.

The sheriff brought the men up to speed with Deputy Larson filling in a few blank spots. They unloaded the sleds and set out for the cabin. It wouldn't take long to reach it on the snowmobiles, but there wouldn't be much daylight left to work with. The dark, gray overcast didn't truly allow much in the way of daylight anyway.

The sheriff led the men in a staggered formation down the snow covered road keeping a vigilant eye out for any sign of man or beast. The wind was brutal coming down off the snowcapped mountain though the snow had let up some. Each member of the team wore the same brightly colored red parka, black helmet and goggles to protect the eyes from the vicious wind and driven snow. They all also wore their service weapons within easy reach and rifles in scabbards on the snowmobiles. They knew that if there was an injured bear around it may get dangerous in a hurry.

Blaine suddenly held up his left hand signaling a stop. He pointed to a tree on the side of the road.

"Wait here."

He turned his sled off the road and drove down the hill coming to a stop on the back side of the tree. Turning off the ignition, he walked around and took a closer look examining it carefully. He could clearly see the damage to the tree and the ruts in the snow and mud. He knew right away that it was the one that Troy had hit with the Jeep.

"Looks like this is where Turner drove off the road. Tree is scarred up quite a bit and these branches didn't break off from the weight of the snow," he told the men as he climbed back on his machine. "Let's get on up to the cabin and see what we can find there."

Rounding a gentle curve in the road, the bridge came in to full view. Sheriff Blaine took the lead and rode up the incline and began crossing followed closely by Billy, then Pete with Noland bringing up the rear. Once on the other side of the lake bridge, the road curved back around and followed the edge of the lake all the way to the cabin. They were only about ten minutes away now and their senses were on high alert, scanning the tree line meticulously.

By the time the small company of officers pulled up to the cabin it was getting dark. A big 4x4 Ford truck sat parked in the driveway and lights were visible on the inside of the cabin. From the looks of it, the truck hadn't moved since the snow first started. There were no tracks around it and the snow was more than a foot deep on the hood and cab.

The sheriff signaled to the deputies to check around the property while he and Larson checked inside. He reached down and turned off the ignition, climbed off and removed his goggles and helmet. Deputy Larson followed suit and they both climbed the stairs. Billy gave a big rap on the door and when no one answered, he nodded to the sheriff and walked around to the back of the house. Sheriff Blaine gave Billy enough time to get around to the back and then rapped on the door once again, this time calling out.

"This is Sheriff Blaine of Hawthorn County. Anyone home?" He reached for the door knob, gave it a quick turn and pushed.

He pulled his sidearm out of its hip holster and slowly walked in. The lights were on in the entire house, but it was eerily silent. He noticed the blood stains right away and the gun lying on the couch. Hearing Billy enter through the back door, he pointed out the blood and motioned for him to check upstairs while he cleared the lower section. A few minutes later they met back in the living room.

"Nothing Sheriff. Nothing, but wet puddles of water on the floor and blood. No sign of any of the men upstairs."

"Nothing outside Sheriff!" Pete said as he pushed through the half closed front door to walk in.

"Stop right there Pete," the Sheriff exclaimed, motioning at the blood on the floor. "What did you find outside?"

"Well, doesn't look like that truck has moved in quite some time. Not since the snow started anyway. Looks like there was a four wheeler or off road vehicle of some kind that left from the front porch area leading toward the mountain and the doors are still wide open on the garage. Those tracks from there seem to be leading out to the driveway. Those are wider so I'm thinking that was probably the Jeep. No other tracks of any kind around the house or perimeter. The snow could've covered anything in a matter of minutes though. We also cleared the garage. Nothing!"

"From the looks of it Sheriff, whoever was bleeding got patched up in the sink. I'm sure all this water is melted snow from their boots, but there's blood on the counter next to the sink along with some scissors and tape. It looks like they left in a hurry. Do you think they were fighting or something?"

"Doesn't look like much of a struggle. Nothing is turned over or out of place. It's odd really! I found blood on the door frame to that back bedroom too. When I went to see Turner at the hospital he was banged up pretty good, but I don't think this blood is his." Nick said.

"Doesn't look like that rifle on the couch has been fired in a while either." Billy said, as he carefully examined the weapon. "No sign of the other two men, but all their gear is still here," he continued, motioning to the front door. "If they're not here, then that means they're out there somewhere!"

"Storm's on top of us now and it's not going to let up anytime soon," the sheriff stated. "Boys, we have one man in the hospital and two missing hunters. We also have a blasted winter snow storm that could turn to white out conditions on us at any time. If we don't find them fast, we may not find them at all. If they're out there and alive, they may not be for long in this weather!"

Chapter 18

Zachariah Blanchard was a tall, lean man with silver hair and steel gray eyes. He was comfortable in his late fifties and in great physical shape. One would not have guessed from the way he was dressed in simple work clothes driving the huge D9 dozer that he was the wealthy owner of Blanchard General Contractors, Inc. He built the business up from nothing to make it the success that it was today. The company had construction contracts all over the country and employed hundreds of people.

Today found him working a site in his hometown area of Hawthorn. Zach grew up in Hawthorn, and married right after college. He and his wife, Megan, were very active residents and a highly respected family. He enjoyed rolling up his sleeves and getting dirty with the work crews when his schedule permitted it. This was one project that he was definitely hands on with.

The project was a new private resort and spa in the mountains overlooking one of the beautiful valleys below. The area was one that had not been developed and would be extremely exclusive and private. The resort was scheduled for completion in eighteen months with plans including a main hotel with one-hundred twelve rooms, several private cabins, a spa, an indoor pool and a great hall for entertaining. Due to the recent snow storm, work was all but shut down on the project, but Zach was on the dozer to clear the access road to allow the workers to make it in and out.

Today, he was working alone. He enjoyed the few times that he could simply climb on the machines and move dirt. It wasn't something that he had the luxury of doing much of these days. He was usually much too busy running the company which left no time to play on the heavy machines. It was peaceful and calming allowing him time to think and destress.

Zach had been staying in one of the trailers on the job site and had sent the work crew home just before the storm had set in. He had opted to stay on site and keep an eye on things himself.

The backup alarm on the giant Cat sounded, Beep, beep, beep, as he dragged his blade to smooth out an area in the frozen roadway before moving on. The snow had stopped for the day, but it had dumped more than two feet over the last few days.

He shifted the heavy duty transmission into forward, readjusted his blade and slowly moved forward pushing earth and snow off the roadway with ease. The roar of the 410hp diesel engine was a testament to the power of the behemoth. The frozen ground and snow was no match for the dozer and easily gave way. Suddenly, something caught Zach's eye causing him to avert his attention farther up the roadway. Something moved on the side of the road. He was sure it was a deer or possibly an elk. Taking time to stop the dozer, he watched the area for it to come into site again. Zach rubbed his eyes in disbelief when the creature stepped out from behind a tree.

The beast was covered from head to foot in heavy black fur, walked upright and was every bit of eight feet tall. It stopped in the middle of the road and turned to look straight at Zach. The beast stood perfectly motionless for a brief moment before taking two giant steps across the road, and was out of site in a matter of seconds.

Zach sat frozen not believing what he just witnessed! He could feel the hair on the back of his neck standing straight up. He was scared and curious at the same time. Snapping out of his gaze, he reached into his coat and pulled out his cell phone and flipped the camera app on. He was too late to get a photo of the beast. He opened the throttle of the dozer and moved forward hoping to get another glimpse of it. He wasn't about to climb down. Not yet anyway.

The squeak of the steel tracks began as soon as he released the clutch. He reached the area where the beast had stood only moments earlier before it crossed the road and disappeared. He stopped the dozer and searched intently, looking the area over for any signs of movement. Seeing none, he climbed out of the cab and cautiously inspected the ground. He was astonished when he discovered the giant footprints in the snow. He snapped some photos of the tracks with his own size eleven boot beside one for relative size comparison. The tracks were almost twice that of his own and he took several photos. No one would ever believe what he had just witnessed. He had heard stories about Sasquatch all his life, but never truly believed in the reality of the beast - until now.

+++

The early season snow storm had blasted the area dumping more than two feet of the white powder covering everything in a soft, wintery blanket. Hawthorn could benefit from it at the ski resorts, but it made for a lot of snow plow miles being driven to clear the highways and main passes. It was more than a fair trade off since the local economy relied mostly on snow.

Sheriff Blaine and his deputies decided to make a sweep of the area and follow the trail that led up into the mountain, presumably the trail that the hunters had taken earlier. They spread out with the sheriff and Larson leading the way and the other two deputies following from further behind. They were all on a heightened sense of alertness due to the circumstances.

As they entered the forested area of the trail, they could distinguish traces of the tracks left behind from the ATV since less snow had fallen on ground under the canopy of trees. After twenty minutes of following the trail up toward the ridge, Larson suddenly threw up his hand and motioned for the others to stop. He walked off the path a short ways while leaving his snowmobile running. When he was finished looking over the terrain, he turned back to the others.

"The ATV stopped up there on the path, then turned back down through the trees and went off the trail. It'll be a little more difficult to follow, but I think I can make out the tracks in the snow well enough."

Nick made a quick decision and instructed his men.

"Noland, you and Pete follow the trail on around. Stay together and watch each other's back. Stay in radio contact. Me and Billy will follow this trail through the woods and see where it leads us," Blaine said. "Keep those radio's handy."

The two deputies rode off together following the trail as instructed. Billy was an expert tracker and could read the signs left on the trail that others couldn't such as how old the trail was, how many tracks had been through the area, to how far apart they may have been if one animal was following another. The sheriff trusted him more than anyone else in that regard.

It was beginning to get dark and they didn't have much time left before they would need to get off the mountain. It was getting much harder to see the trail in the woods and they weren't prepared to stay out in this weather overnight. Nick was about to toggle his radio to check on the others when he heard Billy shout.

"Over there!"

Nick looked in the direction Billy was pointing. It was a red and white ATV smashed up next to a huge pine. They both gunned the throttles and raced toward it. Upon approaching, they could see the vehicle was wrecked badly and had apparently hit the tree. They slowed their snowmobiles and pulled up to the wreck. As soon as they dismounted and began walking over, they both noticed the man laying prone twenty feet away from the wrecked ATV. They ran to him to check on him, but they knew that it was too late.

Nick called the other deputies on the radio and gave them GPS coordinates. When the other men arrived a short time later, the sheriff and Deputy Larson had marked the crime scene and had taken photos. Craig Morton was recognizable only by the identification he had in his pockets. At first glance, Nick considered that the man was the victim of a tragic accident, but further examination lead to more questions than answers. When they had completed all they could, the sheriff addressed them all.

"Fella's, we're going to do everything by the book on this, but we have to be off this mountain soon. This weather is not going to cooperate so we have to be careful. Not sure when this happened and we have no idea how or why or what the circumstances were leading up to it. We know that one man is in the hospital and one other is missing," Nick explained.

+++

The rescue team was able to extract the body the next day, along with what appeared to be a murder weapon - a large, green tree limb about five feet long and four inches around.

Craig Morton had been found covered in blood from an apparent beating. Snow had covered much of the area, but the evidence clearly showed that the missing hunter was killed, brutally beaten to death, rather than from injuries sustained in the crash one could only speculate. 'This changes everything,' the sheriff thought to himself.

Chapter 19

Two days later, Sheriff Blaine turned the wheel of his vehicle and pulled into the hospital parking lot, found a spot near the front, and parked. The weather was still nasty and would be for a while now. He was glad they found the one missing hunter, but was worried about the other one. He clipped his keys on his web belt as he got out of the 4X4 and hurried into the hospital. The search for the missing man was ongoing, but he needed to be the one to talk to Turner first. He entered the hospital by the emergency room doors. The lady at the desk shivered when the door opened and closed allowing the harsh, cold wind in. He asked her if Doctor Jenkins was in his office. She made a quick phone call to the doctor's office and was able to reach his nurse.

"The doctor is with a patient right now. His nurse suggested you could go on back and have a seat in his office while she tracked him down for you. He shouldn't be long."

Nick thanked the receptionist and headed down the hallway. There were several nurses at a station at the end of the hall busy with shuffling papers and making reports. He stopped and asked how Troy Turner in room 112 was doing. The nurse told him that he was doing fine and was resting now. The sheriff wanted to let Troy know as soon as Morton had been found, but the doctor had him under sedation once his fever had broken.

He continued down the hallway that led to Troy's room. He needed to talk to him now and hoped that he was healthy enough to take the news. The search was still on for the other missing man, but the weather was not cooperating. More snowfall and cold temperatures slowed the teams keeping them limited in the scope of their search patterns.

When he walked into the room, Troy turned his way and the sheriff got a good look at his damaged face. Both eyes were black, he had a bandage over the bridge of his nose, multiple scrapes and bruises covered his cheeks and neck, and he had a gauze pad covering what the sheriff knew were several stitches in his forehead.

Troy sat up and greeted the sheriff. "Hey, Sheriff."

"Good morning, Mister Turner. Sorry to disturb you, but I have some news that I thought you should hear from me."

"Oh no, Sheriff, you're not disturbing me. There's nothing to do, but stare at these walls. Any word on Craig and Phil?" Troy asked.

"I'm afraid I have to be the bearer of bad news. I'm sorry to have to tell you this, Mister Turner, but we found your friend, Craig Morton, on the mountain. He's dead."

Troy was taken aback and had to let it sink in a moment before he realized what the sheriff had just told him. He was visibly shaken and his face turned ashen.

"Oh my God! Are you sure it was Craig, Sheriff? I can't believe that...no way."

"I'm afraid so. We made a positive ID on him. I'm really sorry, Mister Turner, but I need to ask you a few questions. There's still no sign of your other friend yet, but my deputies are still searching the area... if he's out there, we'll find him."

"Oh my God, Sheriff, I can't believe it. Not Craig? It was the monster, Sheriff! You've got to listen to me."

"A monster? What are you talking about, Turner? I thought you said it was a bear attack?"

"I don't know what happened, but we left my cabin at the same time. I was coming in for help and he went back looking for Phil. I didn't think anyone would believe me before, but you've got to listen to me now. That wasn't a bear out there. I know this is going to sound crazy, but it's true."

The sheriff looked at Troy more intently now; studying his eyes and facial expressions, looking for any signs that he may be making up a story. Nick was a trained investigator and took pride on being able to know when someone was lying or exaggerating a story to escape trouble.

"You have my attention, " the sheriff replied warily.

"What we saw, what attacked us was...wasn't a bear, it was different," Troy stammered. "I swear it was at least eight or nine feet tall with black hair that covered its entire body. It stood upright, like a man. Walked like a man. Ran like a man only faster than I've ever seen anything run!"

"That sounds like it could've been a bear to me. They can stand up on their back legs and make it seem like they're that tall."

"What?" Troy seemed frustrated with the sheriff's statement. He lay there with eyes wide open staring at the sheriff in consternation. How could he expect anyone to believe such a crazy story?

"My men found him on the mountain yesterday laying not ten feet away from where he wrecked his ATV."

"No, Sheriff! No way! Listen - I know what a bear looks like. This thing that attacked us walked like a man. It was like you and me. It was tall, at least eight or nine feet tall with long arms and...and a face. Not like a bear at all. It didn't have a snout like a bear, but a face like you and me. It just wasn't a bear! It attacked us!" Troy was in a frustrated panic state at this point.

"Alright calm down Mister Turner. Tell me everything you know."

Troy told the sheriff everything he could remember from the night they left the hospital to the moment he woke up in the hospital a day later. The sheriff watched his face as he told his story looking for any signs that he may be confused or lying. He made a few more notes and then asked, "Do you know anywhere that your other friend, Phil Jackson, may have gone to? Maybe he went somewhere else for help? Did he have another vehicle? I've accounted for your Jeep and Mister Morgan's truck and ATV."

"No. That's all there was. He's on foot somewhere. That creature, I don't know what else to call it, Sasquatch? Bigfoot? Whatever you want to call it, it must've gotten him too." Troy paused then continued, "We had no choice, Sheriff. You've gotta believe me! We had no choice!"

"It's just a little hard to believe all of this, Mister Turner. I hope you can understand?" The sheriff said.

Impatiently, he replied, "Yes, of course...I guess. Like I said, we had gone out that night right after we left the hospital because Phil's deer rifle and pack were still out there where he had fallen. Remember when you found him on the road?" Troy asked, but didn't wait for an answer before continuing, "That's when you came along and found him. We wanted to get it on our way home before the weather got really bad."

Nick stood silently while taking notes. He didn't know what to think about all of the things Troy was saying. If he was lying about any of it, he certainly didn't seem like it. Not based on all of the tell-tale signs that people give off when they are. His eyes were focused and made good contact without tipping his hand to the sheriff. He never looked away like he was searching for a way to spin it.

Troy stumbled on, "When we got back to the cabin we drove out there in the ATV and that's when that thing attacked us! It was dark, but we could see it. It threw huge rocks at us. We tried to get away, but we turned the Razor over on its side."

The sheriff interjected, "If you wrecked it, how did you get back to the cabin?"

"We had to cut down a small tree to use for leverage and finally got it back up on its wheels. When we were doing that, it attacked us again. We had my pistol with us, but it stayed out of sight, just hiding in the dark, moving from tree to tree using it as cover. When we got it back up on its wheels we started climbing in, but it got Phil. The creature grabbed him and attacked us and chased us!"

"This thing that was chasing you, it was using trees to hide behind and then it attacked you again?" Nick said.

"Exactly Sheriff," Troy said, "That's why it sounds so crazy. That thing wasn't a bear! It had more intelligence than that. It was...it was hunting us!"

Troy was shaking and his breath was coming in gasps like he was reliving the entire experience. The sheriff knew he had to get him to calm down to get the full story. Intentionally, he lowered his voice and asked slowly, "Son, why do you think it was hunting you?"

"I honestly don't know, Sheriff. I just know we tore out with that thing chasing us. It came after us running on two feet! Does that sound like a bear to you? We went back to the cabin to get more guns to come back for Phil. That's when I got hurt trying to climb onto the roof to knock the snow off the satellite dish. I fell and got busted up pretty good. I knew I had broken some ribs. Craig sent me to town in the Jeep to get help to send back. He went after Phil. He had his guns with him and he wasn't scared, but he didn't see what I did. That thing was huge, Sheriff!"

Still speaking carefully, the sheriff said, "I hope you can understand that your story is a bit...far-fetched. I mean, a Sasquatch hunting you and your buddies down like the deer that you're hunting? You've got to give me something better to go on here. I'm trying desperately to find out what happened and to find your other friend."

"Sheriff, I swear I'm not lying about any of this. It's true!" Troy exclaimed. The look of desperation and fear was clear on his face.

"Okay…it's okay…we'll figure this out. We'll find Phil," the sheriff assured him almost as if he was soothing a child.

As he was leaving he promised they would also get word to any of Craig and Phil's family members back home.

Troy would be in the hospital a few more days. Better for him if he was the sheriff thought. He couldn't let him go back out to the cabin anyway. Not until he had more answers. He would send a deputy over to keep a close eye on him for now.

As he walked out of the room, the doctor called to him from across the nurse's station. Nick stopped and turned.

"Doc, how are ya?" the sheriff asked.

"I'm good, Sheriff. I'm guessing you just saw Turner?"

"Yes – Yes, I did, Doc. We found one of his hunting buddies up on the mountain. He's dead. Looked to be a possible ATV wreck. Still waiting on the M.E.'s report though," Nick said, not wanting to divulge any more than necessary at this time.

"Oh my!" the doctor exclaimed.

"I'm sending a deputy over to keep an eye on our friend here. Hope you don't mind."

"Sure, Sheriff, not a problem," the doctor responded.

The two talked for a few more minutes before the sheriff excused himself and exited the hospital. The wind hit him directly in the face and he hunched his shoulders and moved quicker through the snow covered parking lot. Nick mulled over his conversation with Troy as he walked to his truck. The bitterness of the cold reminded him of his deputies that were still on the mountain searching for the missing man. He had called in assistance from the state police and they were doing all they could, but he had his doubts about finding Phil alive. He got in his truck, backed out, and left the hospital to drive over to the impound yard. He wanted to take another look at the Jeep.

The radio was silent as he pulled up to the curb and parked his patrol unit. He had a set of keys for the yard so he let himself in through the side gate. The impound yard was a partially covered structure, but the snow was still deep around the edges. The Jeep was parked in the back of the lot up against the fence. He spotted the copper colored Wrangler and made his way over to it to get a closer look around the exterior of the vehicle. The Jeep had snow covering it so he scraped some of it off the front bumper.

The damage to the front end was most likely caused by the tree. He could see bark, pine needles and dirt all over the front of it. He had no reason to believe he had hit anything in town. No other reports of damage had come through. He opened the driver's side door and poked around inside. The vehicle was mostly clean with the exception of the blood covered air bag that lay crumpled and dangling from the steering wheel. When he looked at the floor board of the Jeep he could see that there was still mud and water in the driver's side though the passenger side was clean and dry meaning that there were probably no passengers at the time of the incident.

After snapping a few photos with his cell phone camera and. making a few notes, the sheriff locked everything up and headed back to the office. The snow was falling steadily though not as heavily as earlier. The gray sky was relentless and the wind seemed to have a mind of its own. One minute it was howling madly like a thundering herd of horses crashing through the trees and the next it would lay down as calmly as a spring breeze. His thoughts were on the continued search efforts of his deputies.

He needed to get back to the office and check in before heading back out to the Turner property and rejoining the search team. So far, no word had come back regarding the other missing hunter. It had been two days and the sheriff had no promising reason to believe that the missing hunter would be found alive now. The snow storm had left the mountain almost impossible to navigate even on snowmobiles and it didn't seem to be letting up anytime soon.

He arrived back at his office within a few minutes. As he hung up his coat and hat he asked Lindsey to call in one of the patrol deputies. When the deputy arrived, Nick sent him over to the hospital and explained that he was simply to keep an eye on Troy. He then asked Lindsey to have the Jeep sent to the state police lab so their forensics team could go over it.

When the deputy left the office, Lindsey asked the sheriff, "So, what gives Nick?"

"I don't know Linds, I really don't know."

Chapter 20

The sun was shining brightly, though the temperature was hovering deftly just above the freezing mark. The ski slopes were operating at full capacity in Hawthorn now, and would be until the end of the season. All of the fresh snow they'd been getting over the last couple of weeks helped to get the mountain ready for the busiest time of the year for the town. Ski season was what they counted on for the biggest part of the local economy and hunting and fishing was a distant second and third respectively.

"Sheriff, the M.E. just sent the report over on that hunter that was killed out on the Turner place," Deputy Chastain said as he stood in the Sheriff's doorway.

Noland Chastain was a young deputy in his early twenties, tall, lanky and soft spoken. His jet black hair and bushy black eyebrows seemed out of place on such a thin face. He had been with the search crews since they first discovered the body of Craig Morton on the mountain.

Two weeks had passed since the day they discovered the body and the sheriff had ended the search on the mountain for Phil Morton only three days earlier. The snow storm had covered any possible signs of the man's whereabouts in the mountains, if he was even still in the mountains. Search conditions were extremely dangerous in the high country under the best of circumstances.

Sheriff Blaine took the folder from the deputy and quickly flipped through the report. Morton's body had been found in the woods near his wrecked ATV the day of their initial search. The medical examiner's report concluded that he died of blunt force trauma. The interesting part of the report was the suggestion that the blows that killed him came after the wreck of the ATV. His body was severely beaten; he suffered a fractured right clavicle and left radius, humerus, ulna and trochlea. These were all defensive wounds, in the opinion of the medical examiner. He was apparently shielding himself from the blows of the murder weapon, which was a large tree limb, by using his arms. The death blow crushed the skull. There was no doubt that the killer used the tree limb, as forensic evidence clearly showed the bark embedded within the wounds of the victim.

When the sheriff and his deputies found the crash site of the ATV, it looked as if the Razor had been rolled and had taken a beating over the rugged terrain. Photos from the site suggested that the man had been crawling back toward the vehicle when the incident had taken place. The sheriff suspected that the man had been in a struggle, but this report made it concrete. Craig Morton was murdered by someone or something. Morton was a large man, in great shape and didn't seem as if he would be afraid of anyone. The sheriff had two main suspects. One was in the hospital, the other was missing. He also knew that the District Attorney would expect an arrest.

"What do you think, Sheriff?" Chastain asked.

"Turner came into town that night, had wrecked his Jeep, got hurt pretty bad and he swears they were attacked by a Bigfoot," He said, "This report says Morton was beaten to death after he wrecked his ATV which was around the same time frame that Turner got to town. Those injuries could have been caused by the wreck, but the medical examiner says otherwise," Sheriff Blaine replied.

The deputy's eyes widened when he heard the sheriff. He asked, "Do you want us to bring him in?"

"I'll need to call the doc and see when he's going to be released first."

Troy Turner gingerly pulled his boot laces tight and tied them in the familiar knot. He had been in the hospital two long weeks and he was going stir crazy staring at the walls and wondering if Phil may still be alive on the mountain somewhere. It was surreal to think that one of his best friends was dead, possibly the other. Attacked by a beast on the mountain that nobody believed existed.

He slowly straightened back up and began pulling on his red hoodie when Deputy Larson walked in accompanied by another Chastain.

"Mister Turner, I'm sorry, but I have to take you in for questioning sir."

"What? What's this all about, Deputy? Has there been any word on finding Phil."

"No sir. Sorry. Nothing yet. I'm afraid I can't tell you everything, but what I do know is the sheriff asked me to bring you over for questioning concerning the death of Craig Morton," Larson said.

"What? You say that like you think I had something to do with his death? You know I didn't murder Craig!" Troy exclaimed, suddenly in a panic.

"I never said that Mister Turner. I'm sure the sheriff will explain it all in just a bit, but right now I'm afraid that you'll have to come with us," Billy replied.

Clearly frustrated, Troy stared at Larson for a moment. Then, as if coming to a decision, he stated, "Of course, Deputy. Just let me grab my coat. This is all a big mistake though. I had nothing to do with his death."

+++

The search on the mountain for Phil Morton had ended. Teams from the local county sheriff's office, the state police and the state forest service had done everything they could to find the missing man. The early snow storm made the search in the mountains extremely difficult and dangerous for the emergency workers and no evidence had been found suggesting the hunter had been there. After reading the entirety of the report, the sheriff changed the missing person's report to indicate that Phil Morton was wanted for questioning in the death of Craig Morton.

Blaine had seen the three buddy's together and witnessed first-hand their comradery. He didn't feel that either one of them could have killed Morton in such a brutal attack. The strength required to crush a man's skull with a tree limb had to be extreme, and in the weather conditions as they were left a lot more questions than answers. He leaned more toward the wrecked ATV being the culprit because this is the kind of attack that came from pure rage and hatred if, indeed, it was murder. Even he had to admit, one can never predict human behavior in extreme circumstances, but the D.A. had decided they had enough evidence to detain Troy Turner. At least for now, he thought.

Nick sat at his desk when the phone rang. He had been going over the evidence in the case and had expected the phone call, but not quite this quickly. District Attorney Ellen Wain was young and eager. She wasn't originally from Hawthorn, but she had lived in the area for the past six years. She worked for the last five as an Assistant District Attorney and was very successful in prosecuting criminal cases. Elected to the DA's seat last year, she ran on a platform of being tough on criminals. She had sent many to jail for everything from armed robbery to murder. She was hard-hitting and Sheriff Blaine knew she was demanding.

"Sheriff Blaine here."

"Hey, Nick, how are you?" Not waiting for a response, she went on, "Ellen Wain here. I trust that you have a copy of the M.E.'s report on the Craig Morton case?"

"Yes ma'am, I'm looking at it right now." He wondered how she had gotten ahold of a copy of the report so quickly.

"Sheriff, I need more to go on. You've got to find me something I can use here. If this Turner fellow killed his friend, I need clear proof that he did it. Why did he do it? What's the motive? In your initial investigation report you mention that the injuries appear to be consistent to an ATV accident. There seems to be some contradictions here. What's your take?"

"That's what's so puzzling to me, Ellen. I can't find any motive. Not yet anyway. To be completely honest, I've been concentrating our resources on finding the missing man. I've issued a BOLO for him, but nothing yet."

"What's your gut tell you, Nick?"

"My gut tells me that there's more to this story. I don't know what it is yet, but I'm going to find out. The doc released Turner this morning and I have him detained for questioning. So far, it's not proven to be helping and to be honest, I was just about to cut him loose. I'm not sure we have enough to hold him on." Nick said.

"Let's not do that just yet, Nick. I think there's enough evidence now with the Medical Examiners report to hold him, but before I take this further, I want more evidence," she stated flatly. "Find me something solid one way or another."

+++

Jolene stood over the kitchen sink humming a melody while washing dishes. She had cooked breakfast for the family and was cleaning up when she heard the man trying to get out of bed. She quickly dried her hands with a towel and hurried in to the small room when she heard him stumble and fall, too weak from fighting off pneumonia for several days. He was dehydrated and lucky to be alive. He was lying prone next to the bed trying to speak when she entered the room. She gently shushed him and helped him back into the bed.

"You lay right back down there, young man. You're too weak from being half starved. Your body needs rest and lots of water right now," she said soothingly.

She went into the kitchen and retrieved a cup of water then held it to his lips allowing him to sip it slowly and not gulp. The color had come back into his cheeks and he looked much better than when her husband first brought him home days earlier. He had been in and out of consciousness the entire time with fever and pneumonia. He would wake suddenly asking, "Who are you? Where am I?" Then he would mumble incoherently and fall back into a deep sleep. He had no wallet for identification so they didn't know his name or where he was from, but Jolene was certain of one thing. Her husband, Clance Denizen, had saved the young man's life by pulling him out of that frozen lake when he had fallen into it on the other side of the mountain.

+++

Sheriff Blaine was sitting at his desk when Larson brought Troy into his office.

"Mister Turner, have a seat and I'll be with you in just a few minutes." The sheriff gestured to a chair beside his desk. Troy sat down quietly with his hands in his coat pockets and head down. He looked exhausted and distraught. No doubt from the pain medications the doctor had him on as well as the stress of the situation. Nick talked to the deputy for a few minutes outside in the hallway before addressing Troy.

"Mister Turner...Troy... you've got to give me something more to help you with. First, we find your friend where he was killed on the mountain and your other hunting buddy can't be found. We have a statewide BOLO out on him, but no word yet and to be honest, I'm not so sure we will."

"Sheriff, you've got to believe me! I had nothing to do with killing Craig. He was my best friend. I know it sounds crazy, but I know what I saw! Surely when you and your men were out there, you saw 'something'?"

"Nothing that would indicate that a nine-foot tall monster attacked you if that's what you mean."

"No, Sheriff, you've got to believe me." Troy pleaded.

"Look, Mister Turner, I'd like to believe you, but you've got to put yourself in my shoes and I think you can see just how far-fetched your story sounds. Here's what we know for certain. First, your friend Craig Morton was found dead. The M.E. believes that he was killed after the ATV wreck. His head was caved in with a tree limb. Your medical report shows that your hands were badly bloodied. This all happened approximately at the same time give or take an hour here or there. Unless you can give me something else to go on, I'm afraid that I'm going to have to hold you. I personally don't believe you did this, but the D.A. is looking to prosecute."

"Sheriff, I swear to you, I didn't do this. Everything I told you is true," Troy stated.

"Mister Turner, it may be a good idea for you to get the legal advice of an attorney. All the evidence right now is pointing a finger straight at you."

Chapter 21

Phil woke up in his new surroundings with a smile on his face, recalling those first days with the Denizens several weeks ago. Clance pulled Phil from the lake and saved his life by pure chance on that fateful day. The big mountain man would have taken him to the hospital immediately had there been a way to do so as the option to take him inside Troy's cabin, which was only yards away, was out. The two beast's that had attacked Phil and his friends on the mountain were there waiting for him. Clance had a much better chance of evading them by going back over the mountain pass to his own home. Phil found out why it wasn't possible soon after he recovered enough to understand what was going on and where he was. The only road down the mountain pass was blocked by heavy snows and the family had been staying close to the house.

He was in much better health now thanks to Clance's quick thinking and Jolene's nursing skills. Phil told them about the attack on the mountain by the Sasquatch and how he came to fall in to the lake. Clance was worried because the Sasquatch had become increasingly agitated and had been showing signs of aggression for the last few weeks. Phil's story confirmed his feelings.

Clance insisted it was too dangerous to try the trek down the mountain especially with the winter storm slowing them down. Even as the weather loosened its stranglehold on the mountain, Clance wouldn't allow anyone to venture outside alone, not even to the barn to take care of the livestock. Always in pairs with one carrying a rifle and keeping a close watch. The Denizens had no land-line, cell phone or electricity on the mountain.

Clance was a grizzled looking mountain of a man towering over Phil by a good four inches. His shoulders were as wide as the door frame of the large log cabin he called home. He was a powerful man and a man of few words. The others respected him and seemed to know what he wanted of them without being told. It was an odd family, but it seemed to work for them.

Clance's wife, Jolene, was an average woman standing five and a half feet tall with a medium build. However, she was just as strong as any man he'd ever known. She was tough as nails, but also a sweet, doting motherly type when it came to her family, which was very much the opposite of her husband.

Once Phil was able, he helped out around the place as much as he could. He would cut, stack and haul in wood for the fireplace and the kitchen stove. He also helped tend to the livestock outside.

Jolene talked more than the rest of the family and he had lengthy conversations with her when the others weren't around. Clance and Jolene Denizen had two sons, Gavin and Mathew, and a younger daughter named Irene. The oldest boy, Gavin, was twenty-nine and his brother was two years younger. Gavin, being the eldest of the siblings stuck close to Clance when the patriarch ventured out. Mathew usually stayed behind taking care of the place and safe-guarding the women.

Jolene was an educated woman born in Hawthorn, as were their three children. She attended school there and went to college not far away. There, she studied agriculture and graduated with a degree in agricultural sciences. She met her husband, Clancy Denizen, who preferred to be called Clance, soon after graduating. Together, the couple raised their three children on the mountain and Jolene home schooled them during the winter months when the weather was bad and the roads were impassable. There were a couple of times, Jolene told Phil, that one of the kids would leave for a spell, but always seemed to find their way back home. She said that she never wanted to influence their decisions based on her own desires. She and her husband wanted their children to do what made them happy and never stood in their way. While living on the mountain, there were certain expectations of each of them and they all pitched in.

Clance was from the same area and had spent most all of his life in the mountains. He and his wife bought the acreage in the mountains knowing that they wouldn't have access to any of today's modern conveniences this far up. No electricity, rural water or gas extended this far into the mountains, but they actually preferred to live off the grid. They had everything they needed and what they didn't have, they could trade or work for. It wasn't that they were backwards, as Jolene said often; they simply preferred not relying on things they couldn't make for themselves. They had a well with the purest mountain stream water that was cold year round, wood for heat and cooking and oil lamps for light in the house. They grew a large garden and canned vegetables during the summer and fall and hunted wild game for meat.

The daughter, Irene, was a pretty girl with long, dark hair and big brown eyes. Like her mother, she mostly took care of the chores around the house, but she could keep up with her brothers when hunting or fishing. She had a soft smile and a quiet personality when in the company of other family members, but she talked non-stop when alone with Phil. She would ask questions about where he grew up, what he did for a living, the size of his family, what it was like being an Indian, and if he was a good hunter. She was very inquisitive and talked freely about the time that she tried living in town. Phil was always happy to talk about the traditional ways that he was raised. He would tell her stories of learning to fish with a long gig pole, running along the banks of the creeks and rivers where he grew up in Oklahoma and she listened intently to his every word.

She told him about a time she had spent a year living in town. She had a small apartment and worked at a grocery store. She had met a boy and had planned on getting married, but things just didn't work out. She missed home and decided to move back. Her parents welcomed her as if she had never left.

During the early part of his stay at the cabin, Phil asked about the Sasquatch. The big man told him the story of how he first became to be aware of them.

"Several years ago, we had a pretty bad winter. Not that any winter in the mountains is ever good, but this one was a little worse than normal. The snow was deep and the game was scarce. We had plenty of meat put away in the smokehouse and stored in a high-hide to get us through. We had a good harvest that year and had plenty put away in the root cellar. Late one night I heard something out by the smokehouse. I grabbed my rifle and a flashlight and went to check on it. I figured it was a 'possum or 'coon trying to get in. The door to the shed was busted off of the hinges and when I shined my light I heard the most God awful wail! It made my skin crawl. Then that damned beast stepped out of the smokehouse carrying a half side of a hog in one hand. It had to duck way down to get out. When it stood up, it was taller than the shed. That shed is eight foot-tall on the front side!" The big man paused as if remembering the details of the incident before continuing, "I didn't shoot at it. Not that I couldn't have. It looked right at me. I could see that it was just as scared as I was. I pulled my rifle up and aimed, but I couldn't pull the trigger. It looked," the big man paused briefly, "too human."

Phil sat patiently waiting for the elder to continue his story remembering the terror that he felt the night he and his friends were attacked.

Clance began again, "I heard stories all my life and never believed any of 'em. Not 'til then anyway! After that night, I would see it every now and then. Every so often it would come back in the middle of the night and steal some meat out of the shed or maybe even a chicken off the roost. Once, it took one of the goats, but it never seemed to try and do any of us harm, just mostly curious I think. I could always tell when it was nearby as the smell of those things are terrible. The stench of rotted meat and dried blood," he said with a sour look on his face. "When you smell it, it doesn't go away."

"You're right about that; I smelled it when they chased me. It was horrible," Phil said.

"At least you always know when they're around." The big man attempted a half-hearted smile.

"When spring finally started to thaw things out that year, seems like half the mountain was washed away in floods. I had gone down to the lake to catch some fish when I heard something splashing around in the water not far from me. I looked up and saw a small bear cub in the water. That's what I thought it was at first anyway, just a bear cub playing in a small pool of water next to the river. When the water recedes, the fish can get trapped in those pockets and it's easy pickings for bears. I looked everywhere for its momma. A man doesn't want to get between a momma bear and her cub. That's when I saw it."

Clance reflected a moment before continuing, "It was standing just at the edge of the tree line mostly hidden in the shadows. It was just standing there watching me. I looked over at that bear cub again and took a closer look. It stood up and when it did, I saw what it was. It looked like a small child completely covered in fur. It was trying to catch fish with its hands while momma kept a close eye on both it and me."

Clance stopped for a moment to catch his breath while Phil eagerly awaited the rest of the story.

"I had caught a few fish and had 'em in my hand on a stringer, so I threw 'em up on the bank where she could see what I had done, and then I slowly backed out of there. When I got to a fairly safe distance, I saw it move out of the tree line and go to her baby. It was definitely a momma and it was enormous. Stood at least seven feet tall from what I could guess. It grabbed the fish I had thrown up on the bank and then steered the youngster away. My guess is they were having a hard time of it over the winter as both of 'em was fairly thin. I would see more of them over time, but never too close. Over time, I've counted at least ten in their clan. They've always kept their distance until recently. They're a lot bolder now and don't mind you seeing them. It's like they want you to know they're watching you. We've never had any trouble with them, but I'm not stupid either. I don't allow my family to go anywhere alone and never without a rifle, especially the last few months. They used to keep their distance from us and we would do the same, but now I've noticed more than one has been keeping a close eye on us and sticking close to the house,"

Phil asked, "What do you think has them all stirred up now?"

"I don't know, but it can't be good!"

+++

The sunlight reflected off the windshield of the pickup truck as it bounced along the construction site road. The combination of bright sunshine and glaring white snow was blinding enough for the need of dark sunglasses the man wore.

The construction site foreman stood and waited for the truck emblazoned with a Blanchard Contractors logo on the door to come to a stop in front of the office building.

Zach Blanchard turned the ignition switch off and the diesel engine rattled to a submissive silence. He opened the door and greeted his foreman.

"Ronnie, how ya doing?"

"Good, how was the drive up?" the foreman replied, as they shook hands.

"Not bad, the road's in good shape," Zach answered.

Ronnie Tillman was the foreman of the construction project in Hawthorn. He had worked for Zach for several years and the two were close friends. He had proven loyal and dependable and Zach could always count on him. When Ronnie had called two days earlier about vandalism at the work site he suspected it was probably a one-time thing with some drunks that happened to have stumbled upon the place. It was a good hour away from town and there were no houses anywhere near the location. The only way that anyone would have found the construction site was through one of the workmen or by pure chance. When the vandals hit a second time last night, Ronnie called his boss immediately after calling the sheriff's office.

Zach continued as the men walked over to inspect the damage to the office, "I got here as soon as I could. Has the sheriff been out yet?"

"When I called they said he would be out here sometime this morning so I figure anytime now," Ronnie answered.

When the foreman had come in to work early that morning he found that the tool shed had been broken into and the mobile office where they were now standing had been pillaged. One end of the small mobile trailer was knocked off the concrete blocks that held it up and level. The back door had been ripped off and the office had been ransacked and torn apart.

The two men were looking at the damage and mulling over who could have done it when they heard a vehicle coming down the road. The two men went back out to meet the new arrival.

Sheriff Blaine pulled up, parked beside Zach's truck, and stepped out.

"Sheriff, thanks for coming. This is my foreman Ronnie Tillman," Zach greeted him.

"Mister Blanchard, how are you, sir? Glad to meet you, Mister Tillman."

Nick shook hands with the two men and Ronnie filled the sheriff in on all the details he could. When the foreman arrived at the work site that morning he had noticed the damage to the tool shed immediately. It was a large metal pole-barn building that housed the tools used on the site such as welders, torches, generators and tools for working on the heavy machines. The door had been ripped open and the contents inside had been thrown about the building. A large steel cage built to keep explosives had also been torn off the hinges.

"Sheriff, I've gotta tell ya - I've never seen anything like this before. I mean, I've seen a lot of vandalism on work sites during my years, but this is a little weird to me," Ronnie said.

"How so?" the sheriff asked.

"For starters nothing was taken!" Ronnie exclaimed. "Everything was just thrown around and busted up, and the really strange part is in the office. The petty cash funds are all there, albeit all over the floor, but still there. That's over five hundred bucks that we keep on hand in case a fuel card doesn't work or we need to send someone out for something. Just scattered all over the floor, but every penny accounted for!"

"Hmmm," the sheriff began, "Environmentalist maybe? Protesting the development or something, I wouldn't think they would steal money. Could explain why they left it behind."

"Not sure about that. Could be I suppose, but we've never had anything like this happen, it's just real strange," Ronnie said.

The three men walked over to the tool shed and the sheriff took photos of the damage. A large welder had been tipped over and other tools had been thrown about the building. Nick took photos of the metal door that had been torn off the hinges and the contents of the tool cage had been scattered.

Ronnie said, "When we came in this morning and saw all of this, we didn't try to straighten up or anything just in case you needed to see it, but we did check the acetylene and oxygen tanks that were lying on the floor. The caps were still on tight and there didn't seem to be any damage, but we stood them back up. That's all we did though."

"That's fine. So nothing is missing?" Nick asked the men.

"Not a thing, Sheriff," Ronnie replied. "I keep a detailed inventory."

Nick continued taking photos of the building and made some notes then he asked the foreman to show him any other damage. Ronnie pointed him toward the office trailer, and let them over to it. The trailer rested on cinder blocks and was anchored down with metal straps. As Ronnie led them around to the back of the trailer he pointed out where two of the straps had been ripped completely off the trailer and the cinder blocks were scattered beneath. Unfortunately, the work crew had walked all over the site inspecting the damage so there were no tracks or signs distinguishable from theirs.

"How'd they do this I wonder?" the sheriff asked.

"That took some real effort I'll tell ya," the foreman said. He motioned to the ground and pointed out that there were no tracks or ruts where a vehicle rammed into it or pulled on it from any direction in order to pull the anchor straps loose.

Ronnie said, "Those metal bindings are ratcheted down tight and designed to hold up to 2,000 pounds each."

"I take it that you don't have a night watchman?" Nick asked.

"Haven't needed one until now," Zach said, as he turned to his foreman, "Ronnie, have a couple of the men take shifts until I can get someone up here. Why don't you have another trailer brought up and set it up for a security office?"

Nick turned to look at Zach and said, "Good idea, Mister Blanchard. I think I have everything I need. I really don't know what to make of it just yet to be honest. No tracks, no graffiti, nothing taken, no evidence left behind. It's a little puzzling. All I can do right now is to file a report. I do think it would be a good idea to hire a security guard to keep an eye on the place. I will have my deputies make a run up here every so often. Season's in full swing though and we're always short staffed."

"I understand, Nick. Anything you can do at all is welcomed and appreciated." Blanchard said.

"If you need a copy of my report it for insurance, it'll take a couple of days."

"That's fine, Sheriff. I'll walk you to your truck."

The two men left the trailer office and slogged back through the snow and mud to the trucks. The weather was beginning to turn again and the sun was disappearing behind the gray haze of another winter snow. Nick climbed in and started his truck then rolled down his window to say his final good byes when Zach asked him to hold on a minute.

"Sheriff, this is going to sound crazy, but I've got something to show you before you leave," Zach said, as he pulled his cell phone out of his pocket. He scrolled through several photographs before coming to a series that he showed to Nick.

"I didn't want to say anything about this in front of the men, and to be honest, I've not told anyone about this until now. I thought you might like to see this," Blanchard said.

Zach Blanchard was a well-respected man around Hawthorn and the sheriff had no reason to suspect he would make any false claims. When he told him about his experience, it was something that Nick took very seriously.

"I don't scare easily, Nick, and I'm not much on myths and legends, but I know what I saw that day. I know these photos aren't proof of a damned thing, but I've lived in these parts long enough to know the difference between a bear and that thing!"

"Do you think this is what broke into your buildings?" Nick asked.

"I don't know, but it may be. The men had walked around the trailers so much that if they had left any tracks in the snow, they were completely trampled down. I know that thing was huge, and could have easily done this. Also, nothing was missing, just busted up. I'd think that if a bunch of drunks, kids messing around or even protestors would have been up here, they would have at the very least taken the money."

"Can't argue with you on that. Mind sending me those photos?" Nick asked. "I won't say where they came from."

"Sure, I don't mind. They're just pictures in the snow." Zach said.

They spoke a few more minutes before the sheriff put his truck in reverse and headed back to town pondering what Zachariah Blanchard had just shared. *Definitely a new development*, he thought, as he began piecing together the parts of Troy's story that he had all but dismissed.

Chapter 22

Troy lay on a thin mattress in the county jail reading a magazine. It had been weeks since he had been arrested on murder charges and he was growing restless. He would read for a while forcing himself to remain calm, yet pace the floor much of the time like an animal in a cage. He knew no one would believe his story of a Sasquatch attack except maybe the sheriff who seemed to give him the benefit of the doubt. It was a small sliver of hope, but, nonetheless it was still hope.

His cell was small and smelled of mold, but it was warm and quiet. *Nothing that a fifth of vodka couldn't fix*, he thought. The county jail was also where all of the municipal offices were located, including the courthouse. It was an old stone building of a neoclassical design. Tall columns in the front that stood the entire height of the three story design culminating with a triangular pediment that housed a frieze of the liberty scales. A large dome capped the elegant building. The sheriff's offices were located on the back side of the main building in a separate wing. There were only twenty-two cells located here, but just across the street another building held more cells.

Troy's lawyer had visited him earlier that morning to let him know that his hearing date had been pushed back another week because the District Attorney had broken her leg in a skiing accident and needed some time to recover. There had been no further news on the search for Phil. The judge for the case refused him bail at this point because he had only lived in the area for a short time and posed a flight risk.

Troy had very few friends and one of them was missing and another had been killed on the mountain.

He had no visitors the entire time of what he hoped would be a temporary stay other than his attorney. His editor had called him a couple of times to check on him and even offered to fly out and see if he could lend assistance, but Troy refused his visitation citing the fact that the weather was always iffy. He didn't want to impose on him when there really wasn't much he could do to help anyway.

From his cell, Troy could see the main office and interact with the deputies if the hallway door was kept open, which it usually was. There were a few other offenders being held here until they were arraigned, but Troy kept to himself mostly. Once a day, a deputy would escort him to an area out back where he could walk around and get some fresh air. The deputy never paid very close attention to him and he often thought about taking off. He had no idea how he would get back to the mountain and the sheriff would know exactly where to find him anyway, but it was still something that he played out in his mind as a good distraction to pass the time. He knew that he would be exonerated one day soon so he dared not do anything stupid that would foul that up.

He looked up from his magazine when he heard the door open. He saw that it was the sheriff walking straight back to his cell. The sheriff unlocked his cell door, walked over to the bunk where Troy was sitting and took a seat across from him.

"What is it, Sheriff? Did you find Phil?"

"No. Not yet. Sorry," the sheriff said as he sat down across from him, "Tell me again, what did this monster look like?"

+++

Lindsey sat at her desk answering phone calls and posting photos on Facebook, when Nick exited the cells.

She watched him walk straight back to his office and close the door without a word. She knew that look well. The sheriff had something on his mind and wanted to get to the bottom of it. He was on a mission. A few seconds later the red light on the switchboard lit up indicating he was on the phone. She turned back to her desk.

"Norm? Nick Blaine here. Has Pete been around? Need to talk to him."

"Yeah, he's over at the diner now. Went to go get some lunch he said."

"Okay, thanks Norm."

The Blue Rose Diner had been in operation for more than thirty years and sat just off the highway ten miles outside of town. A greasy spoon diner mostly frequented by locals. It was a wonder how it was still open since the new highway that was built a year ago bypassed it completely. Only one customer was there when Nick walked in. The sheriff slid into a seat across from the odd looking patron.

"Pete, how ya doing?"

"What do you want from me, Sheriff? I ain't done nuttin!" Pete spat out indignantly.

The man seated across from the sheriff was a strange looking fellow with long, stringy, salt and pepper hair that looked as if it hadn't seen a thorough washing in weeks. He wore a faded green feed store baseball cap, jeans tucked into buckskin moccasins that were muddy all the way up to his knees and a heavy down-filled blue coat that looked two sizes too large. The thick bottle-cap Government Issue glasses completed the motley ensemble. The sheriff knew him well because Pete had been cross with law enforcement on several occasions. Never for anything more than petty misdemeanors, but Pete certainly wasn't a completely honest and upstanding citizen either.

"Troy Turner, ever met him?" Nick asked.

"No. Never heard of him. Why are you asking me?" Pete replied.

The sheriff watched Pete closely, "He bought old man Reed's place last summer."

"Yeah? So?"

Nick asked, "Ever been out to his place on Hawthorn Lake?"

"Nope. I have no idea where his cabin is."

"Cabin? I never said it was a cabin," Nick said.

"Okay! So I've been there. Just once though. I thought the place was empty and I just wanted to check it out. I didn't take nothing. I swear!" Pete exclaimed.

"Calm down, Pete. I never said you took anything. I'm not here because you're in trouble, but I am here looking for answers," the sheriff explained. "Tell me what you know. Have you ever seen anything strange out there?"

"There wasn't anyone around when I was driving by on my snowmobile one day awhile back and I thought I'd take a look around. I went in the garage for a minute, but once I saw that someone was actually living there, I left. I swear, Sheriff. I didn't take anything. Broke a good pocket knife too, but I didn't steal nothing. I just got back on my sled and left. Never saw nuttin' strange."

"Calm down, Pete, I believe you. This fellow that bought the place, he had two friends come up awhile back and now one is dead and the other one is missing. I have Turner locked up in town on murder charges now," Nick said.

Pete stared Nick in the eye with contempt, "What's that got to do with me? I haven't been back to that place since the day I told you about. I don't know anything about any of that. Surely you don't believe that I had anything to do with that?" Pete asked with an incredulous look on his face, not divulging whether he knew anything about the murder or not.

"No. No I don't, but you did just admit to breaking and entering. It may not have anything at all to do with you, but I think that does make you a definite suspect don't you think?"

"Wait a minute, Sheriff…" Pete trailed off with a look of shock on his face. He sat back in his seat a little more.

"No, 'YOU' wait a minute, Pete. Look here, there's some strange things going on and I need answers and you may have 'em!" Nick said sternly leaning forward from his booth seat. He motioned for Pete to do the same. Speaking in hushed tones, the sheriff explained what he had heard from Troy Turner about the giant, hairy beast. He watched Pete's face carefully as he told him about the three hunters.

When he finished, Pete replied resolutely.

"Sheriff, I tried to tell you two years ago that there was something up there, but you just blew me off. Didn't believe me!"

"Pete, Where were you last night?"

"I was at the garage all night working on my truck. Why?" Pete answered.

"Was anyone there with you?" Nick asked.

"You mean a witness to my whereabouts?" Pete asked.

"Exactly!" Nick replied firmly.

"Yeah, Norm was there. We were working on the truck and drinking beer. I passed out on the shop couch about two this morning."

"Were you up at the construction site on route fourteen at any time?" Nick asked.

"Hell no I wasn't! I haven't been up there since Blanchard first started moving in heavy equipment and clearing land. And besides, I told you we were working on my truck. Transmission's out. There's no way I could've been there."

"How'd you get here to the diner? Its two miles from the garage," Nick asked.

Pete replied nervously, "I rode my sled. I see that look on your face, Sheriff, but you know as well as I do that the tank on my snowmobile isn't half big enough to get me there and back. And why are you even asking about that? Someone steal one of 'ol Blanchard's dozers?"

Pete was clearly getting agitated at the questioning so the sheriff let up. He sat back in his booth seat and relaxed a bit more. After a few seconds of allowing Pete time to calm down, he continued.

"No, Pete, nothing like that at all. And it's not that I didn't believe you before about something being up there, but there was no way I was going to believe that it was a...a Sasquatch. I still don't believe it. A bear maybe, but a Bigfoot, Sasquatch, Yeti...whatever. No! Stories are made up to get in the papers or scare little kids around a campfire all the time. Who would believe it if they've never seen it for themselves? I've lived here all my life and never seen anything like that," Nick said.

Pete leaned forward and with an obdurate look said, "That thing ripped my camper apart with me in it! I shot it with my 12 gauge right in the chest not once, but twice! Those were solid rounds! You know when I aim, I don't miss and I only managed to piss it off! It was at least nine feet tall and strong enough to pick my camper up and throw it down the mountain into the river! I barely walked away with my life! Sheriff, I came to you when I knew you wouldn't believe me and sure enough you blew me off! I never should have even told you about it in the first place."

"I know that, but I didn't have any evidence in your case. After all the rain that we had, it could have been that your camper had simply been washed away with half the mountain or like I said before, it could've been a bear. You know as well as I do that the flow of runoff from the snow melt can get bad so there weren't any footprints, no blood samples, hair...nothing!"

Pete sat back in his seat and stared intently at the sheriff sitting across the table from him.

"Look, Pete, you know that mountain better than anyone. If there is a...'Sasquatch' up there, I want to know where to look."

Pete's eyes lit up. Whether it was with fear or excitement, the sheriff couldn't tell. The little man across from him sat up a little taller, put his hands on the table, and leaned forward.

Pete grinned. "Sheriff, you don't need to ask me. Just go out to that cabin and wait. They'll find you!"

+++

Gavin Denizen suddenly froze in place and grew silent, peering fixedly into the woods behind the cabin. Phil noticed his actions and stopped what he was doing. He quietly walked over to stand beside him. He and Phil had gone out to the barn to feed the livestock and take care of a few chores. Gavin carried a rifle and acted as security while Phil tended to the animals.

Phil had never seen the creatures around the Denizen's cabin as he worked, but he would often see footprints at the corral where the goats were kept. None of the animals were ever taken, though. He didn't have a rifle with him, but when he noticed Gavin's actions, he nervously picked up a hand axe. He held it tightly in his right hand while he stood next to Gavin in the shadow of the barn door.

Phil whispered, "What is it?"

"Out there by that big aspen and that brush pile to the left of it. It's just standing there watching us. There's another one fifty yards behind that one. They're not hiding. I think they want us to see 'em," Gavin whispered.

Phil looked where Gavin had indicated, but could see nothing at first. Then, a small movement caught his eye. At first he couldn't understand what he was seeing, but then it became clear. The monster was standing behind a brush pile that must have been seven or eight feet high. The creature was watching them just as they were watching it. It gave Phil an eerie feeling and he gripped the axe tighter with both hands.

"I've not seen them get this close in the daylight and never more than one," Gavin said.

"What do you think they want?" Phil asked.

"I don't know, but we need to get back to the house and let the others know. It'll be dark soon and I don't want to be out here then." Gavin replied.

The two men slowly moved away from the front door of the barn, pulling it closed behind them and carefully made their way out the back to the house. Clance was at the window with a rifle in his hand when they walked in.

"I just now looked out and saw it. How long has it been there?" the elder asked.

"It's been watching us for about fifteen minutes. I never saw it come up on us. Snuck right up close. I smelled it before I saw it."

"How'd you let it get that close to you without seeing it?" The grizzled mountain man asked.

"Because it didn't want me to until it was ready to be seen!" Gavin answered.

"Mmmm," the big man muttered thoughtfully.

Clance watched the Sasquatch through the kitchen window while the others took positions around the cabin at other windows searching for anything out of the ordinary.

"There's another one out there by the smokehouse," Jolene said softly.

Phil put the axe down and picked up a rifle that Clance had out on the table. He filled his pockets with extra cartridges, walked over to a window, and took up a position being careful not to stand directly in front of it. His knees trembled from fear.

The cabin was well fortified against the harsh winters and was built to sustain the family for long periods of time. Clance was good with his hands and certainly hadn't thrown together a shack to live in. The walls were built with solid pine logs and looked to be able to withstand a major assault without as much as a board out of place. Phil felt safe as long as he was inside, but sure wished he was back at home.

The family had an old 4x4 work truck, a tractor and snowmobiles that they kept well maintained. The snowmobiles were needed in these mountains more so than any other vehicle. When the heavy snows came, the truck was simply not much good at all. When they went hunting, they used the sleds to carry the game back home. All of the vehicles were kept in the large hay barn just across from the family's house.

"They're leaving," Clance said flatly.

"The one on this side is too. What do you think they want, Dad?" Mathew asked.

"Not sure, but they wanted us to know that they were leaving. Otherwise, they wouldn't have let us see them leave at all."

After a few minutes Clance stated, "I'm gonna follow them and see what I can find out."

"I'll get my coat."

"No, Gav, I'm going alone. Less chance they spot me. Everyone stay inside until I get back. Keep the doors bolted and cover the windows. If I ain't back by morning, get everyone off this mountain. Take nothing except the rifles and snowmobiles. And move fast!"

The eldest son knew better than to try and argue with his father. Instead, he began closing the dark curtains on the windows and checking the rifles. He silently watched the elder Denizen put his coat on and slip out the door.

+++

The night dragged on for Troy. He was unable to fall asleep after his conversation with the sheriff earlier that day. In fact, that's all he could think about. The sheriff had told him that the judge set his arraignment for the next morning. That was good news. The bad news came when he said that the District Attorney wanted to go after him with everything they had and firmly believed she would get a conviction. After hearing that, he figured his chances of getting out on bail would be pretty slim.

His attorney had also visited with him for a few hours earlier in the day to go over the details of his story. Once again, he tried to convince Troy to plead self-defense, but Troy maintained his complete innocence. He had been locked up in the county jail for several weeks now and even though the news wasn't good, he felt some relief that his case was finally moving forward.

Troy had no family and his two closest friends were gone. He had no one close to support him. He had always relied on himself throughout his career and never needed anyone. This time was different. He had never been in a situation as dire as he was now and longed for the days that he had his parents to count on. He felt like a small child in trouble and needed them desperately.

When eight o'clock ticked off, he was already dressed and ready. The sheriff had returned that morning and, along with Deputy Larson, they made their way through the labyrinth of hallways to the courtroom where they met his attorney. Once inside, the two officers took their seats directly behind Troy.

Judge Brown was seventy years old, but still as sharp as a tack. When he entered the courtroom he looked it over with a quick glance, took his seat at the bench, and rapped his gavel to bring the room to silence. The court clerk had a brief discussion with him and then she began with a statement of charges. Troy held his breath for what seemed like an eternity trying his best impression at innocence. He had never been in a situation such as this before, not even a speeding ticket or traffic court. He was nervous and his knees were shaking. Once read, the judge asked for a plea by the defense and both Troy and his attorney stood.

"Not guilty, your Honor," his attorney said.

The hearing was short. The judge ordered a jury trial and set a date only three weeks out. Troy's attorney asked for bail and was granted it, but with the condition that he would have to wear an ankle monitor. His attorney whispered to him that with any luck he would be walking out tomorrow. Troy felt this was his first victory, albeit a small one and the relief showed clearly on his face. Being in a ten by twelve jail cell was driving him crazy. He couldn't understand why anyone would intentionally break the law and risk going to jail for any reason.

Chapter 23

It was a little after midnight when the deadbolt on the door of the cabin jiggled. Phil was standing near enough to hear it and breathed a sigh of relief when he heard Clance's voice from outside.

"It's me, open up," Clance said.

Phil moved quickly and met Mathew at the door. Jolene turned the coal oil lamp down low and motioned for the boys to go ahead. Together they pulled the large wooden crossbar beams off, set them aside, and opened the door for Clance. Gavin was standing at the front door with rifle in hand.

"What did you see?" Gavin asked his father.

"Saw that we need to get moving at daybreak. The road off the mountain is blocked by trees and they weren't dead ones. Those trees were purposely knocked down on the road. I think that the two that were here watching us were just trying to lure us out and then ambush us on the road. They're a lot smarter than what I thought," Clance told cabin's occupants.

"Oh my God." Jolene said as she moved closer to her husband with a look of fear of her face. "Why? They've never tried to hurt us before."

"Not sure, but I don't think we're safe here any longer. We need to pack up and be ready to move out at first light. We'll take the snowmobiles out the back way over the mountain."

"Doesn't that take us back down by my buddy's cabin near Hawthorn Lake?" Phil asked.

Clance turned to look at him and said, "Yes, but it's the only other pass off of this mountain. I know it well, but so do those damned beasts! What I'm counting on is that they aren't nearly as smart as they think they are. I think they're all at the road block waiting on us so I'm hoping we can go out the back way before they realize what's happening. We will travel light and fast. Gav, make sure everyone has a rifle and plenty of ammo then check on the snowmobiles and make sure they're plugged in and the tanks are full. Phil, if you don't mind helping?"

The group set about making sure they were packed and ready to go. They would be leaving out in a few hours so Clance suggested they all try to get some rest, but they were all too worried to get much sleep. He went into his bedroom and closed the door. Soon the others could hear him snoring so they remained as quiet as possible going about their business.

There had never been any issues living among the beasts for they rarely showed themselves. They normally ranged in a different area of the mountain and had never bothered anyone.

Phil sat at the kitchen table sipping a hot cup of coffee and thinking about everything that had transpired over the last several weeks. He had no idea if his friends had made it out of the woods that night and back to Troy's cabin. He vaguely remembered being knocked out of the ATV by the Sasquatch and then was running for his life. It all seemed surreal as he sat there in the big, warm cabin. He had heard stories about the Sasquatch since he was a kid, but always thought they were simply stories designed to scare children. His grandmother called it Tsul Kalu which, as he recalled, meant 'sloped giant' in Cherokee.

After a few hours Clance Denizen awoke, got dressed and walked into the main room of the house joining the others. They were dressed and waiting on him. It would be daylight soon and he wanted to be well away from the cabin when the sun came up.

"Are the supplies loaded on the sleds?" Clance asked.

"Yes sir. All loaded and ready to go." Gavin replied.

"I'll slip out first. Give me five minutes and watch the barn door. If it opens up, everyone come out as quickly and quietly as you can. Once everyone is ready to go from the barn, I'm going to start the pickup, drive it to the top of the hill, then get out and let it roll. As soon as I start the truck, you all start the sleds so that the truck engine will help mask the sounds. Soon as you see the truck go down the hill be ready to move. If any of them are out there watching, they may think we're in the truck and give us a little window to get away. They're fast so we'll have to move faster. We only have four sleds. Jo rides with me; Gavin, you and your sister on one then Phil and Mathew can each have one. When I say fast, I mean you better keep up with me, boys!" Clance said.

Clance picked up his rifle, slung it over his shoulder and slipped out the back door. After a few minutes the others saw the barn door open so they all made their way to the barn as instructed. Clance waited on them and when they were ready, he started the truck and they started the snowmobiles. He told them once again to be ready, as soon as he made it back to the barn they would slip out the back way as quietly as possible.

Phil watched the grizzled mountain man drive off in the truck. He pulled on a pair of goggles and adjusted them. He was nervous and scared. He had seen firsthand how powerful these creatures were. He mounted his snowmobile and prepared to go. It was dark inside the barn, but he could see the gray sky outside well enough to navigate by. The lights on the snowmobiles were shut off so that they couldn't be spotted. He went over the instructions in his head. 'Go fast and keep in a straight line.' Clance would lead and he would bring up the rear. If he saw anything at all, he was to flash his headlight on and off. That's all the others would need to be alerted.

He watched the pickup as Clance drove out of the barn and turn down the road. The brake lights shined brightly for a moment and then went off as it started down the hill on its own power. Clance quietly jumped out of the moving vehicle once it was headed downhill and returned to the barn a few minutes later ready to go. He wasted no time climbing on his sled in front of his wife to lead the small troop out the back way. He was followed closely by Gavin, and then Mathew and Phil last in the small convoy.

Clance didn't exaggerate about moving fast. Phil struggled to keep up. He thought he would have no trouble since he spent most of his life riding four-wheelers, but this was different. It was much darker in the woods than he anticipated. The sky may have been gray, but the path in the woods was almost black. He could make out the others in front of him and the shapes of trees as they flew past him, but he couldn't see any detail. Several times he was slapped in the face by tree branches which was alarming enough, but when he almost ran over the top of Mathew that was altogether another level of scary.

They rode for what seemed like a good half hour when Clance pulled up and motioned for the others to stop. The sun was up, but the visibility through the woods was still not good. Clance truly knew his way around and Phil was confident in his ability to get them over the mountain pass.

"It's going to get tight from here on. The pass is narrow in some places, but not too bad. Just take it slow and easy and follow me. Keep a little more distance between us in case I have to pull up short." Clance told them.

The others nodded acknowledgement at the elder's words and moved out following him once again.

Phil watched as each snowmobile pull away and when there was sufficient space, he hit the throttle on his sled and followed behind Mathew. The snowmobile caught traction and immediately lurched forward. It felt good to be moving again. He didn't much care for sitting still; the hair on the back of his neck stood up like thousands of tiny needles.

Just as Clance had warned, the trail became very narrow in parts. Phil's hands held firm to the handle grips of the snowmobile as he maneuvered in and out of the rocky trail. There were many hairpin turns, but it was easier to navigate than he had imagined and it helped that there were fewer trees to block the sunlight. The trail would lead down out of the mountain and very near to Troy's cabin. With any luck, he thought, he would find his friends there and they would be able to get to town and off this blasted mountain. It had been too long and he knew they would all be worried.

Clance led the group up and over a rocky point which seemed to be the very top of the mountain. Phil couldn't see any other higher points when he glanced back over his shoulder to survey the area. It was a beautiful scene as the snow covered much of the rocky outcroppings at the top of the mountain and the fresh white powder hung heavily on the branches of the huge pine trees in the forest below. He hoped to get back into the comfort of that tree line soon. Being out in the open as they were, he felt particularly vulnerable.

The pass opened wide allowing the snowmobiles a short clearing where Clance gunned the throttle and picked up the pace once again opening a large gap between the riders. Gavin fell behind causing Mathew and Phil bunch up in the rear of the formation. Just as Clance reached the edge of the forest line a boulder came crashing down just in front of his sled and he veered sharply behind a fallen pine tree and shot out of sight altogether. Gavin also reacted quickly and sent his sled in a sharp skid following directly behind his father.

Mathew wasn't as lucky. When he turned his snowmobile, the right rudder caught a snag on a rock and flipped the machine. Phil watched it happen directly in front of him and almost hit the same jagged rock, but his quick reaction saved his sled. He hit the brakes hard, turned the rudders, and hit the gas in the opposite direction coming to a sliding stop. In a flash of movement, he grabbed the rifle off his shoulder and got off a snapshot at the creature that he spotted not far away in the rocks. The beast let out a horrific scream and disappeared back into the woods giving Mathew enough time to get back to his snowmobile and get it started. Phil let his rifle fall on his back with the sling holding it in place and turned his snowmobile to catch up with Mathew.

"You okay?" Phil asked.

"Yeah, but my rudder is busted." Mathew replied.

"Jump on!" Phil said.

Mathew climbed on the back of Phil's machine and held on tight. Phil hit the throttle hard and the sled rocketed forward to where he could still see the trail.

"Follow that trail. In a couple hundred yards in, it will turn south and go straight down the ridge line," he barked.

Phil knew to trust him as he had probably been all over this mountain and knew it better than anyone except for his dad and brother.

"Did you hit it?" Mathew asked.

"Not sure really, but if I didn't, he sure knew he was being shot at!" Phil shouted over the whine of the engine.

Snow flew like a rooster tail behind the two as Phil navigated around a clump of trees and raced the engine hard. They easily picked up the trail of the others and in the fresh powder. When they reached another outcropping of large boulders in the trail, he had to slow in order to maneuver through. Mathew kept his rifle ready in case the creature attacked again. They both could see the trail ahead for quite a ways and finally, they saw the other two snowmobiles. Clance had heard the shot and circled back around to check on his youngest son and their new friend. Phil gunned his machine and caught up with them in a matter of seconds.

"What happened?" Clance asked.

"Broke a rudder. Had to leave it behind." Mathew said.

"We heard the shot. Saw you through the trees though and seen that you were moving again. There's some rough going ahead of us, but we need to hurry. Not sure if that was the only one or not." Clance told them.

Clance led the way once again down along a ridge line near the top of the mountain before finding a small pass that led straight down. He turned his machine with Jolene holding tight and the snowmobile leaped down the embankment catching several feet of air. They dropped down with a hard thud and the two fell forward against the tank of the sled. Clance straightened up and glanced back to watch the others come off the steep slope. The other riders were younger and nimbler and they made the leap down more easily, even riding double.

The mountain was relentless in its difficulty and it was a struggle for the group to keep up a fast pace. At times, Phil noticed that the elder Denizen would slow down for a period of time and then speed back up as if he had become suddenly aware of their predicament. He knew it must be tough on the older couple. This was their home and they obviously loved it here in the mountains, but this place was no longer safe. Even under normal circumstances the mountains weren't safe. A person could die from exposure alone, but there were many other dangers always lurking. A person had to respect nature.

The three snowmobiles made their way down the mountain zig zagging between trees and boulders in formation. Phil noticed that there was a massive ledge coming up and instinctively slowed his machine as he looked ahead.

"That's what we call Niagara's big brother!" Mathew said to Phil. "Devil's Backbone. A cliff with a thousand-foot drop straight down. During the snow melt, it's something to see."

"Great!" Phil exclaimed. "I'm assuming that we're not going to jump?"

"No, but we're going to get very close to it!" Mathew explained.

Clance pulled his snowmobile a good hundred yards short of the cliff's edge and waited on the others to pull up. The area was completely clear of any trees, but Phil could see large boulder outcroppings scattered throughout.

"We have to go slow and careful until we get down off this next line of ridges. Avalanches happen here all the time. Ice builds up underneath this snowcap so we need to tread lightly. We're gonna follow this ridge line south for quite a ways before we come to a trail that leads down off the mountain. It comes out near the lake," Clance said.

"You mean the one by my friend's cabin?" Phil asked.

"That's the one. Once we turn down off this ridge, though, you should be in familiar territory. The pass will go on down to another ridge line that runs behind his cabin. There's a lot of switchbacks in this mountain and damn easy to get lost." Clance explained.

Clance and Jolene led the way sledding cautiously along the trail with the others following close behind. Phil could see for hundreds of yards all around as the area was barren of all trees. He could also see the giant pines and hawthorn trees down beneath the cliff that flocked the side of the mountain. He could make out the Lake in the distance below and knew that Troy's cabin was nearby. He looked for the familiar stream of wood smoke from the chimney, but saw none. He prayed it was only because they were so far away, but just as quickly put it out of his mind. He knew he had to stay positive and concentrate on the situation at hand.

Finally, more trees reluctantly began to show up and Phil knew they were getting closer to the place where they would be turning down off the mountain top. They had been riding for most of the day now only stopping to refill the tanks once and that was all the fuel they had remaining. If they ran out, they couldn't get any further on the snowmobiles. The mountain was unbelievably treacherous and even more dangerous when being chased across it. The weather was cooperating nicely, however, and the sun was shining well enough through the clouds that visibility was good though the freezing temperatures were brutal.

Phil felt somewhat relieved when the trail started winding down through the trees. Being out in the open wasn't a comfortable feeling. The cliff was swiftly falling further behind and he concentrated on keeping up with the others. He was tired and breathing hard, but knew they couldn't stop to rest. Mathew hung on, pressed firmly against his back, keeping a look out for the beasts.

Clance suddenly hit the brakes on his sled and grabbed his rifle. Motioning for the others to stay where they were and remain quiet, he dismounted and slowly crept down the path to an overhang where he could see the valley below. Clance trained his weapon on the tree line down and away about five hundred yards, and scanned the entire slope. After a few minutes he had seen everything he needed to and quietly returned to the others who waited tensely.

"We're trapped!" Clance stated flatly.

"What is it?" Jolene asked.

"There's one down there at the bottom of the trail that leads out to the road," Clance pointed out.

"Can we go around it?" Gavin asked, already knowing the answer.

"No. That's the only way out to the road that takes us to town. It's a fifty foot drop off everywhere else. Can't turn around 'cause they already know where we are and by now have us blocked and on our tail - maybe only minutes behind us! We're either going to have to lay low 'til we get an opening, or try to get past him!" Clance proposed. "That one is a smaller, more reddish one. I've seen it before. I think he's a sentry and not the brightest of the clan."

Phil walked over to the older man. "So, what's the plan?"

The big man looked at him tensely before speaking, "We gotta go through it! Kill it if we have to."

Chapter 24

Troy sat patiently and quiet while the sheriff finished up some paperwork concerning his release on bond. His attorney had already been by to see him with instructions not to talk about the case with anyone except him. Troy understood, though secretly didn't care one way or another. He was confident that he would be exonerated. He was completely innocent. He would never hurt anyone, especially one of his best friends. Phil had to be out there somewhere and he would be able to tell the sheriff what really happened and corroborate his story.

Once the sheriff had finished up, he walked Troy down to the booking desk and allowed him to retrieve the personal belongings they collected when he was brought in; his wallet with his driver's license, credit cards and forty-three dollars. The desk sergeant also gave him his cell phone. The battery was dead of course, but at least it still had all of his contacts stored in it.

Sheriff Blaine had agreed to give Troy a ride home because his Jeep's battery was dead and the radiator needed repaired. A local dealership sent a truck over to pick it up, but it would be a week or so before they could get to the repairs, which left Troy on foot. During the middle of ski season, there were no rental cars available. Deputy Larson accompanied them when they left the county jail.

"Sheriff, would you mind terribly if we stop by the market on the way so I can pick up a few things. It's been awhile since I've been out to the cabin, ya know."

"Sure thing," Nick replied.

The three men pulled out of the parking lot and drove through town and stopped at the local supermarket. Troy went inside alone and after fifteen minutes he returned with several plastic bags of groceries that he stowed in the back seat then climbed in.

"I appreciate the ride, Sheriff. This whole thing has got me so unnerved. First, my best friend is killed by something that no one believes in and then I find out my other friend is missing, and now I'm on trial for a murder I didn't commit."

"I understand that it can be unsettling, but believe me, we haven't given up on this investigation. Personally, I'm not sure what to believe, but I do believe that there's more to this than what it looks like on the surface. For the record, I don't believe you did it either."

Troy was glad to hear the sheriff say that. I gave him hope. It was just after 11am when they finally left town. They had to drive through the downtown area of town before turning onto the main highway leading out to the cabin. The weather was clear and sunny though still cold, and the traffic was steady on the highway, mostly busy with skiers making their way to the slopes. Troy wondered what it would be like walking inside the cabin after all this time. He felt a little nauseous thinking about it so he started talking to take his mind off of it.

"Sheriff, have you been back out there since you talked to the real estate developer you mentioned? You said he saw it too." Troy asked.

Nick replied, "Yes, but I'm still not convinced anything is out there besides what we already know. I just haven't seen anything to suggest otherwise."

Deputy Larson perked up listening intently from the front seat. "What do you mean by 'it'" The deputy asked.

Troy explained the story to the deputy. The frustration was clear in Troy's voice. "Surely someone else in this town knows what I'm talking about and surely they've seen it too! I'm not making it up! I swear!"

"I don't think you are at all, Troy. The problem is all the evidence against you. Even though it's all circumstantial there's enough there that convinces the D.A. to take it to trial. Without any cold, hard evidence contrary to that..." The sheriff left the sentence hanging.

The deputy had been listening with curiosity before finally breaking in, "Okay, Sheriff, do you honestly believe that a Sasquatch is out here?"

Troy and the sheriff told the deputy the entire story on the way out to the cabin. Larson listened intently as Nick explained what Zachariah Blanchard had told him and also what he had learned from Pete. By the time the men arrived at the cabin, the deputy had heard everything the sheriff and Troy knew about the case. Troy couldn't tell if the deputy believed any of it or not. He wouldn't have believed any of it himself if he hadn't seen the beast with his own eyes. He was a little leery about having to stay out at the cabin with no vehicle, but the sheriff promised that he would send a deputy out the next day to check on him.

The sheriff pulled up to the front of the big cabin and turned off the ignition. Troy jumped out, gathered his groceries and the three men walked up the steps to the front door together. The sheriff reached for the door knob and found it locked.

"There's a hideaway key under the seat of that porch chair," Troy said.

"Got it," The sheriff replied, as he explained that the place had been locked up since the investigation had concluded some time ago.

The door opened and Troy entered first. He tried the light switch, but the electric had been shut off. Troy put the groceries down and asked to borrow a flashlight. Deputy Larson had one on his web belt and together they made their way through the kitchen to the breaker box in the utility room. Troy flipped the switch that shut off the electric pole and opened up the backup generator. They heard a quiet murmur start up outside and then all of the lights in the cabin slowly came on.

"It runs on propane and it's enough to get through the entire winter as long as I don't run everything all at the same time."

"Nice," the deputy nodded appreciatively. "Guess you need something like that out here."

"I've only turned it on to test it so I'm hoping I don't have to rely on it for much longer. Guess I'll call the utility company tomorrow and see if I can get it turned back on," Troy said.

The two men made their way back into the kitchen where the sheriff was waiting.

"Well, now that you're settled, we're going to head back to town. Like I said, Troy, I'll try to send someone out to check on you in the next day or two."

"Thanks, Sheriff, for everything. I appreciate you and Deputy Larson for all your help."

Troy walked the two officers to the door and watched them get in the truck and pull away. He closed the front door and collapsed on the sofa with his head in his hands. He sat there for several minutes thinking about everything that had transpired over the course of the last several weeks when it suddenly occurred to him why it was that the old man that he bought the place from took his first offer and moved out as quickly as he did. *Son of a bitch could have warned me,* he thought. What kind of person does that knowing what he knew?

Troy felt his stomach growl and remembered that he hadn't yet put his groceries away. When he walked into the kitchen, he spotted the blood on the sink and remembered that Craig had cut his hand badly the night they had wrecked the ATV. He didn't realize just how much he had bled on the floor and counter tops. He quickly put the groceries away, walked into the laundry room and found the bottle of bleach. He made up a bucket of bleach water, opened the kitchen window above the sink, and set about cleaning up the blood stains.

+++

Phil thought about Clance's plan while they waited. The creature below had the only trail to the road blocked effectively. There was just no way around it and too much distance to cross. He knew firsthand how huge these things were, how fast they could move, and how ferocious they were when angered. It was much too far away for any of their rifles to be effective enough to put the beast down. The plan was to draw the Sasquatch away from the trail. Clance would ride down alone and get the beast's attention. Once he was certain that it was chasing him, he would signal the others to make a run for the pass with three gunshots. With any luck, they would have enough time to reach the safety of Troy's cabin before the creature figured out where they were. In the meantime, he would try to lose it in the woods and meet them there. If he couldn't lose it, he hoped he could kill it.

It sounded like a realistic plan, but Phil worried that the old man wasn't as skilled and athletic enough to pull it off. Even Gavin tried to reason with Clance, but the big man wouldn't have it. He said that it was his duty to protect the family and the look on his face quieted any further argument. They waited nervously as the big mountain man settled his rifle on his shoulder and prepared for the run. He was resolute and his confident demeanor was calming to their fears. They worried that if they didn't hurry, the rest of the creatures would be on top of them any moment.

As Clance talked quietly with his wife, Phil suddenly knew what he needed to do. He took a deep breath, turned to look at Mathew behind him and said, "I'm sorry about this, Matt., but this is my fault."

Mathew was suddenly caught off guard when he felt Phil's hand on his chest shoving him off of the snowmobile and safely into the soft snow. When he realized what was happening, Phil was hurtling straight ahead at the beast several hundred yards below.

The wind was brutally cold against his face burning Phil's skin even through the protective gear he wore. Snow flew behind the sled like a rooster tail as he gunned the throttle toward the tree line. He couldn't see where the giant beast was exactly, but he knew it had to be hiding somewhere near the trail in order for Clance to have spotted it in his rifle scope. When he was within a hundred yards, he stopped the snow mobile and pretended to be in distress in order to get the creature's attention just as Clance had planned on doing. He left the engine running on the sled, but dismounted and took a few steps away toward the trees.

"I know you're out there, big ugly!" he yelled. "Want to come out and play now?"

Phil had his rifle on a sling across his back, but now pulled it into his hands in front of him and held it aloft.

"Come on out, big ugly, here I am so come get me!" He shouted again.

Suddenly he caught a glimpse of movement in the darkness of the trees. He knew it had to be the creature. It stayed hidden in the woods, watching and waiting for Phil's next move. Phil scanned the area and made a quick plan and thought to himself, *these things seem to hunt in pairs so I bet that the other one on top of the ridge is his partner. Jeez, I pray it is!*

"I hope you're all alone you big, ugly bastard!" he shouted as he slung the rifle back around his back, climbed on the snowmobile, and raced toward the tree line. When he was fifty yards away he saw a slight movement in the same area. He brought the snowmobile to a sliding stop, swung his rifle around from his back to bring it to bear in front of him, and fired off three rapid shots straight at the Sasquatch. The shots were meant to get the attention of the monster, but also to signal the Denizens that it was now time to make their escape, just as Clance's plan called for.

Phil gunned the engine straight ahead for twenty more yards. Suddenly the creature stepped out onto the trail and with a menacing scream threw a huge rock barely missing Phil's machine. Phil cut hard to the right and veered off the trail. He hit the throttle hard and followed the edge of the tree line through a large open field. The beast with long, reddish black fur gave chase, but used the safety of the trees to stay hidden when possible. Phil's heart was in his throat and his adrenaline kicked in as he raced the sled away from the trail in order to give the others an opening to escape. He planned on looping back around once the Denizens had a chance to get past and then he would rejoin them at the cabin. As long as he could stay in the open field he had a speed on his side, but if he had to go in the woods, that advantage was gone. He prayed that he had a smooth track for a very long way.

+++

"Sheriff, do you believe any of this? I mean about Sasquatch and all?"

"I don't know, Billy, but I'll tell ya, a lot of people do. A lot of highly respectable people too. Folks that you wouldn't think would ever make up something like this that could potentially ruin their name," the sheriff replied.

"I know, but it still seems strange. Honestly, I don't believe that Turner could have done it either. I don't think he's big enough or strong enough to have bested that other fella. He was a big man and looked like he kept in good shape. He had a good forty or fifty pounds on Turner. The whole thing just seems unlikely and I still don't see any motive," Billy explained.

The two men grew silent and thoughtful as they drove along the snow-covered road. Billy stared off into the trees, alone with his thoughts as the sheriff looked ahead as he drove down the picturesque trail that led from Troy's cabin to the main highway. They had left Troy just minutes earlier and figured to get back to the office before dark. It was the end of a cold, brisk day, but the sun still shined brightly and the views were absolutely stunning in the mountains.

The sheriff rolled his window down a little and lit up a cigarette. Reaching over the laptop, he turned the radio on at a low volume. A tune by Randy Travis came on the oldies station, but neither man paid much attention to it as they were lost in their own thoughts.

Billy realized just how tired he was from having worked a double shift, leaned back in his seat, and closed his eyes. He had just dozed off when he was suddenly catapulted into the dash.

"Sorry, Billy," the sheriff said. "I Just heard three gun shots. Didn't mean to slam on the brakes so hard. "

"Where did they come from?" Billy asked, once he got his bearings.

"Not sure," The sheriff replied as he reached down and turned on the emergency lights overhead.

Nick put the truck in park, quickly stepped out and looked around. Billy got out on his side and came around.

"Couldn't tell which direction they came from the way sound echoes around these mountains. They were faint, but distinct. Three in a row."

"You don't think it was Turner do you?" Larson asked.

"Nah, the cabin's quite a ways away and he doesn't have a vehicle. Couldn't have made it this far on foot this fast. We've had dozens of people up here combing this entire mountain. Weeks later we hear three gun shots just as we drop Turner off? I want to know who's out there!" The sheriff said firmly.

The sheriff climbed back in the truck and hit the siren a couple of times hoping to illicit a response. The 'Woop Woop' was extremely loud as it echoed across the snow covered countryside. Whoever was out there may be able to hear them or spot the bright blue and red lights down below.

The two men stood there for quite some time watching and listening for any further signs. They knew there was no way they could possibly track down the source of the gunshots without the aid of snowmobiles – not over this terrain.

I'll see if I can get Lindsey on the radio and let her know what's going on. I don't like the feel of this."

Billy jumped in the truck, picked up the radio mic and attempted to call the station, but there was no return.

"Doesn't seem like anyone can hear us right now, but if you want to go on out to the highway it shouldn't be too far 'til we can get a clear signal. These mountains are a pain in the ass sometimes," Billy suggested.

"She knows where we are. If we're not back soon, she'll send someone out. Let's head back to Turner's and check things out there. We're not that far away and if that's our missing hunter, we need to bring him in," the sheriff said.

Billy hurried back around to his side. "Yeah, and it'll start getting dark soon," he called out.

When they got back in the truck the sheriff turned around and headed back to the cabin with the windows down so that they could listen for any more gunshots. It was bitterly cold and when the sun sets, it would drop well below freezing. Billy shivered from the wind blowing in the through the windows so he reached over and turned the heater up. Whoever was on that ridge should be getting out of there too he thought.

As they drove along the sheriff said, "I couldn't tell where those shots came from exactly, but my bet is from that switchback ridge up there."

"You could be right, but that's still a long ways from here." Billy replied.

Suddenly several shots echoed across the mountain valley. They were farther away, but this time both men heard it. The sheriff hit the gas on the big four wheel drive truck and sped back to Troy's cabin.

Chapter 25

Troy was scrubbing the floor with the bleach water when he heard the three gun shots. They were nearby. Not close, but close enough that he knew they were coming from somewhere on his property. He dropped his cleaning brush, stood up and hurried to the back door. Stepping out into the cold wind he looked up at the tree line behind the cabin. It could've been Phil. He still hadn't been located and he hoped that he was still safe somewhere.

The sun was still up, but would soon be setting. When it did, it would get dark very fast. He didn't have a snowmobile and he certainly had no desire to go up on that mountain alone and on foot. Maybe it was the sheriff, he thought. If it was the sheriff, what the hell was he shooting at?

He turned and went back inside. There wasn't anything he could do at the moment. His cell phone was dead, so he plugged it in to recharge then turned back to the floor. He needed to get it cleaned and get a fire going before dark. With the kitchen window open and now the back door, it was cold enough in the house that his teeth were starting to chatter. It would take some time for the heater to get the house back up to a comfortable temperature. He finished the floor, cleaned the wall then checked all through the house once again for all the places where Craig had been. Once he was satisfied he had everything cleaned, he grabbed his coat and went outside to get some firewood off the porch. He was just about to walk out the door when he remembered he didn't have any guns left in the house. The sheriff said that all the weapons in the house were confiscated and taken for testing. He looked around and found a hunting knife in Craig's packs and strapped it on his belt loop. He hadn't heard anything since the three gunshots and knew it wasn't much defense anyway, but at least it was something. He would be sure to drop the heavy wooden beams across the doors and keep them bolted.

He carried in several arm loads of wood and kept a close eye out for any sign of trouble. Once he had enough inside to keep it going for a couple of days, he built a big roaring fire and turned the heater down low so that it would only turn on if it reached seventy degrees inside or colder. The fire would keep the house above that most of the time which should be perfect, he thought. The generator would keep the lights on in the house and the appliances working with no trouble. The cabin was naturally insulated and the fireplace could heat the entire house very well if all the interior doors remained open. It was a well-constructed home and insulated for the extreme northern climate.

The entire time that Troy was working his thoughts kept going back to the gunshots. He hadn't seen or heard anything else since then, but he walked outside to the front porch and looked around. If that was Phil up there, he may be lost, he thought.

I should leave the outside lights on for him in case he needs help. He thought.

He hurried back inside and flipped the switches, including the ones for the string of lights that led down to the boat dock. The whole place lit up like a Christmas tree. He realized then just how dark it was getting. The sun was beginning its descent over the mountain and when he looked up he could no longer make out individual details on the trees. They were fading to a dark mass surrounding the cabin.

A cold shiver ran down his spine. He hurried back inside and bolted the doors. He made his way through the house checking for any weapons the deputies may have missed. He would feel better if he knew he had something to use as protection besides a small hunting knife. 'Damn,' he thought, 'why did they take everything and leave me no way to defend myself out here?'

He made sure the crossbar was on the doors upstairs. After searching his bedroom he noticed his laptop lying on the dresser. He flipped the screen up, but it was dead. He carried it down to the kitchen where the charge cord remained in the outlet. He plugged it in and sat on a bar stool while it booted up. He reached over and hit the reset switch on the wireless router. Just in case, he chuckled to himself. Never know about technology, maybe I can get a signal.

After a few minutes, the laptop whirled awake and began booting up. His stomach growled hungrily and he remembered he still hadn't eaten yet. He busied himself making a sandwich and something to drink then sat back down at the counter. The laptop was going through several updates.

"Figures," he said to himself. He left it alone and went to the sofa to finish eating.

Ten minutes later he heard the computer ding several times "What was that?" He wondered out loud. He walked back to the counter, put his finger on the touch pad and woke the computer up. Then it occurred to him: that was the email notification. He opened the app up and looked at his emails. There were several in his inbox including dozens of spam ones. He laughed to himself and thought it odd that of all the times for the internet to actually work, this would be the one.

He quickly downloaded the emails to an offline archive just in case the connection was lost. Once he had them all moved over, he finished eating as he went through each one. It was easy to do so as he could delete just about everything that wasn't from his editor. He didn't have many people that he emailed directly; mostly these were from different shopping websites that he was a member of. After a few minutes he noticed that the internet reception had gone to almost nothing again. At least it worked for a few minutes, he thought. So maybe it'll be back on again tomorrow if the weather is clear or if it's less windy. His mind drifted back to the gunshots and his friend still out there on that mountain somewhere.

+++

Phil gunned the engine of the powerful snowmobile and led his pursuer down a long, gently sloping hill. The creature was careful to stay mostly hidden in the trees and Phil was careful not to let it get too close. The beast was fast and nimble, but was no match for the speedy sled. Part of him wanted to stop and take a shot at it, but the rational side of him knew he had to lose it quickly and get turned back to the trail that led to the cabin.

When he got to a rocky point where the field met the trees and narrowed down to a small glade, he recognized exactly where he was. He remembered that if he went straight down the tree line at this point there was a sharp drop about two hundred yards further in. There was no way to get around it; he had to turn back and find the trail the Denizens took. Hopefully it came out on the road that led to Troy's house, but he knew he would lose a race with the Sasquatch before he ever made it to the road.

Another hill was coming up fast, but he had no idea what was on the other side of it. If it were tall enough, maybe once he got over the top of it he could turn around before the beast made it through the woods to parallel him. He could fool the monster into thinking he had continued on and then out run it back to the trail and catch up with the Denizens at the cabin. They weren't far from it and that would be the safest place. It was built like a fortress with huge, heavy wooden logs.

Nothing would be able to break it down, not even a monstrous Sasquatch.

+++

Clance saw what Phil did, but it was too late to stop him. He reacted the only way he could.

"Jo, get on with us. You boys ride together. Gav, keep that rifle handy and watch our backs. Follow close behind us. We only have one shot at this."

The group did as the elder instructed. As soon as they heard Phil's three shots, Clance hit the throttle with his family following closely behind. Phil was leading the Sasquatch away from them to give them a chance to escape, and Clance was determined to make sure they did exactly that. He knew the way to the cabin and it wouldn't take them long to get there as long as there were no other Sasquatch in the area. He didn't think there would be; he had hunted and lived around them for many years so he knew the lone sentry was only to guard against intruders and to warn the others of approaching danger.

+++

Phil crested the hill at breakneck speed catching several feet of air and immediately realized his mistake. Standing directly in his path was the eight-foot tall menacing beast. It spread its arms out wide and let out a tremendous roar. *Son of a bitch tricked me*, Phil thought, thinking through his options in a split second. He nearly panicked and hit the brakes, but clarity took over and he thought better of it.

He gunned the throttle hard and sped straight at it. At the last possible second, Phil turned the rudders sharply and leaned all of his weight to the side sending a sheet of snow and ice toward the hair covered giant. In one swift motion, he performed an arcing one-eighty, hit the throttle hard and sped away. The beast stood still for a few seconds in stunned silence then let out another roar. Phil heard the beast's frustration as he sped away.

When he looked back over his shoulder he saw the creature still standing there. He let go of the throttle, hitting the brakes at the same time, spun his rifle off his back, and took aim with the carbine. He took only a split second to aim and fire, and then fired again and again until the gun was empty. The beast screamed on the first shot and Phil knew he hit it. At that range, he couldn't miss. The other shots also found their mark. The beast went down on a knee then finally crumpled with a loud, mournful wail. It reminded Phil of the deeply resonating and very low tone of the dinosaurs he heard in a movie once. An odd memory at a time like this, he thought. It was eerie and unnerving when the Sasquatch made its last gasp and lay motionless.

On impulse and curiosity, he climbed off the snowmobile and started to walk over to it. It was lying face down in the snow less than fifty yards away, but then he thought better of it. He needed to catch up to the Denizens before any of the others found him.

+++

It took only a few minutes for the Denizen's to cross the open, snow covered range and get to the relative safety of the woods. Once they reached the edge of the clearing, the trail became tighter and more twisted around the trees and rocks. The wind wasn't as bad with the big trees acting as a windbreak. Clance kept the group moving fast through the dense forest. The trail was narrow, but easily navigable. They had to slow to round a tight curve. Just as Clance let off the throttle, he heard several more rifle shots and slowed to a stop.

"Did you boys hear that?" Clance asked.

"We heard it. Maybe he killed it?" Mathew replied.

"Soon as we get your mom and sister to the cabin we'll come back for him."

Clance hit the throttle and took off at a fast pace. The boys understood what he meant. They knew Phil was good with a rifle so he had a fighting chance, but right now, they had to get the rest of the family to safety before they could be of any help to him.

As they laced their way down through the forest trail they caught a glance of lights through the trees. The valley wasn't far below now and they should reach Troy's cabin safely. With any luck, they would be able to get inside quickly. There was no way to be certain that anyone would be home, but it was their only chance at this point. It was dark in the tree line and they had to use the headlights on the sleds. Clance felt comfort in knowing that the cabin was this close. He had to get his family to safety. If Phil had killed one of the Sasquatch clan members, there would be hell to pay.

They passed through the roughest part of the trail and came to a clearing near a small pond. It was less than a mile to the cabin now. Clance made a quick decision and veered off the path. He knew a quicker way; it was a small game trail, but it was big enough to let them through easily. It led to the backside of the lake and brought them down almost directly behind the cabin. It was the way he came when he would go to the lake and where he had rescued Phil. It was also further away from the main trail, but he hoped Phil would be able to follow their sled tracks easily enough.

The group weaved through the trees and glided silently over the snow with no further incidents. The air was crisp and cold, but void of heavy wind making the engines of the snowmobiles the only sound. They were fairly quiet when they weren't running them hard. Ten minutes later, the lights of the cabin came into full view.

The entire valley was lit up and it would be hard to miss high up on the ridge line. The trail zig-zagged down and Clance pulled straight up to the front steps of the house and met Troy Turner standing in the doorway.

"Are you Turner?" Clance asked quickly as he stepped off the snowmobile with his wife and daughter.

"Uh - yes I am. Who are you?" Troy replied.

+++

It was beginning to get dark and the trek over the mountain had taken its toll on him. He was exhausted. The adrenaline that pumped through his body had him literally shaking with fear and excitement as the creature lay dead behind him. He climbed back on the sled and took long, deep breaths until he had calmed his nerves. Once he regained his composure he reached into his coat pocket for extra rounds and reloaded his rifle. He slung it on his back then reached down to the handle bars and started to hit the throttle. That's when he heard it.

A distant scream on the mountain top above him that sent chills down his spine. It was drawn out and sounded like pure rage and could only have come from one of the beasts. He took one last look at the beast lying behind him then turned his search to the mountain above him. Seeing nothing, he hit the throttle and circled back close to the tree line. He found his old trail and followed it until he came to the point where the tree line connected with the switchback of the ridge line that made a natural trail down. He picked out the tracks of the other snowmobiles and followed them as quickly as he dared. As he bounced over the trail dodging trees, rocks, and brush he thought he heard another scream on the mountain. He opened up the throttle and picked up more speed.

Chapter 26

The sheriff drove as fast as he dared down the snow covered dirt road that led to Troy's cabin. He kept the emergency lights on just in case someone in the woods needed help. They may be able to spot the vehicle and know which way to go to find the road if they were lost. It didn't take long for them to reach the bridge over the lake. As they crossed over it they could see that Troy had every light in the house turned on.

Billy said, "Wow, you see all those lights from the cabin down to the boat dock? Looks like you could land a plane there!"

"Ain't that the truth," the sheriff murmured as he studied the area. When they pulled up to the house they saw that Troy wasn't alone. Nick stopped the truck and they both got out and met the entire group at the front of the house. He recognized Clance Denizen and his family.

Clance was the first to speak, "Sheriff, glad you're here, but you may not be. You're not gonna believe this, but we all need to get loaded in your truck and get the hell out of here as fast as we can, but we have to wait on Phil."

"What's that Clance?" The sheriff asked.

"Phil Morton. He's out there," Clance said.

"He's alive?" Troy asked excitedly.

Clance nodded then replied, "He was when we left him twenty minutes ago." He said, then pointing to indicate the mountain he said, "He led one of those damned beasts away from us so that we could get away and get down here. It had the trail down to the road blocked."

"What are you talking about, Clance?" the sheriff asked.

Billy was starting to get nervous and fidgety. He silently studied the faces of everyone around him not sure what to believe. He looked around into the darkness as Clance told them the story and instinctively he let one hand slowly fall to his holstered weapon. He had no idea what was happening, but he would be ready.

Clance explained the current circumstances and the dire need for getting out of the valley. The sheriff ordered everyone to get into the truck. While the men helped the women into the vehicle, Billy was the first to spot it and shout out.

"Sheriff, someone's coming up the road. That's gotta be Him!"

The single headlight of a snowmobile bounced along the road at a breakneck speed from where they had just come. The group could hear the rider shouting, but couldn't make out what he was saying until he skidded to a stop in front of them all and jumped off the sled in one swift motion.

Phil shouted, "Everyone, get inside! Now! They're right behind me!"

"Let's get in truck and get off this mountain," Jolene exclaimed in a loud, shaky voice.

"There's no time and the road's blocked now!" Phil exclaimed, "I just followed the sheriff's lights and the whole damn mountain is right on my ass. I killed the one on the ridge and the others are pissed and not far behind me."

The men quickly moved into action and gathered the emergency supplies from the truck and carried them inside. Troy closed the front door and then bolted it with the heavy wooden crossbars. Everyone had a weapon except Troy. The sheriff handed him one of the twelve gauge shotguns from the truck with a box of slugs.

"They're only accurate at close range. Hope you don't need it!"

"Me either!" Troy said.

Once everyone was armed, the sheriff and Clance checked out all of the flashlights to make sure they were working and handed them out. He directed the deputy upstairs.

"Get up there and stay out of sight and let us know if you see anything moving! Clance, what do you think?"

Clance said, "My boys can set up in that room there and each one cover a window. The place is lit up pretty damn bright, should be able to see anything that gets within a hundred yards. I'll go up on the deck with your deputy, Sheriff. Scope on this rifle will come in handy."

The sheriff continued his instructions, "Sounds good! Troy, you and Phil take the room where you can watch the front and east side. Be careful not to get too close to a window."

In all of his years in law enforcement, Nick had never been in a situation like this. He had seen a lot of things, but this was one that no one would ever believe. One thing he knew for certain, Clance Denizen was not a man to lie and he certainly wasn't a man that scared easily. He was an eccentric mountain man, though honest as the day was long and Nick knew it. If he was worried about whatever it was out there, then he had cause to worry too.

Everyone moved quickly and took up their assigned positions. Before Troy moved away, Nick asked him,

"Troy, do you have a working phone?" The sheriff asked.

No, Sheriff. It only works if the internet does and it's been down all evening. It worked for a few minutes earlier when you first brought me home and then nothing," Troy replied.

"Try again!" The sheriff demanded. "Radio is out of range. It's no good."

There were no stars or moon to light up the night sky so it was pitch black on the mountain. The lights shined brightly off the soft white snow and played eerie shadows through the trees when the wind blew the lights hanging from the electric wire. It was quiet. Unnervingly quiet! The only sound was the wind blowing down from the mountain and across the frozen lake. Every now and then it would blow the boat around at the dock and they could hear the aluminum bang against a post and ring hollow.

The men had taken stock of all the weapons and ammo. They were, in Clance's opinion, woefully under powered for what was about to take place. Each man watched intently at their respective positions and was obviously on edge. They had turned the lights off inside the house so that they wouldn't be silhouetted through the windows. Not that they expected a Sasquatch to fire a rifle, but they wanted to retain their night vision without being blinded.

After several minutes of waiting with no signs of the Sasquatch, Billy whispered to Clance,

"Maybe they're not coming. Maybe he scared them off when he killed that one on top of the ridge."

"Nah, they're coming. They're just watching us right now - waiting." Clance was matter of fact with no sound of fear or trembling in his voice.

"For what?" Billy asked.

"Just sizing up their prey before the hunt," Clance replied.

More silence.

Sheriff Blaine walked from the living room window he was watching to the stairs and called out to the big mountain man.

"Clance, how many do you think we're dealing with?"

Clance moved off the deck and into the bedroom before answering him.

"Can't say for sure, Sheriff, but I've counted at least nine or ten through the years. They don't all look alike. Some are really tall, but I've seen a few others that were only about as big as me. Some have reddish, brown fur all over 'em and some are black as the night. They blend in to their surroundings and are hard to see. If they don't want you to see them, you won't."

"If he's right and he killed one of them up on the ridge..." Nick let that last thought trail off and the two men shared a knowing look. There would be hell to pay after killing one of the clan. They moved back to their positions without another word.

Chapter 27

Troy worked diligently on the internet connection, but was having no luck. He restarted the modem several times in hopes that it would pick up the signal, but it could never establish a connection longer than a few seconds.

"Signal's too weak, Sheriff. I'll keep trying," he called out.

Almost two hours had ticked away, but it felt like an eternity to the inhabitants of the cabin. Clance and Billy took turns coming inside to warm up. They had a perfect spot on the deck where they could see from one side of the house all the way to the other. They couldn't see in the back of the house, though. The back was the least guarded side of the cabin, but it was also the most protected with only one small kitchen window and a heavy wooden door. It would take a locomotive to break it down. The cabin was their best defensive position if they had to defend their ground at all.

Clance turned his head slowly when he thought he spotted something moving near the boat dock. It was several hundred feet away, but he knew he saw something. The movement was different than the moving shadows caused by the blowing light bulbs. He knew not to look directly at it because his vision would blur so he opened his eyes wide and took in everything. Suddenly, he saw it again! There was no mistaking what he was looking at. A huge Sasquatch was skulking near the shoreline. Immediately Clance knew what they were going to do. He quietly alerted Billy, then moved inside and called downstairs.

"Turn off all of the lights, in fifteen seconds!" Clance told them.

Troy clambered from his position at the counter, counted down, then quickly shut off the lights. The sheriff had seen the movement from his position as well. They both knew the Sasquatch were moving for the lights. They were going to try and knock them out, but Clance's quick reaction was just in time to surprise the Sasquatch and maybe cause them some confusion.

"What do we do now?" Gavin shouted from the bedroom.

His father called out, "Give 'em thirty seconds then turn 'em on again. Be ready to shoot and only at what you can see and hit! Don't miss and don't waste ammo!"

Clance quickly returned to the deck and carefully made his way to the edge crawling on his hands and knees through the snow piled on it. He and the deputy took up prone positions and waited. The others waited anxiously below with their weapons at the ready.

Troy counted down quietly to himself. When he counted thirty seconds he threw the light switches on. Clance was the first to fire. A huge, hulking Sasquatch had gotten very close to the house and carried two large rocks, one in each hand. The beast screamed before letting go with one of the rocks. The mountain man's shot rang true and hit the beast in the upper torso just as it let go the rock. It screamed in agony and rage when the bullet found its mark then threw the other rock. The bullet had caused too much damage and the beast's strength failed it. The rock fell short of its intended target. It turned to flee, but was severely injured from the large caliber bullet that had lodged in its chest slowing its retreat. Clance fired again; the beast stumbled and went down on a knee for a brief moment then moved over a small embankment and out of sight.

Suddenly, the cabin shook from a deluge of large rocks booming against the walls and reverberating throughout. The Sasquatch had surrounded the cabin and were close enough now to cause serious damage. Gavin spotted one near the garage and opened fire with his rifle through the bedroom window. The bark of the big bore rifle was deafening in the bedroom where he and his brother took refuge, but the adrenaline was pumping through his veins and he fired twice more. The beast went down with a mournful howl and Gavin continued firing until his rifle was empty and he had to reload. The beast was down, but Gavin couldn't take his eyes off of it.

"I got one!" he shouted just as a huge rock banged into the side of the house near him causing him to flinch back from the open window.

The attack became more ferocious as the rocks pelted the walls smashing windows and shaking the house. Photos that hung on the walls were jarred off and crashed to the floor. The cabin held firm even though the pounding seemed to last forever. Each time the walls were hit, the entire cabin shook to the foundation and the people inside felt the vibrations. The huge rocks pounding the house from all sides sounded like a hail storm on a tin roof. The screams from the beasts were terrifying and echoed through the dark mountain valley.

One of the lights hanging on the line leading down to the dock was suddenly knocked out sending a shower of sparks spraying into the night then quickly disappearing into the darkness. The two yard lights on tall electric poles and the outside porch lights on the cabin were still bright enough that the defenders could still make out targets - when they got close enough and showed themselves.

Billy turned just in time to see a large rock smash into the light above the garage. He quickly turned his aim in the direction it came from, found a target and fired three times in succession with his shotgun. He heard the creature scream and thought he may have hit it, but couldn't tell for certain. He rolled from his position and moved to the back of the deck just as another large rock shattered the deck railing where he had been laying. Splinters pierced his cheek.

Clance grabbed Billy's arm and pointed to the vehicle below.

"There's one behind the truck, if he gives you a target, empty everything you've got!" he shouted.

They were most vulnerable being out on the deck, but they also had the best vantage point to see them coming. Billy waited tensely, but the beast never showed itself. Several more rocks found their mark on the upper deck of the cabin forcing the two men to move closer to the door. Clance ducked inside with Billy in tow. Just as Billy turned to slide the heavy wooden door into place, a rock smashed through one of the French door panels and slammed into his shoulder knocking him to the floor.

"Turn off the lights!" Clance shouted to anyone that could hear him below as he helped Billy up and bolted the doors.

He knew they had to turn them out before the beasts found them all and knocked them out. They might be able to use the trick at least one more time. If the lights weren't shining, maybe the Sasquatch wouldn't see where they were. If they were lucky, they may save a few.

Troy threw the breaker plunging the cabin into complete darkness. The sheriff also had seen the monster behind his truck just as it went dark. He quickly reached into his pocket and hit the remote button to unlock the doors. The vehicle gave out a 'chirp chirp' and the entry lights came on. The Sasquatch had stepped out thinking it was in the relative safety of darkness only to be caught out in the open. With a scream it jumped back and ran toward the tree line, but not before Nick was able to get off a shot.

Just as suddenly as the assault started on the lakeside cabin, it stopped. The Sasquatch seemed to disappear as quickly as they came and the mountain valley became eerily quiet once again. The defenders had held out against the assault and had beaten back the attack of the Sasquatch. They could rest now, but for how long, they wondered. They knew they could wait it out for quite some time in the comfort and safety of the cabin if they were careful. The fire was burning and the cabin was warm, even with the generator turned off, but with most of the glass in the windows shattered it would soon get cold.

It wouldn't take long until Linsdey would start to worry about us and send in the cavalry. All they had to do was survive the night, the sheriff thought, as he walked around the cabin checking on everyone else. He walked into the bedroom where Gavin and Mathew were standing guard. They were shining their flashlights in the area of the yard where Gavin had shot the Sasquatch, but there was no body lying there. Blood was everywhere and they could see where the creature was dragged away or had crawled to safety. They knew it was either wounded badly or had been killed.

"I know it's dead, Sheriff." Mathew said, "There's no way that that thing could take a half a dozen slugs like that and live! I hit it in the chest at least once if not twice. No way could it have survived!"

"One thing's for sure, you hit it! That's a lot of blood out there. Either way, it's out of this fight!" The sheriff responded.

The men took the opportunity to reload and count their remaining ammunition. They were all still in decent shape since they had only fired when a target had presented itself. They waited quietly and watched through the broken windows for any sign that the Sasquatch would attack again. Several long minutes went by with no further hostilities though they could hear what sounded like whoops from the distant woods. Troy and Phil were in the bedroom of the lower floor. They were each at corner window watching intently out into the darkness, nervously waiting for the next volley. Troy was exceptionally nervous as he glanced over at Phil. He couldn't see his face in the darkness, but could make out his silhouette from the fireplace light reflecting off the glazed, wooden logs of the home. In the fast pace of the evening, he never had much of a chance at conversation, only a brief greeting.

Almost hesitantly, Troy said, "I think that was just the first attack, right? Just feeling us out to see what they're up against? If three of 'em were hit and maybe dead or dying, maybe they'll think twice about attacking again?"

"That makes a total of four! The one I shot on the ridge is dead. There was no mistaking that. I emptied my gun on it and it took every shot to bring it down! But it WAS down!" Phil insisted.

"I wonder just how many there are?" Troy asked.

"I dunno. Hey, Troy, where's Craig?" Phil asked.

Chapter 28

Shadows from the firelight flickered about the cabin dancing on the walls and ceiling while the crackle of the cinder burning popped in a melodic and almost hypnotic manner. It was peaceful and calming to the group that sat in silence, watching and waiting.

"Who's doing that?" The sheriff suddenly asked, disturbing the silence. He explained he was hearing a thumping that sounded like someone nervously tapping on the cabin floor with their foot.

The sheriff had been looking out through one of the windows in the front room for any sign of the Sasquatch. Everyone was clearly on edge. It had been at least an hour and nothing had been seen of the beasts except for whoops and calls in the woods earlier.

Jolene had made coffee for everyone and Billy stood near the fireplace sipping a cup. He planned on heading back upstairs once he warmed up.

"Stop doing what, Sheriff? I'm not doing anything," Billy said.

"That tapping on the wall! It's making me nervous."

"But I'm not..."

The others heard the sounds too. Clance had come downstairs to get some coffee and was just on his way back up. He stopped, sat his cup down and walked to the front doors to listen closer.

"That's the Sasquatch. They're using limbs to knock on trees. It's a way they communicate I think. I've been hearing it faintly for a few minutes now. Guess it didn't register until you pointed it out. Not sure if they're calling in more of the damn things or signaling another attack. Either way I'd say we'd better get ready for anything! I'm gonna sneak back onto the deck and keep watch. Turner, throw the lights on again if you hear me shoot!"

Clance slowly and quietly unbolted the huge doors and crept back out on to the deck with Billy following closely behind. The glass in one of the doors had been broken out when the large rock busted through it, but the heavy wooden barn style door itself was solid. Clance instructed Billy that if they had to retreat back inside, the first thing they had to do, no matter what, would be to slide the heavy wooden barn door in place and secure it with the crossbar. It was built to withstand the elements, but also to keep out curious bears rummaging for food. These mountains were full of bears, big cats, and wolves that wouldn't pass up a chance at an easy meal. Folks that built their homes out here knew how to keep all animals, big and small, out. They just hoped that with the aid of their rifles and the heavy wooden doors, they could also keep the Sasquatch out!

In the bedroom below, Troy was explaining everything that had happened since Phil had been knocked out of the ATV on that night in the woods. He told Phil of the search for him, the trip into town, his hospital stay, and subsequent arrest for the murder of Craig. When he was done relaying everything, he let the impact of his words hang. Phil had no idea that Craig had been killed and was in complete shock. The two of them had grown up together, went to college together, went on many big game hunts together. It was a huge blow. Phil sat down on the bed in the dark room. Troy could hear his breathing catch from time to time as his friend choked back tears.

"I'm sorry I wasn't able to get back here for you. I was in pretty bad shape after I fell in the lake. If it hadn't been for Clance, I wouldn't be here. It took a few weeks for the fever to go down and I was in and out, but once I woke up and realized where I was, the damned things were on us and kept us pinned down close to the cabin."

"No, Phil. I know why you weren't here. I'm just sorry that we weren't able to double back and find you. We were forced to retreat back to the cabin to get weapons and we had no idea where you could have been. We searched for you, but it was like a needle in a haystack in all that chaos. Then after I woke up in the hospital I told the sheriff. They had dozens of people combing the mountain for you, but no one ever found a trace of you. Winter storms didn't help either. I have no idea what could've provoked these damn things. I just can't figure it out!"

The two men sat quietly with their thoughts to themselves. The silence was broken suddenly when Clance shouted down to everyone to be ready. The windows of the cabin were small to protect against the harsh winters, but they still provided plenty of area to watch from. The night air was bitter cold as it blew in through the open windows. They were scared and nervous, but ready for a fight. Troy moved back over to the breaker box in case he heard shooting and had to throw the light switch on again. As he moved in the darkness, he tripped over the leg of the bed and fell. The butt of his shotgun slammed hard on the wooden floor and discharged. The boom of the weapon was deafening in the small room and startled the occupants in the cabin. There was a loud and enraged scream at the abandoned window where Troy had just been. One of the Sasquatch had somehow gotten close enough to reach in. Finding nothing except empty space, the creature roared in anger and attempted to climb inside. Phil turned and fired at point blank range hitting the beast in the shoulder and again in a giant, hairy hand. He kept levering rounds in and fired several more times, but the beast kept trying to come through the small window. Troy regained his footing and he also began firing at the monster. They couldn't see the beast, but fired only from sound of the terrible and enraged screaming.

Jolene hurried to the light switches and turned them on just as another gunshot, much louder than the others, echoed through the cabin, dropping the beast and ending the shrieks.

The sheriff had heard the commotion and ran to the doorway. Shining his flashlight with one hand and aiming his weapon with the other he took careful aim and let go with the .454 Casull. The firearm exploded and nearly took his hand off with it from the recoil. It was a huge hand canon used for stopping bears. It did its job in this case, dropping the Sasquatch deftly to the ground. He checked on the two men in the bedroom then quickly moved back to his position in the front room and looked around for any others.

"Clance? Billy? You guys okay?" The sheriff called out.

"Yeah we're good. Everyone down there okay?"

"We're good," the sheriff called back.

Phil said, "We never saw it or heard the damn thing. It looks clear now. Must've been a scout they sent in. This is crazy! I can't believe how intelligent these things are. Sneaky bastards! "

"Cover me fellas, I'm going out to get a closer look at this thing," Nick said.

The sheriff held his flashlight in his left hand and the Casull in the right and slowly made his way off the front steps and around to the side of the house. Both Troy and Phil were watching from all directions for any signs that others may be around while they kept their weapons trained on the giant Sasquatch lying prone under the window.

Nick could see the eyes of the beast and knew a death stare when he saw it. The creature was dead. He heard a low, mournful cry from somewhere deep in the woods. It was far enough away that he wasn't too worried at the moment. He reached into his pocket and withdrew his cell phone. He opened up the camera app and began taking photos of the creature and then finally he took a few moments of video footage with close ups of the creature's face.

Clance walked down the side steps from the deck and stood beside him.

"I know this one. I've seen him watching me before when I ran my traps. He walked with a gate unlike the others. Never showed signs of aggression, but never showed any signs of being friendly either. I think he was one of their hunters, but not the leader."

The two men stood and stared at the enormous creature for a moment in silence and amazement. The creature was at least seven and a half feet tall and they estimated it weighed about four-hundred pounds. Its arms were long, muscular and thin, as were its legs. The entire body of the Sasquatch was covered in solid black fur and smelled terrible. The sheriff looked over at Clance.

He said, "They're gonna come in to get him ya know"

Chapter 29

Troy and Phil were at their positions covering the windows in the bedroom. Gavin and Mathew were set up in the other room nearest the garage which was the point that made the nearest cover for the Sasquatch and most vulnerable for the cabin because of the blind spots. The lower bedrooms of the cabin were on the corners of the house and each one had a small window on each side. From their vantage point, they had a clear line of fire on the rear of the cabin, both sides and the front.

The sheriff remained in the living room guarding the front of the house. The front door was located in the center of the room. A small window on each side flanked the door and gave him a clear line of site to most of the front porch area. His truck was parked in front beside the other four by four that was owned by Craig. He knew the vehicles had sustained some damage from the first attack, but wasn't too worried about it. He wondered how he would ever explain this - provided they made it out of the ordeal alive!

Jolene and her daughter, who were well versed in the use of any rifle just as well if not better than many men, were keeping an eye on the back door in the kitchen. There was a small window over the sink where they could see out, but it wasn't open. The kitchen was at the opposite end of the living room so the sheriff was nearby if needed, as well as any one of the other men in the lower bedrooms. They were all ready for the expected attack.

The wood knocking and the howling had stopped. It seemed like an eternity had gone by when Troy noticed the red LED clock on the kitchen counter showed it to be only a little after midnight. The sun wouldn't be up for several more hours. Secretly, he wondered if they would they survive night.

Seconds counted down and everyone remained on edge. Clance was again in a prone position on top of the deck with his rifle and two pistols ready for whatever came at them. He was an expert marksman as was any man there, but when in the heat of battle even the best could be flustered and scared enough to miss at point blank range. Clance Denizen wasn't one of those men.

Billy stood at the edge of the doorway on the upper deck with the shotgun and his forty-five caliber Glock side arm. He had two high capacity clips in his web belt and one in the pistol. He was shaking so badly that he literally felt his teeth chatter. He didn't know if it was from the cold or simply out of fear. He never would have thought that something like this could happen. He had always been skeptical of stories of Sasquatch or Bigfoot. He had never seen proof; only stories. Until now!

"Keep a good watch, Billy. I'm gonna go down and see about some more coffee. It's gonna be a long night!"

"You bet," Billy said through chattering teeth.

Clance slowly crawfished back from the edge of the deck and retreated inside the cabin. The sheriff heard him walking down the stairs and went over to meet him.

"Pretty quiet, huh, Clance? Maybe they'll leave us alone now," Nick said.

"All that silence worries me. Gonna grab some coffee. You want some?" Clance asked.

The two men poured their coffee and walked back over to the front windows where they could stand and still keep watch.

"So what do you think got these things all pissed off anyway?" The sheriff asked.

"I'm not sure. It has to be something though. Too many years we've coexisted and they've never bothered us," Clance answered.

"I talked to Zach Blanchard the other day. He's building a new resort up on route fourteen. Apparently, he's had several break-ins where the place was just ransacked. Busted up real bad, but nothing ever taken. He suspects that it may have been the Sasquatch. He told me he seen one near there when he was on the dozer one day. Showed me some pictures of footprints he had taken with his cell phone."

"That's smack dab in the middle of their hunting grounds, Sheriff. They can't be none too happy about that. That may be what the problem is. Blanchard had no way of knowing what kind of hell he was stirring up!" Clance said.

"That would explain a lot, Clance," the sheriff stated.

"So it would seem," Clance said.

"Had to be the Squatch! They usually stay way up in the mountains where people never go. Only come down to hunt when winters get bad. Now that he's building on their hunting grounds, they're retaliating! This may get worse before it gets better, Sheriff. They never hurt me or my family before. Always left us alone, until now. Now I think we're all lucky to be alive and we'll be damn lucky to survive this at all," Clance said firmly.

Clance finished his coffee in silence and moved back upstairs and resumed his position at the edge where he could keep a close watch. It had been quiet for too long and that made them all nervous. He hadn't been lying in his prone position long when he caught movement out of the corner of his eye and slowly maneuvered the muzzle of his rifle to cover the area. He quietly whispered to Billy to be ready, he had one in his sights. He took careful aim, let out half his breath and squeezed the trigger. The roar of the big bore rifle startled the others into action, but they could see no targets yet. The lights were still burning brightly outside, shining on the snow covered ground. They had lines of vision for quite a ways. The only worry was near the trucks and the garage where the beasts could be gathering and hiding behind. After a few moments of silence, they heard the bark of Clance's rifle again.

One of the boys yelled out, "I don't see anything!"

Just as Clance's second shot rang out the rocks began raining down on the roof and the walls again, like a thunderstorm had broken loose on top of the house. Two of the Sasquatch had been moving in on the house, slowly crawling underneath the snow pack using it as camouflage. They were dragging something that they had filled with rocks. Clance saw movement from the first one, but held his fire. He wanted to make sure that he had a good count of how many were there. When he spotted only one other, he turned his attention back to the first one that he had a better field of view of and fired.

The beast was hit and shrieked in a rage. It began pelting the cabin with the rocks, trying to hit the place where the threat was coming from. Clance rolled on the deck and changed positions just as a large rock splintered the railing above him. Rocks were raining down on the cabin and the vehicles outside from all directions. Staying in a prone position, he put the cross hairs of his scope on the creature's head and fired. His first shot missed as the creature was thrashing about wildly forcing him to reload. His next shot was true and ended the life of one more Sasquatch. The second beast dropped the rocks it was carrying and rushed the cabin, shrieking in fury.

Troy saw it running towards the front of the cabin and fired his shotgun at the same time that Clance, Billy and the sheriff did. The beast made it to the porch and slammed hard into the front door. Clance and Billy could no longer see what was happening beneath them and relied on the others to stop the threat. Neither of them could leave their positions unguarded.

The cabin walls shook from the pounding and the shrieking screams of the beast was deafening as it battered against the door in a blind rage. The heavy crossbar held firmly though and the door stood strong. Through the chaos, the sheriff finally had a clear view of the huge beast and fired his weapon. The huge slug from the weapon found its mark and the Sasquatch stumbled dazed and confused. In the next instant, it began clawing madly at its chest trying desperately to make the burning stop. This gave the sheriff another opportunity to fire again through the small window. The creature made another lunge at the door just as the weapon bucked violently in Nick's hand. The slug tore through its chest and it stopped for a brief moment breathing heavily and clawing at the gaping wounds.

Gavin saw the beast rush the cabin, but didn't have a clear shot from his position. He took the butt of his rifle and broke out the remaining glass shards from the window as quickly as he could. Leaning halfway out, he was finally able to get a clear view of the chaos and brought his rifle up. When the sheriff's second shot stunned the Sasquatch and caused it to pause, Gavin let loose with a rain of bullets pelting it and dropping it hard to the porch floor.

The chaotic melee' was deafening. The sheriff's ears were ringing from the discharge of the weapons and the shrieking of the beast, but he could hear a high pitched scream in his head. Somehow it was different than before. Suddenly, the realization hit him that the sound that he was hearing wasn't in his head, but coming from somewhere else. He snapped out of his battle haze and back into the moment.

Jolene! She was screaming from the other end of the house. She had been watching out the window for any signs of the assailants when one of the creatures busted through the small kitchen window with a long, hairy arm and grabbed her by the front of her coat causing her to drop the rifle she had been holding. She fought to pull away from the grip, but the creature was too strong.

Nick turned and ran through the living room to get to her as did both Gavin and Mathew. Gavin reached her first, pulled a huge bowie knife from a sheath on his side as he ran, and threw himself at the creature's arm. He put himself in between his mother and the window and began slashing at its unprotected flesh. The Sasquatch screamed and lashed about so badly that no one could get a shot off. The chaos was maddening and caused everyone to rush to the scene. The attacker had to let go of the small woman to fend off Gavin and his sharp blade. When he did, Jolene fell to the floor in a crumpled heap.

Mathew, not being able to get a clear shot at the creature in the kitchen, threw the crossbar off the back door barricade, opened it, and fired his weapon. In a flash, another Sasquatch found an opening and rushed the door. Mathew never saw it as the beast hit him and knocked him hard into the kitchen wall. He dropped his rifle, crumpled to the floor and lay unmoving. The sheriff reached the back door just as the monster tried stepping inside and let go with another round driving the beast back out into the night. When the door was clear, he dragged Mathew safely back out of the way while keeping an eye on the door.

Irene still had her rifle in her hand, but could not bring herself to shoot. She stood still, frozen in terror. The screaming of the giant beast as Gavin slashed at it was deafening. Suddenly, her father's big hands grabbed her and quickly moved her out of the way.

Clance turned to his wife who lay on the floor. He quickly picked her up and carried her to the sofa near the fireplace. Gavin still fought the beast through the window with his big hunting knife. Clance could see that the boy was no match for the Monster. He kissed his wife's forehead then ran for the open door out into the night.

Nick was angling for a shot inside the kitchen, but had to hold his fire once Clance ran outside after the enraged monster. He couldn't afford to fire blindly in fear of hitting the man.

The beast at the window was throwing Gavin around trying to shake him off of its arm. The knife was inflicting major damage to it and it was bleeding profusely, causing the floor to become slick. The putrid smell of the animal was terrible and it was everything Gavin could do to keep a hold on the creature. His knife blade repeatedly found flesh and finally the Sasquatch let go and jerked its arm back out.

Nick heard Clance screaming at the creature just outside the door and ran to help him. His feet slipped on the blood and snow just as Gavin moved toward the door and the men got tangled up and fell in the slick mess.

BOOM! BOOM! BOOM! BOOM! BOOM! BOOM! BOOM! BOOM! BOOM! BOOM! BOOM! BOOM! BOOM! BOOM! BOOM!

When the men were able to untangle themselves they burst out the back door, just as the reports of a large handgun emptying a full clip in a matter of seconds ended. The outside lights shined enough to see the monstrous beast collapse in a raging shriek on top of Clance. The other was lying nearby. Both of the assailants were dead! Nick put two more slugs from the Casull into each of the Sasquatch bodies, just to make sure after helping Clance back up on his feet.

The Sasquatch was huge and reddish brown in color and the fur was matted with mud, blood, and snow. The stench of the beast was nauseating and was enough to make even the grizzled old mountain man heave. Together, Nick and Gavin helped the elder Denizen into the house. The ferocity of the attack left everyone in complete shock and thankful to be alive.

Billy, Troy and Phil had held their positions during the melee', but now that it was over and quiet again they met the others in the living room. Mathew had already gotten back on his feet, picked up his rifle and sat at the counter on a bar stool waiting on the others. He had a deep gash across his forehead, but shook off any assistance, saying it probably looked worse than it really was.

The sheriff was able to close the back door and drop the crossbar back in place. The small band of warriors found some clean wash cloths and began quietly dressing wounds and taking stock. There was no conversation, just methodical triage.

Jolene was shaken up and in shock, but otherwise fine. Gavin had several bumps and bruises though nothing that wouldn't heal given enough time. The one that was most worrisome was Clance who suffered the most grievous of injuries. Among the claw marks on his face, chest, and arms he seemed to have a few broken ribs and a busted arm. Nick set the bone with Troy's help and then helped dressed all of his wounds. A few of the claw marks were deep and nasty, and he knew they would require stitches.

The rag tag ensemble sat quietly in the early morning solitude of the mountain and discussed what to do when daylight came. It was only a few hours off now. They felt certain that they could hold off any further attacks.

Billy stood in the living room with his back to the group looking out through the busted window at the two Sasquatch that lay dead under the front yard light. His eyes were glazed over and his shoulders slumped as if he had been carrying a ton of weight on his back. He was exhausted from being so incredibly tense all night. He turned to look at the others.

"How many have we killed now?" He asked.

The question made the others stop what they were doing and look up at him. After a moment or two of silent contemplation, Clance spoke in a slow and strained voice, "Seven... by my count."

Phil was down on one knee leaning on his rifle. He slowly stood up and looked around the room studying everyone's faces. "Yeah, I think seven is right."

The sheriff stood up from where he was helping Jolene dress a wound on Clance's shoulder. "Wait a minute. Clance said before that he's counted about nine or ten of 'em through the years. Maybe there's only a few left now and they'll leave us alone? Maybe it's all over and we can get out of here now?"

Phil replied, "If there is another one or two out there, we're still not safe! We'd better keep our guard up. It may not be over at all! We're safe inside the cabin for now. I vote we stay at least until daylight."

The others all agreed and began making sure that all the doors were secured in order to wait it out. The sheriff built up the fire and had the others close off the doors to the other rooms and hang blankets over the exposed windows so the heat could stay isolated. Most of the windows were busted out from the rocks and were letting the cold in. He had it blazing warm in the living room in no time.

Clance was resting as comfortably as he could with his wife sat at his side. Everything was quiet and still and the group finally began to relax.

Gavin suggested they turn the inside lights off, but leave the ones on outside to keep watch. Troy agreed and switched them off. He grabbed a thick wool blanket out of the closet and went upstairs to the deck. He would keep watch there while Phil patrolled the rooms below, watching through the windows on each side of the house. When he got to the top of the staircase and opened the door, he could see several huge rocks that had been thrown by the creatures and remained on the deck. He knew it was a ridiculous thought, but he wondered how much it would cost him to repair all of the damage to his house. His mind swirled with thoughts of the last few months leading up to this moment. After all he'd been through, it still wasn't over. Despondently, he started thinking it would be a miracle if any of them survived this ordeal. He found a spot against the wall, pulled his blanket tighter about his shoulders and slumped down on the deck with his rifle in his lap. He was exhausted.

+++

Sheriff Nick Blaine's head bobbed with drowsy fatigue causing him to wake with a nervous start. His immediate reaction was to reach for his gun. He felt like he had just nodded off for a brief second and had caught himself, but when he glanced around the room he saw that everyone else was asleep. He relaxed, taking long deep breaths, he let the tension fade. With a big yawn, he stretched his legs out, stood up and walked over to the coffee pot. He was feeling every muscle in his body ache with pain as he filled his cup, and he moved over to the window.

The coffee cup shattered on the floor and Gavin, who had fallen asleep in the recliner, woke suddenly and jumped up ready for action with his rifle in his hand. "What is it? What's going on?" He asked.

"They're gone!" The sheriff exclaimed.

The cabin was suddenly bustling with activity as the men scrambled to see what was happening. Everyone had fallen asleep in the quiet aftermath of the night's battle including Troy. He suddenly woke when he heard the shouts down below. He let the heavy wool blanket fall to the deck when he jumped up. He guessed that the sun had been up for a good hour now as he slept. He walked over to the edge of the deck railing and peered down below, drawing a deep breath of the morning air into his lungs. It was bitter cold, but the sun was shining. The wind blew a sharp gust of cold air into his face and caused his eyes to water. He wiped the moisture away and rubbed his eyes. When he was able, he looked all around the area below and instantly knew something was wrong. He turned to head downstairs, but instantly froze. What he saw made him shiver to the bone. Giant footprints could be clearly seen in the snow on the steps and in places on the deck. The Sasquatch had been up here - watching him while he slept!

"They're all gone," Gavin shouted.

"Yeah, the two out back are gone too," Mathew stated.

Gavin came back into the living room and reported that the one at the corner of the house was also gone. None of the beasts that they had killed in the night were still there. They all stood silently in disbelief. There had to be several more of the creatures around in order to have taken all the bodies so quickly, but nobody had seen or heard a thing.

Mathew, who was standing near the front door of the cabin, suddenly turned and shouted out excitedly, "Sheriff, there's trucks coming up the road with their lights flashing."

Nick hurried outside to the porch in time to watch three vehicles that looked to be state police cross the bridge and turn toward the house. He told everyone to put their rifles and handguns down so that they wouldn't have any of their visitors worried about coming up on the scene. Everyone did as instructed and came out to the front porch to watch them slide to a halt in front of the cabin.

The lead vehicle was driven by Deputy Chastain, followed by a state trooper SUV, and then an ambulance with two paramedics. The deputy jumped out and hustled around his truck quickstepping to the front porch. He slowed when he noticed the sheriff's truck and the other four-wheel drive sitting next to the driveway. He let out a long, slow whistle. The vehicles had busted windows and obvious dents all over them that looked like they had been in a hail storm of boulders. Rocks were strewn about everywhere and some still lay on top of the vehicles. When he looked back up he noticed the cabin windows were busted out as well and rocks were still lying on the roof, the porch, and all over the front yard. He nearly fell as he stumbled over one. With panic starting to set in, he asked, "Sheriff? Are you okay? What's going on?"

"You're not going to believe us, Noland, but I'll explain everything. Right now we have an injured man inside. Let's get that gurney in here, fellas." Nick called out.

The two paramedics rushed to the back of their ambulance, retrieved their medical equipment and hurried to the cabin. The state troopers who were following behind the deputy noticed the blood stains in the snow and cautiously approached with their hands on their weapons.

"What the hell happened here, Nick?" a trooper asked.

"Long story, Tom. Just damn glad to see you!" Nick replied.

Chapter 30

"So, what are you going to do now, Troy?" the sheriff asked.

It had been a few weeks since the ordeal on the mountain. The District Attorney had agreed to drop all charges against Troy and the ankle bracelet had been removed. The story had been circulating around the country and reporters had been clamoring to get the inside scoop. Hawthorn may have been a ski resort town, but now it was inundated with every type of 'Bigfoot' hunter imaginable. Film crews had to be reprimanded by the sheriff's deputies for trespassing on private property. Everyone wanted to see where this alleged attack took place.

"I'm not real sure, Sheriff," Troy said. "I'm headed to Oklahoma with Phil for a while, not sure how long I'll stay. Craig didn't have any family, except a few cousins that he really never talked to, but we wanted to go help settle his estate. He didn't have much, but he may have had a will or something."

"I guess you have everything you need then?" Nick asked.

"Yes sir. Phil and I got everything packed and loaded into Craig's truck. We'll drive it down. I've made arrangements to have my Jeep stored until I return. I wanted to stop by and let you know what's going on. We've secured the cabin and, of course, you know about the gate. Who knows if it'll help or not," Troy explained.

"I know we've had a hell of a time trying to keep people out of there. The new gates can only stop the honest ones, but for every honest person that won't cut a lock on a gate, there's a half a dozen who will," Nick replied.

"I'll most likely be back in a few weeks, but who knows. I've been thinking about selling the place. I've had a hundred offers on it, mostly from quacks and nut jobs who just want it to make some kind of Bigfoot business out of it or something, but I'm not interested in selling the place right now," Troy said.

"I understand. I'm sure the folks around town appreciate your thoughts on not selling out just yet. Personally, I hope you come back and stick around," the sheriff said with a smile.

"So tell me, Sheriff. Do you think it's over? Do you think we've seen the last of 'em," Troy asked.

"Who's to say? I hope so. I think what drove them down in the first place was the encroachment on their hunting grounds. When Blanchard started building up on that part of the mountain they had to cut roads right through the middle of it. It must've made 'em angry so they struck back. There's just no way of knowing for sure I suppose, but it seems a likely theory. I'm sure it will die down soon," Nick said.

"I appreciate that, Sheriff. I love the place, I really do, but I'm just not sure about living alone out there anymore. After going through everything I just did..." He left the thought lingering.

"I understand, Troy. Listen, you take care and when you get back into town, drop by and see me," the sheriff said as he stood to shake hands.

"Sure will, Sheriff. Take care."

Troy turned and walked out of the sheriff's office and made his way out to the big Ford truck where Phil waited in the passenger seat. The town was much busier with all the new traffic. People were flocking to the area in hopes of catching a glimpse of 'Sasquatch'. Troy and Phil had packed up all of Craig's belongings and planned to take them back home. Troy was going to stay with Phil for a few weeks and possibly longer until he decided what he was going to do about the cabin. Phil urged him not to make any hasty decisions right now and encouraged him to wait until spring. The cabin wasn't going anywhere and hopefully all of the Sasquatch hunters would be gone by then and life could get back to some sort of normalcy.

The Denizens were staying in town at a relative's house for now. Troy and Phil had visited with them a few times since the ordeal. Clance was recovering in the Hawthorn Memorial Hospital from his wounds. He would have a nasty scar across his face and several other ones on his neck and shoulders, but he would recover fully. Jolene never talked much when they stopped by. She simply sat and stared at her husband and kept her thoughts private. The attack through the window had scared her more than anything she could have ever imagined. Troy couldn't blame her. It was a brutal attack and they were all lucky to be alive. Had it not been for her husband flinging himself out the back door of the cabin when the creature attacked, the beasts may have gotten in and hurt a lot more people, maybe even killing someone? Clance Denizen had saved them all by sacrificing himself. Troy felt a great deal of admiration for the mountain man.

Phil seemed to enjoy the company of Irene Denizen and Troy saw a few glances pass between them that certainly seemed like more than a simple 'hello' look. *Maybe that's why Phil doesn't want me to sell the place and move away*, Troy thought.

In the days that followed the rescue, the state police along with the sheriff's department and the state wildlife department all combed the mountain on snowmobiles and helicopters searching for any sign of the creatures. The photos that the sheriff got on his cell phone were the only evidence of what the beasts looked like. Those photos had already circulated across the continent via Facebook and every other social media website. Many non-believers called it an elaborate hoax.

Others were skeptical, but for the most part believed that 'something' happened, just not sure what exactly. Giant footprints were found; casts were made, and sent to anthropologists for study. A few samples of blood and hair were collected as well and sent to labs for testing. It was all a flurry of activity and one that the locals wished would go away.

Troy put his seatbelt on, shifted into drive and pulled away from the curb.

+++

The sheriff sat at his desk reading the morning paper when Lindsey walked in the front door of the office. He glanced up at her when she said good morning. He returned her greeting and continued reading the paper. When he was finished, he shuffled the paper back into a semblance of the original fold and discarded it in the trash can with obvious disgust.

"I wouldn't worry about what they're saying in the funny papers, Sheriff. It'll run its course before long and then some other story will take its place."

"I know, Linds, but this town is already being bombarded with skiers and now we have Sasquatch hunters all over the mountain to deal with, too!"

"Look at it like this, Sheriff. It should be good for business and good business during an election year can't be a bad thing!"

The sheriff gave a half smile and said, "Well, maybe you're right. I'm just really thankful for you, Linsdey. Without your quick thinking when you got that email from Turner, none of us may be here to tell about it."

'No worries, Nick. I honestly thought nothing about it that night you didn't come back to the office before my shift ended. Wasn't a need to honestly. You've always done that, but when I saw you never came in at all by the next morning I knew something was wrong! That's when I noticed that email come through from him and to be perfectly truthful here...I didn't notice that the date stamp on it was over three months old!"

"Three months old? What do you mean?" The sheriff asked.

"The way I figure, Sheriff, is that Troy sent that email on the first night that they were attacked. It just didn't go through because of his internet connection being down. And then when he was released nearly three months later and went back home, he must have got the internet back on and all of his emails went through at that time. So you see, that email that saved your bacon was an old one! Sorry no pun intended with the bacon comment, Sheriff." Lindsey said with a laugh.

The End

A note from the author

More and more authors are self-publishing every day. With over 4 million titles on Amazon, gaining a presence in the world of booklovers can be a daunting task for new authors. Thus, reviews generated by readers become an important factor. The thoughtful feedback provided not only helps to create exposure for authors in such a robust market; it also helps the author hone their craft.

It is my hope that my stories will instill a sense of wonder, excitement and eagerness for more when finishing one of my novels. If you enjoyed this book, please consider posting a review on Amazon and Goodreads. It only takes a moment and is very much appreciated. You have my thanks and gratitude.

Paul G Buckner

About the Author

Paul G Buckner is a Native American author, musician, an amateur photographer and an avid outdoorsman. The oral tradition of his Cherokee family drove him to collect folktales and stories of those he met in his travels across the U.S. Many of these stories have been passed down through many generations. It is these stories that provide inspiration for his writing.

Paul grew up in the foothills of the Ozark Mountains and as a young boy spent many summers in the woods or on the lakes, creeks and rivers hunting, fishing and camping. Those experiences led to a deep respect for the outdoors, traditional ways and the natural environment. You will see this respect reflected in his writing.

He attended Northeastern State University where he graduated with a B.S. in Business Management and a Masters of Business Administration. He spent several years developing curriculum and teaching business management principles to Native American non-profit groups as well as volunteering countless hours of community services.

Please be sure to follow Paul on his social media sites

www.pgbuckner.com
www.facebook.com/AuthorPaulBuckner
Twitter @authorbuckner
Instagram #tazredrock
Email him directly at pgbuckner@yahoo.com

Made in the USA
San Bernardino, CA
11 December 2016